SHE'S LIKE THE WIND

CARRIE ELKS

"I'm Nate Crawford. I believe you have my daughter here."

"What's her name?" the cop asked, looking up from where he was sitting behind the desk. There was a full wall of glass between him and Nate, and in front of it, resting on the shelf, were clear plastic holders full of information leaflets.

Suffering from Domestic Abuse? We Can Help.

Information for Victims of Crime.

Seattle PD Strategic Plan – Have Your Say

Nate lifted his gaze from the counter and met the cop's stare. "Her name's Riley. She's sixteen years old."

"Riley Crawford?"

"That's right." Nate nodded.

"Okay, take a seat. Somebody will be with you soon."

He followed the cop's directions to the bank of chairs at the far end of the room. They were empty save for an old man who was muttering to himself, and a young woman who was shouting into her cellphone. Neither of them paid him any attention, thank god. Maybe it was normal for a guy wearing full evening dress to walk into the Seattle Police Department to pick up his daughter.

Sighing, Nate pulled out his cellphone. Four missed calls – all from Stephanie. He wasn't inclined to listen to them right now. He pretty much knew what they were going to say.

Where the hell was he?

"Hanging around in a police station on a Friday night," he muttered to himself. "Where else?"

"Mr. Crawford?" the desk sergeant called out. "Your daughter's on her way out. We just need you to sign a few forms."

Nate stood and pushed his phone back into his pocket, pulling at the sleeves of his dinner jacket until they covered his white dress shirt. At the desk, the sergeant pushed the pieces of paper toward him and asked him to sign and date each one.

"Is she being charged?" Nate asked, catching the sergeant's eye.

"Not this time. But she's gotten lucky. Really lucky. This is the second time we've brought her in. Let's not make the third time a charm."

Nate nodded and said nothing. Because what was there to say? He wanted to get her home and pour himself a glass of whiskey – large – and try to block this all out of his mind.

That's your problem, the little voice in his head reminded him. *You seem to be able to deal with every problem in the world except your daughter.*

Strange how it sounded exactly like the family counselor they'd been seeing since Riley had come to live with him in Seattle. Even his own inner voice was criticizing him.

Yeah, well it could join the line. Right now Riley and Stephanie were fighting for first place.

He scrawled his name across the white paper with a tattered pen that was fixed to the desk with a piece of string, presumably to stop somebody from pocketing it. Just as he pushed the signed documents back through the narrow gap between the desk and the glass he heard the doors opening next to him.

Riley was standing in the doorway wearing the grey and pink checkered skirt and white blouse mandated by her very-expensive private school. Her hair was pulled back into a messy ponytail. Her blue eyes – so like his – widened when she saw her father.

"I'm sorry..." she muttered, chewing the corner of her lip.

"Save it for later." His voice was as short as his temper. He glanced at the desk sergeant. "Are we done here?"

"Yep." The sergeant didn't lift his gaze from his computer screen.

Nate rolled his head to try to loosen the tight muscles in his neck, but it didn't help one bit. He was too tense, too angry, too hyped up to relax them.

Maybe that whiskey would help.

Sighing, he inclined his head at his daughter, then at the station doors. "Let's go."

For once she didn't argue, as she followed him quietly, the hard soles of her shoes tapping against the tiled floor. As the electric doors opened and Nate stepped onto the sidewalk he glanced at his watch.

Eight forty-five p.m. Was it really that early? Damn, it was turning out to be a long night.

Nate pressed the button for the gate, idling the engine of his Lexus as he waited for the mechanism to whirr them open. Riley hadn't said a word on the journey home. Hadn't even leaned in to change the radio to something she preferred as she usually did. Instead she was staring out of the windshield, her eyes still as wide as dinner plates, her arms crossed tightly over her chest.

When the gates opened he pulled into the driveway, glancing up at the imposing lake house he'd bought three years earlier. It was huge, modern, and backed onto Lake Union, and for two and a half of those three years it had suited him perfectly.

There was another car parked in the driveway, and Nate bit down a groan when he saw it. He didn't have to look to know that Stephanie was sitting in the driver's seat of the sleek silver Mercedes. The car was vibrating – from the engine, he hoped, rather than Stephanie's anger. He pulled up his own car and switched the engine off, closing his eyes for a moment to try to get some kind of control. What was it he'd said about a long night?

Right now it felt more like a long year.

"Go inside and go straight to bed," Nate told Riley as they climbed out of the car. "We'll talk about this in the morning."

She opened her mouth to reply then clearly thought better of it, pressing her lips shut and stomping up the driveway. From the corner of his eye Nate saw Stephanie open her car door and step out, just as Riley opened the front door and escaped inside the house.

He took a deep breath and walked over to where Stephanie was standing, her arms folded across her chest in exactly the way Riley's had been earlier.

"That's a nice dress," he said, glancing at the silver floor-length gown Stephanie was wearing.

"It cost me five hundred dollars. Plus another two hundred for my hair and make-up, not to mention the gala tickets. So far I figure I'm out almost a thousand thanks to you."

He noticed her nostrils flaring. That wasn't good at all.

"I'll pay you back."

"That's not the point." She shook her head. "The point is you made me a promise and you reneged. You made me look like an idiot in front of all my friends. Do you know how long I was sitting in my apartment waiting for you to pick me up? In the end I had to take a cab."

"It was an emergency. As you can see, I was ready to come and pick you up." He glanced down at his evening clothes. "Then I got a phone call."

"So your phone was working then?" Stephanie said acidly. "I was beginning to wonder."

A breeze blew in from the lake, ruffling Nate's hair and making Stephanie shiver. "You want to come inside?" he asked her. "It's getting cold out here."

"It depends."

"On what?" Nate frowned.

"On whether we're going to have a decent discussion about this or if you're going to put me off again."

Nate's jaw tightened. "Let's just go inside and get warm."

Five minutes later he was carrying two mugs of coffee into the living room. So much for that whiskey. Stephanie was sitting on the corner of his pale cream leather sofa, her legs angled to the side. She was staring out of the huge picture windows that looked out onto the lake. The dark water was dappled with the colored lights of Seattle as they reflected on the surface. He could see greens and reds, blues and pinks, all dancing in the water. Above them towered the Seattle skyline, silhouetted against the dark blue sky. For a moment Nate let the sight soothe him, before he brought his attention back to Stephanie.

She was glaring up at him, her eyes narrowed. He offered her the coffee but she shook her head, so he put it on the large square table in front of her.

"I really am sorry about tonight," he said, sitting down opposite her.

She looked as tightly wound as he felt. "It's not just tonight though, is it? How many times have you stood me up or changed your plans at the last minute since *she* came to stay?" Even her voice was stretched thin. "Things were great between us until then."

"When you're talking about my daughter I'd prefer you use her name." Nate's voice was quiet, but he couldn't hide the anger in it. "And you know what she's been through. What do you expect me to do? Ignore her because we had a prior engagement?"

"Yes. That's exactly what I expect." Stephanie's eyes flashed. "We've been going out for two years, Nate. We were talking about moving in together before..." she trailed off. "Before Riley came to stay. And now you're treating me like crap."

"I'm sorry." He couldn't think of anything else to say. Especially without making things worse.

"That's not good enough." Stephanie shook her head. "Do you know how many offers I've turned down since I've been with you? How many guys have begged me to go out on dates with them? I'm a prize, and you're losing me. If you want to keep me I need to see change."

Nate took a sip of his coffee, surveying her over the rim of his cup. "What you see is what you get, Stephanie. You always knew I had a child."

"So you're not going to change?"

He gave a humorless laugh. "What exactly do you expect me to change?"

"You could send Riley to live with your sister. You said they always got along well."

Nate's mouth dropped open. "Seriously? You think I should send my troubled, grieving daughter away because she's an inconvenience to *you*?"

"I'm just pointing out that this isn't working. Not for any of us. And it was working just fine before she came. Logic dictates that the problem lies with her."

"You *are* serious. You're asking me to choose between you and my daughter."

"I'm asking you to honor your commitments." She pressed her lips together in a firm line.

"I *am* honoring my commitments. I became a father long before I met you. That's the only commitment I'll never break."

"So that's it? You're not even going to fight for me?"

Nate closed his eyes, pinching the bridge of his nose between his thumb and forefinger. He could feel the beginnings of a headache, slowly throbbing its way up to maximum. "It's been a hell of a day, Stephanie," he said, his voice tight. "And tomorrow's probably going to be even worse. I'm just asking you to give me some space to sort things out."

"Space?" Her voice rose up an octave. "What kind of space? Are you breaking up with me?"

He slowly opened his eyes and took a deep breath in. His immediate reaction was to tell her no, of course he wasn't breaking up with her. She was looking at him expectantly, waiting for that exact response.

But for some reason he couldn't give it.

Though the living room was a large expanse of open space – exactly the way he liked it – right now he felt as though all the walls were closing in on him. His mind was a whirl of Riley's latest problems and Stephanie's demands, not to mention everything that was going on with his business. There were complications everywhere and with each day that passed they seemed to be getting worse.

"Yes, that's exactly what I'm saying."

Stephanie's mouth dropped open. Out of the two of them, he wasn't sure who was more surprised by his response. But then a sense of relief washed over him – a feeling he hadn't experienced in the longest of times. When he'd mentioned space he'd been thinking of a few days, a week at the most.

But right now, Stephanie's suggestion sounded like the only viable option. He'd spent months trying to please everybody and in the end nobody was happy.

Nate caught her eye; trying to ignore the hurt he could see sparkling there. This situation was doing none of them any good – and it was time they all faced it. Yes, he was a bastard, and yes she was going to hate him, but right now he had to concentrate on his daughter, not his girlfriend.

"I'm sorry, Stephanie," he said, his voice low but full of certainty. "I think it's time we agreed to bring our relationship to an end."

Ally Sutton's mouth fell open as she stared at her phone. Slowly, she brought her gaze up to where her two friends, Ember and Brooke, were staring at her with equally gaping mouths.

"He's sold the café?" Ember asked. "Seriously?"

"I can't believe you just hung up on him," Brooke said, reaching for Ally's hand and squeezing it tightly. "Good for you, honey."

Ally blinked, though there were no tears in her eyes. Just disappointment that only got worse when she saw on the phone screen that her father was trying to call her again. She quickly rejected the call and set her phone back down on the table.

"You're not going to answer?" Ember asked.

Ally shook her head. "If I talk to him I'm going to end up saying something I shouldn't." She sighed, dropping her head into her hands as the screen went dark.

"Maybe it's for the best," Brooke agreed. "I wouldn't have anything nice to say to him, either. Hopefully he'll get the message and give you some space."

Just as Brooke finished speaking, the screen lit up for a third time.

Ember pulled Ally's phone toward her and keyed in the code. They all knew each other's codes by heart; they had since they were at school. Her friends had her back. They always did. She trusted them with her life *and* her phone.

It began to buzz again. "It's still your dad," Ember told her.

"Don't answer it," Ally said quickly. "Not yet."

"I'm not. I'm just going to put him on block. His calls won't register and his voicemails will go to a separate folder. That way you can listen to them when you're ready, rather than when you're angry." Ember ran her fingers across the screen and looked up. "There. Give yourself a few days. That way you might still have a relationship at the end of it." She passed Ally back the phone.

Ally took it from her, sliding it into her purse. Even without the threat of her dad constantly lighting it up, she still didn't want to look at it.

She didn't want to think about anything at all.

She glanced around the café that she'd known for her whole life. Her throat tightened as she took in the blue cushioned seats and the scratched metal tables. How many times had she sat at them with a coloring book and her favorite strawberry milkshake as a kid? Then, as she grew older the coloring book was replaced by her cellphone, and the milkshake by a coffee.

She'd pretty much grown up in this place. And now she was the manager, which meant not only was her childhood being sold off to the highest bidder, but her job was too.

"I guess I should polish up my résumé," she said, giving her best friends a grim smile. Some of her blonde hair had escaped the topknot she'd tied it in, and she tucked the stray strands behind her ear.

"You're losing your job too?" Brooke's eyes filled with tears. "Oh honey..."

"He didn't exactly say that," Ally admitted. "But I'm not sure I want to work here once it's sold."

"What will you do?" Ember asked. She'd always been the sensible one. A kindergarten teacher at the local school, she was an expert at making plans.

"I don't know. Who would want to employ a twenty-seven-year old woman who's never done anything but manage her father's café?" Ally asked. "I'm not like you, I don't have a college degree. All I know how to do is serve breakfast."

"That's not true. You're still young, you can do anything you want. Even go back to college." Brooke gave her a soft smile.

"I know *you* went back to school, and you're great at it," Ally said. "You kick ass at juggling everything. But school's not for me. I wouldn't know what to study anyway." She slumped in her seat. She could never do what Brooke did. She was way too squeamish to train to be a vet. She had no idea what she was going to do at all. Maybe cross the road and work at the Angel Sands Diner, like the failure she was?

The café door opened, letting in a warm breeze. Ally looked up to see Lorne Daniels shuffling in. He was wearing a pair of bright floral board shorts that revealed his thin, weatherworn legs. On his top half was a denim shirt with the sleeves cut off, leaving a white frayed edge. For as long as she could remember, Lorne had run the surf shop next door to the café – and for all that time he'd been her father's best friend.

"Hey." She smiled at him. It wasn't his fault her dad was being a jerk. "You want a coffee?"

Lorne nodded at Ember and Brooke. "Mornin', ladies." Then he turned to Ally. "Your dad called. He wants you to call him back."

From the corner of her eye she could see Ember bite down a smile. This was one of the problems of living in such a small town – everybody knew your business. In five minutes time Frank Megassey from the hardware store would probably come in with the same message, along with Deenie Russell from the bookshop.

Luckily, Ally only had to raise her head to see the upside of living in Angel Sands. The amazing beach and the beautiful ocean, sparkling like it was full of a thousand diamonds. You won some, you lost some, but overall there was nowhere else she'd rather live.

"I'll call him back soon," Ally said, smiling at Lorne. He was one of her favorite people. She always took him a coffee as soon as she opened up in the morning and the two of them would sit on the sidewalk and watch the sun come up, sipping at their drinks until their first customers arrived.

Another thing she'd miss if she left this place.

"Don't leave it too long, he's worried about you."

"Well he should be," Brooke said. "We're all worried about her."

Lorne clicked his tongue and nodded, his leathery face giving nothing away. "I know you're hurtin', sweetheart, but he's your dad. He's made mistakes and he knows that. But at the end of the day blood is blood."

Ally felt the lump in her throat grow to the size of a rock. There was a part of her that knew Lorne was right. "Yeah, well he hasn't acted like that recently. I've been trying to keep this place going while he's been living it up halfway across the world. And after all I've done he's selling it right from beneath me."

"He's got his reasons I'm sure." Lorne shifted awkwardly on his feet. "He loves you, that much I know. I'll let him know you'll call him when you're ready, but don't leave it too long."

Ally nodded. Her chest felt too full of emotion to say anything. Anger, sadness, fear of the future, they were all mixing together and making her heart ache. She wanted to get out of here. To pull on her running shoes and head up the coast to where the mountains began, stretching her muscles and pushing her lungs until she could think of nothing else. Running was her happy place, the one thing that helped her manage her thoughts and get through the day. And right now she needed it more than ever.

Everything was changing, and she didn't like it one little bit.

"You okay?" Nate asked Riley, glancing at her out of the corner of his eye. They were parked outside of her new school, the car surrounded by students rushing by as they headed for their first class. The sky above them was a sparkling blue, the air outside warmer than it ever was in Seattle, yet his daughter's face had the look of a storm.

"I could have driven," Riley told him. "I bet I'm the only junior who has to rely on her dad to get her to school."

"After what you did to your last car, I think you're safer with me or the bus."

"It was an accident." She didn't need to add 'duh' but he heard it anyway.

"I know." Nate could feel the frustration rise in him. This was supposed to be a new start for both of them, yet they were already arguing. He closed his eyes, his lids turning red beneath the bright sun, and took a deep breath.

"Do you know where you're going?" he asked.

"To the office to pick up my schedule." Riley had her hand on the door handle. "And then I'll head to the bathroom and kill myself before you do it for me."

"You're being over dramatic."

Riley's brow furrowed. "Seriously? You think I'm dramatic? You've just dragged me thousands of miles away from everything I know. I'm sixteen years old and I don't have a single friend here. I can't believe you're punishing me like this." She huffed out a lungful of air. "It's not fair."

"Hey, I'm new here, too. And I don't know anybody either. I've got to go to this coffee shop and introduce myself to all the staff and they're bound to hate me before I've even opened my mouth. Maybe we can compare our terrible days later over some pizza?"

That was empathy, right? The family psychologist had told him he needed to show it, even if it was harder than anything else he'd ever done.

"The difference is, you had the choice whether to move to this crappy town. I didn't. You made the decision for me, the same way everybody does, and I just have to go with it. Do you know what it's like to move schools in your junior year? Everybody already has their friends. Nobody's interested in a new girl. They're just going to look at me as if I'm some weirdo. Thanks, Dad."

Nate felt his heart rate begin to rise. "Ri..."

"I'm going to be late. I'll see you this afternoon." This time when she grabbed the handle, she opened the door.

"Are you okay catching the bus home?"

Riley gave a grunt as she climbed out of the car.

"Okay, well have a good day..." But she'd already slammed the door and was stomping up the sidewalk, her backpack slung over one shoulder, and her long hair falling over her face.

"See you later, Dad. Good luck at the new shop," Nate muttered, then pressed the button of his Lexus to start up the engine.

Yep, he was really killing it at this dad thing.

There was something special about running early in the morning. The sun was barely up, and most of the small beach town of Angel Sands was still asleep as Ally pounded her way down the boardwalk, her breath steady and her muscles strong in spite of the ten miles she'd completed. She still had a couple more miles in her – she could feel it – maybe a run up and down the beach would finish things off nicely.

Stopping by the café, she pulled her running shoes and socks off, and stuffed them by the front entrance. Like the rest of the shops on the boardwalk, it was shut up and silent. In an hour they'd all be opening up and the customers would begin to trickle in, but right now the boardwalk and beach belonged to the surfers and runners.

Yep, it was definitely her favorite time of day.

The sun had begun to rise behind the cliffs that bordered Angel Sands to the east, the bright orange rays stretching across the sleeping town. Ally launched her body forward, her long legs stretching as she pounded her way across the beach, the unforgiving sand making her thighs ache and her breath come faster.

God, she needed this. To forget about everything for a while. Her head was too full of thoughts about the café closing and trying to decide her next steps – the nothingness that running brought was welcome.

When she reached Paxton's Pier, she took a deep breath, leaning on a wooden post as she looked out at the sparkling blue ocean beyond. A small crew of fishermen were loading up their boats to sail out for that day's catch, calling to each other and laughing. A familiar bearded figure was walking up the boarded slats, his hands stuffed in the pockets of his cut-off jeans, a captain's hat jauntily angled on the top of his overgrown hair. She lifted her hand to wave, and Griffin waved back. She'd gotten to know him ever since her best friend, Ember, had started dating his own best friend, Lucas. They'd got on like a house on fire, enough for Ember to ask her if there was anything going on.

"No there isn't," Ally had said, wrinkling her nose up. "We're friends, that's all."

"Well you can't blame me for asking," Ember had said, grinning. "You're usually the first to see the romantic possibilities in everything. I'm only doing you a favor by pointing it out."

Ember had been right in one respect. Though Ally was only interested in Griff as a buddy, she usually *was* the first to spot the chemistry when her friends met a guy. It was so much easier with other people than it was with herself. She believed in love, she really did.

But maybe not for herself. If there was a Mr. Right out there for her, he was hiding so hard he deserved a medal. She'd almost given up hope of meeting him.

She made it back to the boardwalk half an hour before opening time. Lorne Daniels was already opening up the Forever Summer Surf Shop, next to the Beach Café. She smiled as she watched him clip the front doors open. He glanced at her as if he could feel the warmth of it, and squeezed his eyes together to block out the brightness of the morning sunrise.

"Mornin'." He nodded at her. "Looks like it's going to be another warm one."

He always said that, as though the weather in Angel Sands was anything else.

"Should be good for business," she replied, nodding at him. "Did you make it out for a surf this morning?"

"With these old bones?" he asked her. "No, ma'am. I decided to have an extra half hour in bed. You've got enough energy for the both of us." His tone was teasing.

"Speaking of which, I should go and grab my shoes." Ally glanced over at the café she'd been working in for the past ten years. "I need a shower before I open up. The time ran away with me this morning."

Lorne cleared his throat, still staring at her. "Have you spoken with your dad?"

"Since he told me about the sale? No." Ally looked down at her feet; they were covered in sand. She wiggled her toes to try and brush it off. "I haven't called him back yet." Or listened to the voicemails he'd left in the special folder. She was still too hurt, too angry to hear them. Ember had been right, she should wait for a week or two until she felt better.

He was her dad. She wanted to get over this, not burn any bridges between them.

"You should talk to him." Lorne's voice was kind but firm. "At least so you know what's going on with the sale. Frank Megassey said he saw some out of town contractors eyeing the place up yesterday. Do you know if the sale's completed yet?"

Ally felt a shiver work it's way down her spine, in spite of the warm weather. "I've no idea." Maybe she should listen to those voicemails when she went home to shower. "I'm guessing it will take a while, though."

"I wouldn't be so sure."

"There's not much I can do about it. But I'll keep you updated if I hear anything." That's how it worked here in Angel Sands. Either you told people what was going on or they made assumptions. "I'd better go," she said, glancing at her watch. "I'll bring you a coffee as soon as I've opened up. You still taking three sugars?"

"Of course."

Ally smiled. Lorne's wife was in a constant battle to try and reduce his sugar intake. She'd asked Ally to only put two sugars into his coffee, but he'd realized right away. "I'll bring you a cake too, if you promise not to tell Marcie."

Lorne touched the side of his nose with the tip of his crooked finger. "Don't worry, your secret's safe with me."

A minute later, Ally walked around the side of the Beach Café, stooping down to wipe the sand off her feet as she reached for the shoes and socks she'd stashed behind the trashcan.

But there was no sign of them.

Ally frowned. She quickly scanned the rest of the deck, wondering if she'd put them somewhere else. But as soon as she turned the corner, all thoughts of her shoes disappeared. The main door to the café was wide open.

She licked her lips, the taste of saltwater lingering on her tongue as she peered inside the open door.

"Jeff is that you?" she called out, wondering if the chef had made it in early for once. She walked inside the café, the tiles cold against her bare feet, and called out again, her voice stronger this time. "Did you steal my shoes?"

A loud bang came from the kitchen, before the door swung open revealing a dark-haired man wearing a pair of tailored grey pants and a white shirt, the sleeves rolled up to reveal his tanned forearms. He reached up to run a hand through his thick brown hair, slowly lowering his gaze from her face, down past her spandex-clad body, his brows rising up as he spotted her bare feet.

Nope, that definitely wasn't Jeff.

She followed his gaze, grimacing at how long overdue her pedicure was. When she looked back up, the man was still staring at her.

Their eyes met with a clash.

She opened her mouth to ask him who he was, then snapped it closed again. Because in her heart she knew. This dark-haired, smoothly dressed man with a suit that seemed to love every inch of him was the new owner of the beach café.

"Uh, hi. Can I help you?" Nate said to the blonde who was giving him the strangest of stares. "We're not really open yet, so I can't offer you a coffee."

She shook her head, her brow still pulled down into a frown. He could see two tiny lines furrowed deep into the skin between her eyes. Christ, she was pretty, with those big blue eyes and golden hair.

"Are you okay?" he asked when she hadn't replied.

"Um, yeah." She let out a mouthful of air. "I work here." He watched as she bit her lip then released it again. "My name's Ally."

"You're Ally Sutton? The manager?" Damn. This wasn't exactly how he'd intended to introduce himself. "I'm Nate Crawford. I just bought this place." He reached his hand out to her. She gave him the hastiest of shakes, as though she was afraid to touch him.

She stared down at her palm for a moment, as if he'd burned it, before bringing her gaze up to his. "I don't suppose you know where my shoes are, do you?"

"Your shoes?" His mouth turned suddenly dry.

"I left them on the deck," she told him, "but they're gone."

"Those were yours?" he asked, his eyes widening. "I thought they were trash. I threw them in the can out front." He pulled at the collar of his shirt. Was it getting hot in here? "I'm sorry, they looked really old and beat up. I didn't think..."

"They're worn in. Not beat up," she almost snapped. Her frown deepened, if that was even possible. "It takes weeks to get them to feel right." She turned on her heel – her bare heel – and walked back to the doors, stepping out onto the deck where the trashcan stood. Nate followed her, stopping behind as she peered in, a frown on her lips, staring at her shoes resting on a layer of wrappers and peelings.

Nate stared at the shoes over her shoulder. They really were beaten up. She couldn't blame him for thinking they were abandoned.

Could she?

"I can't believe you threw them away." Okay, she could totally blame him. She shook her head again, and looked straight at him, and looked straight at him, their gazes colliding once again. "I guess I'll have to find something to cover my feet with and walk home."

"I can give you a ride," he offered, feeling terrible. This wasn't exactly how he'd planned meeting his first staff member. And the manager at that. "My car's in the lot over there." He pointed at his dark blue Lexus, keeping his voice as conciliatory as he could.

Damn, this was a bad start. He'd arrived early so he could take a good look around without any of the staff following him or trying to explain why the oil was so dirty or the coffee grounds were reused five times. Once done with his perusal of the café, he'd planned to let himself out and sit on the deck, waiting for the manager and the cook to arrive, then introduce himself formally before they all went in.

But instead he'd been caught in the act. And even worse he'd thrown the poor woman's shoes away. Christ, he was an idiot. "I can reimburse you for the shoes," he said, grabbing his wallet from the back pocket of his pants. "How much were they?"

"I don't want your money. I can buy my own shoes." Her

tone was resolute. She stared back at him, unblinking. He couldn't help but be impressed by the way she stood her ground.

"Can we start this all again in a little while? After you've gone home and gotten some shoes?" He pointedly looked at her feet again. "Once the rest of the staff are here we'll have a meeting."

"But we need to open this place up. Customers will be arriving soon. They'll want the coffee to be hot and ready for them. We'll lose business if they see it's closed up." She glanced at her watch. "Damn, I'm already late."

"It's okay, I didn't intend for us to open today anyway. We'll probably need to close for a week or two while the renovations happen and we train some more staff. I'll drop you at home and you can take your time getting ready. There's no need to rush."

She looked down again, as though she'd only just remembered she was wearing spandex. A crop top and tight shorts that clung to her, accentuating every curve. He looked away, determined not to be *that* guy. Even if she was crazily attractive, with her glowing, tan skin, her pink cheeks, and her sun-kissed blonde hair twisted up into a knot.

"You're closing it? For a week! Or two!" She blinked as though the sun had hit her eyes. "But what about our customers? We never close."

He looked at her for a moment – only from the face up. He figured that was safe enough. "Ally, I really appreciate your commitment to customer service," he began, trying to find the right words to encourage her out of there. He needed to be able to look below eye height at some point in time that day. "But the customers will understand. They might even be excited. It's not every day Déjà Brew moves into town."

A flash of recognition passed her eyes. "That's who bought this place? Déjà Brew?"

"You've heard of them?"

"Who hasn't?" Ally asked. "They're like the McDonalds of coffee." Her eyes widened as soon as she'd said it. "Oh god, that's your company, isn't it? You own Déjà Brew? I'm sorry." She lifted her hand to cover her mouth, and her face – already pink from her running – deepened in color. "But seriously, you're planning on changing this place?" She shook her head a little, as though trying to jolt her thoughts down. "Are you renaming it too, or will it still be the Beach Café?"

"All our outlets are called Déjà Brew. Our customers like that." He shrugged. "And you're right, we do try to offer our customers the same experience, too. It doesn't matter if they're in Seattle, Sacramento, or Angel Sands. They know their latte is going to taste good." He smiled. "It's a formula but it works."

"It won't work in Angel Sands," Ally told him. Was that a smug tone he could hear in her voice?

"Of course it will. It works everywhere."

"Did you look around town the last time you were here?" Ally asked, sounding impassioned. "Did you spot any chain stores among all the boutiques and bakeries?"

"No," Nate conceded, his voice low.

"And there's a good reason for that. The locals and the tourists don't like them. They prefer one-of-a-kind places, like this café and the surf shop next door. They love looking for books in a little independent shop that's run by the same woman who's owned it for the past forty years."

"Ally," Nate said, his voice even, "I promise you I know what I'm doing. Your customers are going to love the new outlet, and so will all the new customers we attract. But I need your help with this. You know the town and you know this place." He gestured at the café with his hand. "You're the most important member of the team." He pulled the keys out of his pocket and walked toward the door. "Let me take you home and we can start again later."

"I can walk." She sounded defeated. "It's not that far."

"In bare feet?"

She wiggled her toes. "Yeah."

He opened his mouth to argue, then shut it. He had enough experience to know when he was defeated.

"If you're sure..."

"Of course I am. What's the worst that can happen?"

✺ 3 ✺

Well at least now she knew what the worst was, and she was still trying to clean it off her feet under the hot spray of her showerhead. Who knew gum could stick that much? After a few attempts at trying to yank the big wad of sticky goo from her bare sole, she'd resorted to jabbing at it with the end of her razor. It finally fell off in a huge lump in the shower tub. She tried not to heave as she lifted it up with the tips of her fingers and threw it in the bathroom trashcan.

On the bright side it wasn't glass. Or something a dog had squeezed out. And anyway, it was worth it to have walked out of the café with her head held high.

Or as high as it could be when you're walking in bare feet and you have no idea if you'll have a job in a couple of weeks time.

She climbed out of the shower, wrapping a towel around her body and using a second one to dry the spray off her long hair. She twisted it into a turban and walked down the hallway to her bedroom, yanking her closet door open to try and decide what to wear.

In front of her hung the same old clothes. Shorts and

24

denim skirts, t-shirts and tanks. A couple of sweaters that were only dragged out on the rare occasion the temperature dipped. She'd once had a raincoat that had stayed on its hanger for two years before she'd donated it to Goodwill, tags still attached.

In the end she picked a pair of navy shorts and a blue striped top that knotted at the waist. And when she'd pulled them on and managed to coax her damp hair into a messy topknot, she sat down on the bed and stared at herself in the mirror her mom had fixed to the wall when they'd first moved into this place twenty years ago. She could remember them looking around it, and her mom being so proud to be able to afford their own place with her wage from Newtons' Pharmaceuticals. And at the time all Ally could think of was the fact it was a condo, and there was no swimming pool.

Looking back, she regretted that day so much. Hated that she'd failed to understand how hard her mom must have worked to keep a roof over their heads. And she'd never had a chance to tell her that. Instead, she'd lost her mom when she was still a hormone-ridden, sullen teenager, too busy rolling her eyes to see her mom for who she really was. Her passing was sudden and shocking, and Ally thought about her every day.

For years after her mom's death, while she'd lived with her dad in his bungalow over on the other side of town, they'd rented the condo out. Her mom's insurance had paid some of the mortgage off, but they'd relied on the rental income to cover the rest. When Ally had left school and started working at the café, she'd decided to move back in to the condo. Her wages weren't amazing, but they were enough to cover what was left of the loan and the additional bills she had to pay every month.

Without them she wouldn't be able to live here anymore. She pulled her legs up close to her chest, wrapping her arms around her knees, trying to comfort herself. Having to move out of this place would cut her like a knife. It was her one connection left to her mom. She could sit in the kitchen and remember how it used to feel as she finished her assignments at the square table when her mom rushed in from work and would immediately throw some food in the stove. Then there were the Christmases – the ones when it was her mom's year to have Ally for the big day itself and they'd stay up late on Christmas Eve watching movie after movie. By that point Ally knew the truth about Santa, but her mom never batted an eyelid. She'd tell Ally to go and put her stocking out at the foot of her bed, and when Ally walked into her bedroom she'd see a new pair of pajamas waiting for her on her bed, a little note from Santa attached.

She still bought herself a new pair of pajamas every year, putting them out on Christmas Eve in memory of her mom. Nobody else knew about that, not even Brooke or Ember. It was a secret, *their* secret, and she kept it between herself and her mom.

If she was really honest, the thought of having to move out of this condo was one of the things that was motivating her to get dressed and walk back to the Beach Café. She needed a job, and right now that was her best option.

The other thing? It was the café itself. Like her home, it had been such a huge part of her life ever since she was a child. And now that her dad had left, it was her only connection left to the life she used to live. She'd lost her mother, and her dad showed no signs of coming back to town. The Beach Café felt like the only thing she had left.

Except it wasn't hers, was it? It now belonged to Déjà Brew and its handsome owner. She closed her eyes for a moment, remembering how dismissive he'd been of the café and it's history. He hadn't wanted to hear her explanations, even though she'd worked there for the past ten years. He'd made it perfectly clear that he didn't care about the culture in Angel Sands, or what the locals preferred.

In fact, Mr. Déjà Brew wasn't interested in her opinion at all. And wasn't that just a kick in the teeth?

———

Nate was on a phone call to the building company who were booked to do the refurbishments when the door to the café opened. He looked up to see an old man walking in, wearing a pair of baggy surf shorts and what looked like it used to be a white t-shirt before it became grey thanks to over-washing.

"I'm sorry, we're closed right now," Nate told him.

"So I see. You the new owner?" The old man had his arms folded across his chest the same way Riley had the previous day. Nate tried not to smile at the comparison.

"That's right. Nate Crawford." He held out his hand. The man looked at it for a moment. Then he reached out his own hand and gave Nate's a brief shake.

"I'm Lorne Daniels. I own the surf shop next door." Though his tone was neutral, his eyes were narrowed.

Ah, a fellow business owner. Nate had learned to tread carefully there. You couldn't tell if they were the type to embrace change or be fearful of it. Plus there was the Déjà Brew brand – that always polarized opinion.

"It's good to meet you, sir. I hope we don't cause you any problems by being closed for the next couple of weeks. I know a lot of business around here rely on footfall, but I can guarantee that once we're open I have plans to increase our traffic by fifty percent. That should hopefully spill out to the rest of the shops, too."

"I don't care about the footfall. I have enough turnover to keep things going. I want to know your intentions toward Ally Sutton."

27

"I'm sorry?" Nate's brows knitted together. "I don't have any intentions toward her. I mean she's a beautiful woman and everything, but she's really not my type." Had Lorne spotted him taking a surreptitious look at Ally when she'd been standing in front of him with all her spandex-clad glory?

"I don't mean *those* sort of intentions," Lorne replied. Though his face remained expressionless, Nate could have sworn there was a twinkle in the old man's eyes. "I mean are you going to keep her employed here? That girl's like a daughter to me. I want to make sure she's taken care of. In fact, there are a lot of people in Angel Sands who feel the same."

"She'll stay working at the new coffee shop. I promised her father."

"Huh. And I suppose you'll be leaving town as soon as the café is up and running then?"

"No, sir," Nate said. "I plan to stay around while my daughter finishes high school. After that I'll be heading back to Seattle."

"You and the wife?"

"It's just me and Riley."

Lorne gave another 'huh'. It really was halfway between a hum and a choke. Nate had to look twice to see he was okay. "That's what they all say," the old man muttered.

Nate frowned. "That it's just them and Riley?"

"No. That they're only in town for a little while. But what *they* don't know," Lorne said, leaning closer, as though he had the best secret to tell. "And what *you* don't know either, Mr. Crawford, is that once this place has its hooks in you, you'll never want to leave."

"Is that right?"

"Yes, sir. I suppose you've heard the story of the angel?"

Um, no he hadn't. Nate didn't particularly want to hear it now either. He wanted to go back into the shop and get things ready for the staff meeting he was planning to have, and later the renovation company would arrive, ready to begin work on the place.

"That's how this town came to be built, you know," Lorne said, even though Nate hadn't had a chance to reply. "A lost man was looking for somewhere to call home. His name was Captain Paxton and he was sailing around these shores looking for a place to anchor up. Then he looked into the sky and saw an angel hovering ahead, her arm stretched out and pointing to this very bay. And though his entire crew thought it was too dangerous, too rocky and too shallow, he steered his ship inward and came to rest just where Paxton's Pier is today." Lorne nodded his head. "And even if you can't see her, the angel's been showing lost people their way home ever since."

That was all very well, but this wasn't Nate's home. It was just a place he hoped Riley would be able to see out school for the next year and a half. Without flunking out, without getting kicked out, and preferably without being thrown into jail.

"That's a good story."

Lorne shook his head. "It's a stupid story. Everybody knows Captain Paxton was a drunk."

"He was?" This conversation was more than confusing. Nate wanted it to end, and soon.

"Yes, but that's a story for another day. Okay, then. As long as we're clear on everything." Lorne nodded, more to himself than Nate. "You understand?"

"Sure," Nate lied. "Completely."

"Well have a good day. And remember to treat Ally right." With that, Lorne turned on his heel and left, walking out a lot faster than he'd walked in.

Nate took a deep breath and shook his head, because, seriously?

He wasn't sure what just happened.

A crowd had gathered on the boardwalk by the time Ally made it back to the Beach Café, a much bigger one than she'd seen waiting for a coffee in a long time. She smiled at Deenie Russell, long-time owner of Books on the Beach, and Deenie waved back.

"We were just looking for you. Are you okay, sweetheart?" Deenie reached out for Ally's hand and squeezed it.

"Is it true that you're closing up the café for a few weeks?" Frank Megassey asked, staring at the sign Nate Crawford must have pasted on the locked door to the café. "For renovations? Nobody's asked me about helping with materials."

And from the dark tone in his voice he wasn't happy about it one bit. Everybody in Angel Sands knew that Frank supplied the best materials and tools. He knew about every renovation in town.

Except this one, it would seem.

"It's just for a couple of weeks," Ally said, staring at the closed doors. "The new owner wants to brighten the place up. It's been a long time since those walls saw a lick of paint."

"Who's the new owner?" Frank asked, inclining his head to try and look through the glass. "Do I know him?"

"Or her," Deenie said, shooting Frank a dark look.

"I don't think so. It's been bought by a chain," Ally told him, trying to keep her voice as upbeat as possible. She might have told Nate what she thought about his plans, but that didn't mean anybody else needed to know. "You might have heard of them. Déjà Brew."

"I told you." Lorne raised his eyebrows at Frank. "See, I'm not such an old liar after all."

"Déjà Brew?" Frank repeated, rubbing his thick beard

with his fingers. "Drink it once and we guarantee you'll be back?"

"You've seen those ads too? They're catchy as hell, aren't they?" Deenie said. She turned her warm eyes on Ally. "What does this mean for you, honey?"

"There's a job for me in the new place if I want it."

"And do you want it?"

Ally forced her lips into a smile, deciding a lie might be better than the truth. "Yes, I do. This could be a great opportunity for Angel Sands. The tourists are going to love it." Think positive, right? That way she might even begin to believe it herself.

Maybe.

She reached for the door handle, curling her fingers around the metal, feeling the warmth of it against her palm. For a second she remained still, her chest tightening at the thought of all the changes that were happening. From the youngest age she'd seen that as a bad thing.

Changes meant people left her. They meant she'd be pushed this way and that, like a piece of jetsam floating in the ocean.

Opening her lips, she took a jagged breath in, and squared her shoulders. She wasn't that little girl anymore, and there was no need to be afraid. She was surrounded by friends. Nothing bad was going to happen.

"Well here goes nothing," she whispered to herself, pushing open the door.

It was time to face the future – *her future* – and whatever it was, she could handle that.

"You're giving us two weeks off?" Jeff's face lit up as he leaned forward and grinned at Nate. "Seriously? That's fantastic." He paused for a moment then frowned. "Wait, I'm still gonna get paid, right?"

"Yes, you'll be paid. And you'll need to come in toward the end of the second week for training along with the new staff. I want us to hit the ground running when we open."

It was funny how easy it was to gain the loyalty of some people. Jeff looked as though all his Christmases had come at once. Ally, on the other hand, was biting her lip at what he'd just said. As though he'd told her she was fired rather than offering two weeks paid leave.

He couldn't work her out at all.

"Sure, great. Can I go now?" Jeff stood up and rubbed his hands together, a big smile splitting his face. "See you in a couple of weeks. Thanks for the time off, Mr. Crawford. You sure are a great boss."

It might have been Nate's imagination, but he thought he saw Ally shudder at this. "Yeah, sure, you can leave now. I'll send some paperwork through the mail to you. And I'll call you with the dates for training."

Whether Jeff heard or not, Nate wasn't sure. The cook was already halfway out the door by the time Nate finished speaking. As the door closed behind him, Nate turned to look at the woman sitting opposite him. Her elbows were resting on the table, and there was the strangest expression on her face. She was impossible to read.

God she was pretty, though. Not that he should be noticing – she was an employee. And after the debacle with Stephanie, he was pretty much done with relationships for life. What woman in her right mind would want to get involved with a guy with a teenager? Ally Sutton might have a body to die for in that spandex running gear, but he was a grown up, he could push that out of his mind.

"Is everything okay?" he asked her.

He noticed she was drumming her fingers on her thighs

beneath the table. "Um, yeah, it's fine." Her whole body started to move to the rhythm. "Are you sure you don't want me here?" she asked him. "Won't you need someone to show you where everything is? The electric box, the water supply, all that jazz? I'll happily hang around to help."

"Your father's lawyer sent us the plans for the place. They include all the utility points. I have a whole team of people who plan out the renovations and liaise with our construction companies. They have it under control." That didn't make her look any happier. The smile slipped from Nate's lips. "Seriously, Ally, if anybody deserves a break it's you. I looked at the staff rosters before I bought this place and I saw how many hours you'd been putting in."

She shifted in her chair, her fingers still drumming. "I like working," she said. "I don't believe in doing anything half-baked."

Yeah, he could see that about her. And it only made her more attractive. Another good reason for her to take two weeks off so he could concentrate on getting the latest Déjà Brew up and running, without being distracted by those lithe, tanned legs.

He cleared his throat. "You won't be doing anything half baked," he reassured her. "Once we're up and running I'm going to need all of your energy and concentration. I won't have the ability to be spending a lot of time here, so I'm going to need to trust you. That means that when we start training in a week's time, I need you well rested and ready to learn. So go home, relax, and enjoy your break."

He stood up and waited for her to do the same. When she did, he walked slightly ahead of her, gesturing to the door. She followed silently, opening it up, still unlocked from when Jeff had made his speedy escape, and turned back to look at him.

"Go on," he said, giving her an encouraging nod.

Nate had spent most of his life surrounded by women in one way or another, but he'd never quite understood them. Chuckling softly, he walked back to the counter and rolled open the plans the building contractors had couriered over, making sure everything was ready for the construction team.

Later that night, Nate lifted a whiskey glass to his lips, taking a moment to smell the aroma of the warm grain before tipping his head back and letting the liquor coat his tongue. He'd been working since the early afternoon, setting up his office at the back of the house, chairing two video conferences with his staff in Seattle, and making phone call after phone call to try and trouble shoot some zoning issues.

He'd stopped at seven, long enough to ask Riley if she wanted something to eat, to which she'd shrugged and slumped down on the sectional sofa, closing her eyes as though to make a point.

He'd ordered pizza. She hadn't come when he called, but when he went out to pour himself a drink twenty minutes ago, he noticed three slices had disappeared. At least she was eating – that was one thing to be grateful for.

Nate glanced at the framed photograph on his desk. It had followed him from office to office for years, starting in the cramped room above his first coffee shop, before moving on to bigger rooms as his business grew. For the past four years it had been on his large polished oak desk in downtown Seattle, where he'd had the best view over the city.

It was a photograph of a small child with a huge gap-toothed smile. That's how he remembered Riley as a little girl – she laughed so much and so loudly you couldn't help but join in. He could have closed his eyes and picked her out just from hearing her chuckles. When was the last time he'd heard those?

In those days he'd only seen her on the weekends and during the holidays. He'd leave the coffee shop early on Friday afternoon and make the drive north to Mount Vernon, where Riley lived with her mom, and pick her up before turning right around to take her back to Seattle. On Saturday she'd help him open the shop, laying out the pastries with concerted effort, remembering not to lick her gloved fingers in between each one.

She'd long since stopped coming with him to work. In the past couple of years, she'd barely wanted to come and visit with him in Seattle at all. He'd understood her reluctance – all her friends were in Mount Vernon, along with the gymnastics studio she trained at four times a week. What thirty-something old father could compete with that?

And then suddenly, shockingly, they were forced together. Two people who had only ever spent short periods of time with each other. Along with this massive grief that his daughter carried with her and Nate had no idea how to deal with.

Nor did Riley. So she did everything she could to show the world she was angry at it. And now they'd moved almost a thousand miles south to California. It had felt like a good idea swapping the city for the beach. Taking Riley to a much smaller town that had less crime and a lot more fresh air. But his daughter clearly disagreed. He should be used to that by now – they disagreed on pretty much everything. And yet he couldn't help but feel frustrated at their lack of understanding.

He drained his glass, standing up and carrying it out of the office to the kitchen, where he put it in the dishwasher drawer. Then he closed the pizza box, sliding it into the refrigerator in case Riley decided to creep down for a midnight snack. He shook his head at the contents of the fridge – everything in there looked unhealthy. A trip to the grocery store was in their very near future.

He might be failing her in every other way, but he could at least look after her nutrition.

Flicking the lights off in the hallway, he set the alarm for the doors, softly padding down the hallway to his bedroom. Riley's room was two doors down from his – he'd deliberately given her that room so she could have some privacy. He stopped outside it, breathing softly as he wondered whether to knock on her door or not.

Then he heard it. A loud sob followed by a shuddering breath and it cut right through him. Nate swallowed hard, his chest aching. He knocked on the door and pushed it open. Riley was curled up on her bed, her body shaking as she cried, her hands covering her face in an attempt to muffle the sound.

This time he didn't hesitate for a moment. He walked right over and scooped her up, holding his daughter against his chest, stroking her hair as she wept. He dropped his face into her hair, whispering that it was okay, that *she* was okay, mumbling little tiny words that didn't seem like enough at all.

And right then she was the same little girl he'd once known. The one who clung to him when she was scared, and jumped into his arms when she was happy. And right now, she was desperately sad and he had no idea how to make things better.

But he'd promised himself that he wouldn't stop trying.

❧ 4 ❧

Ally pulled up short on the sand and bent in two, her lungs working overtime as she gasped for air.

Three days. That's all it had been since she'd last worked at the café, and yet it was long enough to feel like she was going crazy. She'd cleaned her condo from top to bottom, and the local Goodwill had been the lucky recipient of six huge bags full of clothes and accessories she'd managed to clear out in her desperate attempts to keep herself busy.

Her whole body ached, not only from the constant activity at home, but also from the grueling runs she'd been going on, each one longer than the last. Yet none of them had managed to remove the constant fizzing from her veins. That's how she used to try and describe it to her mom when she was little. It was as though somebody had removed all the blood from her and replaced it with bottles of soda, the liquid making her limbs feel jittery and desperate to keep moving.

She'd been eight when that feeling first started. Her pediatrician had run test after test before referring her to the child psychologist, suggesting it may be a psychosomatic response to her parents' then recent divorce. But her mom had baulked at the psychologist's suggestion of putting Ally on medication, choosing instead to try and help her daughter with a combination of exercise and meditation. For the most part she'd succeeded, too. Though Ally had been more active than the average child, her energy had been manageable.

It was only in recent years that it had gotten worse again. And right now it was almost excruciating to stand still for too long. She had to keep moving or she'd explode.

Her phone ringing was a welcome distraction. She grabbed it immediately, a warm feeling washing over her when she saw Ember's name on the screen.

"Hey." She couldn't help but smile. Ember did that to people.

"Hey. Are you okay?" Ember asked. "I thought I'd give you a call while I have a break." Ember worked as a Kindergarten teacher at Angel Sands Elementary School. A glance at Ally's watch told her it was lunch time there. "I stopped by at your place after work last night but you weren't there."

"I was probably at Goodwill." For her third visit. "Or maybe I was running."

"You can't have been running. You went out yesterday morning, remember? Lucas said he saw you on the beach."

And that's exactly where she was right now. Unlacing her shoes ready to run all the way over to Silver Bay and back again to feel the rush of air through her lungs. "I've been running twice a day," she admitted. "It's too lovely out here to be cooped up indoors all day."

Ember laughed. "Tell me about it. The children are driving me crazy. I could barely get their attention this morning. They were too busy looking out of the window to listen to me."

Ally knew exactly how they felt. She could remember the agony of having to sit still at school, completely unable to concentrate on what the teacher was saying at the front of the class. No wonder she'd had to work so hard to keep up her grades. And thank goodness for athletics club. Not to mention gymnastics and swim team.

"Have you heard how the renovations are going at the café?" Ember asked.

Ally glanced to her left. Okay, so she just happened to run past the café at least twice a day. And if she peeked in through the windows to see how they were going? Well that was just natural, wasn't it?

She pulled her socks off, stuffing them into her brand new running shoes, then carried them over to Lorne's surf shop – her latest hiding place, which happened to be very far from any trashcans. She was still upset about that. Still upset about everything really. In just a few days it felt as though her life had been turned upside down. And though she'd spent half of them running as fast as she could, she couldn't get over the thought that in reality she'd just been going backward.

"They've ripped everything out," Ally said, her throat aching at the thought. "All the old tables and chairs were taken away in a dumpster." Along with all those years and memories. Those booths, lined with tattered benches, had been a staple of her childhood. She'd sat there and watched as her dad served customers as a child. As a teenager he'd let her stand on the other side of the counter, filling up mugs with hot coffee and taking orders for Jeff to cook up in the kitchen.

"Oh sweets. That must be hard," Ember clucked sympathetically. Even though she'd been through her own troubles in the past few years – first with her fiancé, Will, leaving her after years of living together, followed quickly by Ember's beloved father dying so suddenly – she still worried more about other people than she did for herself.

That was one of the reasons why Ally was so happy her

CARRIE ELKS

friend had found love again with Lucas Russell, a lieutenant in the fire department. He took care of her, the way Ember took care of everybody else, and it was a beautiful thing to see.

"It's okay," Ally said, swallowing hard. "It needed a makeover anyway. I would have done it years ago if I could've afforded it." She took a step back, her feet sinking into the warm sand, and glanced over toward the café. Not that you could tell it was that anymore. Along with the furniture and the kitchen equipment, the signage on the front had also met its fate in the dumper truck. Now the building was bare, the old white paint half-peeled off where the signs had been removed.

It was hard to believe that in another few days the Beach Café – or Déjà Brew as it was now – would be ready for training to begin, before opening to the public.

Just a few more days. That's all she needed to get through before she'd be working again.

From the corner of her eye she saw the door open, and a loud cacophony of banging and drilling spilled out. Nate Crawford walked through the doorway, his phone held to his ear, his hand pressed against his other one in an effort to hear what the caller was saying. He wasn't wearing a shirt and dress pants today. In their place were a pair of jeans and a t-shirt that seemed to cling to every ridge of his body, and for a moment she couldn't help but stare at him.

"I guess I'd better go," Ember said down the line, bringing Ally's attention back to their conversation. "I need to get the classroom ready for this afternoon's lessons. Hey, did you want to meet up this weekend? We should take advantage of the fact you won't be working for once."

"Yeah, sure." Ally's reply was half-hearted. She was still staring at the man who had turned her life upside down. He'd walked away from the café and was leaning against the wall between the beach and the parking lot.

There was something about him that drew her in. Every time she looked at him she felt a little rush of pleasure, followed by a warming sensation that flooded her veins. And for a moment she didn't feel restless at all. As though she could have stood in the same place all day watching him.

Ugh. Stalkerish much? She shook her head at herself. Maybe it was seeing a man running the café again that was unsettling her. Reminding her of when her father was constantly behind the counter. Yeah, better not to delve down into that too much. The last thing she needed was a daddy-complex.

After Ember ended the call, Ally slid her phone back into the band fixed with Velcro around her bicep. Then she glanced back at her boss for one final time, leaning down to stretch out her leg muscles. But this time his head was up and he was looking right at her. The shock of their gazes connecting was like an electric prod to her skin. Her heart started to hammer in spite of the fact she hadn't moved at all.

Unlike Ally, Nate didn't look embarrassed to be caught looking. Instead he gave her a nod and walked in the opposite direction, as if he'd barely noticed her at all.

Licking her dry lips, she turned around and began to stretch, the soles of her feet pushing against the rough sand as warm gusts of air caressed her skin. Within moments her mind would be beautifully, achingly blank, and not full of Nate Crawford and the new café. And that was just the way she wanted it, because she was thinking about him way too often for her own good.

"She's sick?" Nate repeated, his brows pulling down into a frown. "What's wrong with her?" He had to shout to make himself heard. Until he'd taken this call he hadn't realized how loud the construction work was – he'd become immune to it after days of banging and drilling. He made a mental note to apologize to all the other business owners surrounding him. They'd been more than understanding about all the mess surrounding the café.

"Yes, Mr. Crawford," the school nurse replied. "She says she has a headache and feels dizzy. We've given her some pain medication and let her rest for the past half hour, but it doesn't seem to be getting any better. Hopefully taking her home will help." She sounded more sympathetic than Nate felt right then. Riley had been perfectly fine when she'd left for school that morning. Well enough to have a shouting match with him when he'd told her that he still wasn't getting her a car and she'd have to catch the bus home for the fore-seeable future.

Nate sighed. "Okay, I'll come over and pick her up." He ended the call and glanced at his watch. He had an hour before the building inspector was due to take a look at the work they'd done so far. Just enough time to pick Riley up and drop her off at home. Not enough for them to get into another screaming match. That was a win at least.

All the while he'd been talking, he'd been staring out at the beach. Well, not the beach exactly. If he was honest, his gaze was firmly on the woman warming her muscles up on the sand about twenty yards away from him. She was leaning forward, her hands clasped around her ankle as she stretched out her quadriceps.

Christ, she was flexible. Her entire body was perfectly formed. From her long, lean legs that led up to the flare of her hips, dipping into her small waist that was only accentuated by the spandex shorts she was wearing.

What she wasn't wearing, he noticed, were shoes. A flash

of guilt went through him again as he remembered throwing her last pair away. He wondered where she stashed them now? Not anywhere near the café, he was sure of that.

She looked up at him, her eyes widening as her gaze caught his. His breath caught in his throat, and for a moment nothing else registered. Not the sound of the construction work in the café, nor the softer splash of the ocean as it kissed against the shore. It was just the two of them alone on the beach.

Dear God, he was seeing things that weren't there. And even if they were, they shouldn't be. He gave her a quick nod, trying to dismiss the heat that was rushing through his veins. Turning away, he began to walk toward the parking lot, ready to drive to the high school and pick up Riley.

By the time he turned back, Ally had started to run, the muscles in her thighs tensing as she made her way down to the water's edge. He watched her for a moment, impressed by her strength as well as the form of her body.

Shaking his head at himself, he turned back to the car. He wasn't some hormonal teenager. And he had enough things to worry about, with Riley and the café, not to mention being thousands of miles away from his growing business. The last thing he needed to be doing was admiring Ally Sutton's muscles.

And with that thought, he tried to push her straight out of his mind. Whether it worked, remained to be seen.

Ally loved this part of the beach, where the buildings and the tourists gave way to nature. She ran past the dunes and skipped over the rocks, heading toward the tiny cove where she used to come for picnics with Brooke and Ember. The three of them would stuff themselves full of whatever they'd managed to grab from their parents' kitchens, barely able to eat because they were all talking too fast about whatever the latest school gossip was, or more often, about their crush of the month.

Ember used to bring her iPod and speakers with her – that was back in the days before they had smartphones to keep them company. They'd play music and dance themselves silly without fear of anybody seeing them. Ally smiled, remembering how Ember would fling out her arms and spin until she dropped.

Those were good times. She missed them. Now they were too busy to spend more than a few hours together. Ember had her relationship with Lucas, and Brooke had her son, Nicholas, to take care of, and on top of that they were both so busy with their jobs and school. Ally's eyes began to sting and she blinked, blaming the salty air that carried up from the water.

She came to a stop in the middle of the cove, stretching out her arms, and feeling her chest open as her fingertips reached out into the air. Then she spun herself around the way that Ember always used to, starting slow, before turning faster, her hands whooshing through the air as her body turned in circles.

She'd forgotten how it felt to be this free. To not care about the fact she was getting dizzy, nor that any moment she'd be too lightheaded to remain upright. Instead, she kept turning, her body leaning to the left, the air escaping her mouth in a shout of joy.

By the time she fell over her blood was rushing through her ears, echoing the sound of the waves crashing into shore. She collapsed on her back, flinging her limbs out in a starfish position, feeling her body still moving in circles even though she'd stopped.

As the sound of her rushing blood died down, it was

replaced by something strange and high pitched. Ally cocked her eye open, glancing out of the corner. She saw a young girl standing there, laughing her head off at this adult who'd spun herself until she'd felt sick.

"Glad I amused you," Ally said, not feeling quite stable enough to sit up yet.

The girl shook her head and laughed again. Ally opened her other eye and attempted to focus on her. She looked a little familiar, but she couldn't quite place her. "Do I know you?" Ally asked.

"Nope." The girl shook her head. "I'm new in town."

Slowly, Ally sat up. Her stomach was still lurching. "Then you probably don't know that this is our town dance. Everybody who lives here has to do it."

"Bullshit."

Ally blinked. "Okay, so I *might* be making that bit up. But don't you ever want to spin until everything else disappears?"

"All the time." The girl sat down and pulled her knees to her chest, circling her arms around them. "But what I'd really like to do is spin myself out of town and back home. Wherever the hell that is."

The girl sounded despondent. If only Brooke was here. Or Ember. Both of her friends were so much better at talking to children than Ally was. She was more used to taking their food orders and telling them to get their feet off the benches.

"Don't you like it here?" Ally asked, grasping for anything to say to the girl. "I'm Ally by the way."

"Riley," the girl replied. "And no, I don't like it here. I prefer Seattle where there's actually something to do. Do you know all everybody talks about is the beach? When they're going to sunbathe or surf, or go and grab an ice cream from the parlor. If you took the sand away there would be nothing to do at all."

"There's the mountains," Ally pointed out. "Lots of people go hiking up there."

"But what about the movies and the mall?" Riley replied. "What about hanging around and going out to eat together? There's nothing fun to do around here."

"Déjà Brew is opening up an outlet at the beach," Ally said. "I've heard it's pretty popular with kids."

The girl let out a strangled scream that made Ally jump. "Do you know how much I *hate* Déjà Brew?" Riley asked, her nose wrinkling up. "I hate it with the power of a thousand angry demons."

"Wow," Ally replied, her brows rising up. "That's a lot of hate. What did the place ever do to you?"

"My dad owns it." Riley shrugged. "Isn't that enough?"

Ally felt the air rush out of her lungs. "You're Nate Crawford's daughter?"

Riley frowned, tipping her head to the side. "How do you know my dad?"

"I work for him."

The girl's lips twitched. "At Déjà Brew? Oh god, what on Earth did you do to deserve that? Torture kids? Kill a cat?"

"Is he that bad?" Ally asked, biting down a smile. There was something about this girl that she liked.

Riley leaned forward, her voice lowering. "He's much, much worse. Take my word for it. Run as fast as you can. And whatever you do, don't look back."

This time Ally couldn't stop herself from grinning. She loved the way teenage girls were so dramatic – she could remember being that way herself. Maybe she still was sometimes; ignoring her dad's calls being a case in point. "Well I guess I should be going now," she said, standing up and brushing the sand off her. "I have another couple of miles to run." She nodded at the girl. "I'll see you around, Riley."

Riley finally smiled, and it lit up her face. "Not if I see you first. And definitely not at Déjà Brew."

Ally raised her eyebrows, lifting her hand in a goodbye. And as she left, ready to continue her run, she could see Riley begin to spin around the same way Ally had done only ten minutes earlier.

It was strange how happy that made her feel.

❦ 5 ❧

"**Y**ou're early." Nate pulled the door to the café open. She wasn't expecting him to have a smile on his face, but there it was, wide and natural. Ally was momentarily disarmed. She had to curl her fingers up and dig her nails into her palms to snap herself out of it.

"I thought it would be good to make the right impression, since it's my first day," she said as Nate stepped aside to let her pass. Her bare arm brushed against his, and for a second she felt the warmth of his skin through the thin fabric of his shirt. But then her attention was taken by the interior of the shop, and she looked around with wide eyes.

Everything had changed. The walls were painted a deep matte blue, and the floors were freshly laid with polished walnut planks. There was a new counter, too, deep black with a shiny steel top.

"What do you think?" he asked. She felt her mouth go dry. It looked amazing, and yet her heart ached at the sight.

"It's nice," she said, her voice thick. "You've done a great job."

He was still looking at her, she noticed. His eyes scanned

her face as if he was searching for something more. She tried to swallow down the emotion that was coursing up inside her. Now wasn't the time to mourn the demise of her dad's old café. It was time to look forward.

She glanced over at the counter again, noticing the huge espresso machine placed behind it. She'd never seen such a big one – it was a stainless steel monster. Even worse, it looked complicated as hell.

Nate glanced behind him, as though he was following her gaze. "Shall I take you through the equipment?" he asked her.

"*You're* doing the training?" Ally widened her eyes. She hadn't expected him to be the one to show her the ropes. But a glance around the café told her it was only the two of them in there.

"Yeah. It'll be a lot easier for you to learn if somebody shows you. We have corporate videos, of course, and manuals. But I have a couple of spare hours so..." He shrugged, trailing off.

"Will the other staff be joining us?"

"No. Once I train you, it'll be your job to train them. They'll be coming in later this week, ready to open on Monday. But as the manager, you're the most important one right now."

She tried to ignore the little shiver that snaked down her spine at the thought of them being alone in here. It didn't matter how good he looked with his sleeves rolled up to reveal his golden skin, or how every time he looked at her she felt her body heat all over. He was her boss. He owned the whole damn company, after all. And she was way too old for crushes.

Shaking her head at herself, she squared her shoulders and followed him over to the counter.

"Have you ever used a machine like this before?" he asked

as they walked. "I don't remember seeing one in the inventory."

"We used to have an automatic machine," she told him, taking the apron he offered her and knotting it behind her waist. "But it looked nothing like this." She took a deep breath, deciding to be frank with him. "If I'm being completely honest, I don't know that much about coffee. We ordered ours in from the same place for years. I used to scoop it into the filter and let it brew. If it smelled good and strong then it worked."

Nate was silent for a moment. She looked down, embarrassed at her own admission. But then he cleared his throat, and she felt the warmth of his stare on her face without even having to look.

"Why don't we start with the basics?" he suggested. "In fact, grab a seat." He pointed at a stool. "I'll give you a brief history of the coffee bean."

"Seriously?" Her lip curled into a half-smile.

He shrugged. "Why not? We've got all day."

Really? He'd said earlier they only had a couple of hours. Refraining from commenting on that, she did as she was told, sitting on the stool next to the counter, as Nate reached below and pulled out three jars of beans.

"Did you know the word coffee comes from the Arabic for 'wine of the bean'?" he asked her, opening one of the jars and tipping some out into his palm. "Once you get to know all the different varieties you'll understand how similar to wine it is. There's a different bean for every kind of palate." He dropped a single bean into her hand, and curled her fingers over it. "This one's a light roasted bean from Brazil."

"It feels oily."

"It's the roast," he said. "Lift it to your nose. Tell me what you smell."

She held the bean to her face, inhaling it in. For a second

she closed her eyes. "It's almost nutty," she said, letting the aroma take over her senses.

"Now try it."

"Try it?" She looked up at him, her voice full of questions.

He nodded. "Put it in your mouth."

Nate stared at her intently as she opened her lips and pushed the bean onto her tongue.

"What can you taste?" he asked.

"It has an earthy flavor," she said softly, her eyes still connected to his.

"What else?" His voice lowered. He'd moved close enough for her to hear his breath.

"It's sweeter than I thought."

"It's not as strong as some of the darker roasts," he said. "But it has more caffeine than they do."

He held another bean out. "This one's a medium roast from Ethiopia," he told her. "Can you tell the difference between this and the last one?" he asked, placing it onto her palm.

She slipped it into her mouth, and closed her eyes. It was better that way. Less personal. Something about it being just the two of them was making her senses feel raw. As if he could see right through her and knew how attractive she thought he was.

"It's not as oily," she whispered, rolling the bean around her tongue. "And it has more pep to it. It almost tastes fruity."

When she opened her eyes, she saw his lips curl up into a smile. "You've got a good palate," he told her, nodding slowly. "Not everybody can tell the difference."

She flushed at his approval. "You're a good teacher. You make it seem easy."

He opened his mouth to say something, then obviously thought better of it, turning around to grab a tiny glass cup from where they were stacked on the side. "Now, I'm going to show you how a good espresso should look."

He turned and placed the cup on the machine, then pulled at the lever above until it came loose. "This is the porta filter," he said, turning to show it to her. It's where we put the coffee in." He held it beneath another machine – this one full of beans. When he pressed a button it started grinding them, and coffee powder spilled into the filter.

She watched as he pressed it down with something he called a 'temper' before he put it back in the espresso machine. There was something about his easy competence that made her lean forward, her eyes glued to the movement of his hands as he fixed the porta filter back in.

He pressed a button and the water was forced through the filter, pushing out a deep colored coffee.

"You can't leave an espresso standing for more than thirty seconds," he told her, turning to place the cup in front of her. "That doesn't give you much time to either serve it or make up whatever drink the customer has ordered. Speed is of the essence."

"What happens if you leave it for longer?"

"You have to throw it away and start again." He shrugged. "Believe me, we go through a lot. Can you see the three layers?"

"Yes," she said, smiling. "It's darker at the bottom. Then a little lighter, and at the top it's almost white."

"The top part is called the crema. If you get these three layers you know you've made a good espresso. If there's no crema you try again."

"You want to taste it?" he asked, his fingertips brushing hers.

She nodded, lifting the cup to her lips. She could feel the heat steaming up, as it misted the top of the glass. She blew at the surface before slowly tipping it up and letting the hot, black liquid coat her tongue.

Nate leaned his elbows on the counter, his face inches from hers. "What do you think?" he asked.

"It's exquisite."

His eyes caught hers again. It was crazy how often it was happening. Even crazier the way her heart hammered every time it did. Neither of them moved, blinked or even breathed. For a moment everything was still.

And then it was like a curtain had been pulled down. Nate pulled his gaze from hers and pushed himself away from the counter, taking her cup and rinsing it under the sink. "Okay, it's your turn to make one," he said, still looking away.

Oh God, this time she'd really embarrassed herself. No wonder he pulled away, he must have seen the way she was staring at him. Gritting her teeth, Ally stood and walked around the counter, tightening her apron as she made her way to the imposing espresso machine. She felt better with a few feet between them – enough space to be able to breathe. She swallowed hard and told herself to stop being so weird. He was her boss. That was all. Maybe she should behave like an adult without embarrassing herself for once.

"Wish me luck," she said, still not looking at him. She had a feeling she was going to need it.

***

Nate watched as Ally pulled the porta filter from the machine and slid it beneath the coffee dispenser the way he'd shown her. There was at least four feet between them right now, he'd made sure to hang back as far as he could, but right then it didn't seem far enough.

He felt an overwhelming urge to touch her. He had to hold tightly to the counter to stop himself from doing it.

Christ. He blew out a mouthful of air and took a step back. Best to keep the distance between them. He was her boss, for God's sake.

Not to mention old enough to be her father. Or a much older brother, at least. Somehow that didn't make it feel any better.

Ally pushed the filter back into the machine and pressed the button. But instead of forcing the water through the coffee grounds, the steam pushed the filter off where Ally hadn't fixed it on properly, and coffee grounds flew everywhere. "Oh shit." She grabbed a wet cloth and wiped it all down, glancing over at Nate with a rueful smile.

"It's okay," he said, glad of the diversion. "It happens. Try again."

This time the coffee came out when she hit the button, filling the little glass cup with dark liquid. She glanced at her watch and then at the cup before picking it up and carrying it over to him. "You have twenty seconds before it's no good," she told him.

He lifted it up, inspecting it. "Three layers," he murmured. Then he brought it to his lips and drank from the cup, letting the warm, nutty flavor envelope his tongue.

Her eyes were full of anticipation as she waited for his verdict, the same way Riley used to look when she was a kid, holding a drawing out for his inspection. "It's good," he told her.

"Really?" she asked. "You like it?" Her lips curled up into a huge grin, and she clapped her hands together with delight.

"Yeah. I think you've got the hang of espresso. Now let's move on to the steamed milk. I'll show you the difference between cappuccinos, lattes, and flat whites."

"This is so much more fun than I thought it would be," she told him, that smile still curling her full lips.

She was right. In spite of the need that was thrumming in

his veins, he realized he was having more fun than he'd experienced in a long while. "I don't get a chance to use the machines very often," he admitted. "Normally the only equipment I spend my day on is the laptop. I've missed doing this." Back when he'd had his first coffee shop, Nate had spent most of his life attached to an espresso machine, but it had been years since he'd done more than have a little play with them.

"I guess that's what happens when you rise to the top. You stop doing the thing you actually love and get to watch all your employees do it instead."

"Yep. You're not wrong." A wistful expression crossed his face.

"Maybe it's a good thing you came to Angel Sands, then," Ally said. "You can relax and have fun for a change."

The corner of his lip quirked up. "Yeah, maybe."

Ally took the cup back from him and turned around to rinse it. Nate watched as she bent over to turn on the faucet, her blonde hair flowing over her shoulders. "I met your daughter the other day," she said, her back still to him. "She seems nice. Is she settling in okay?"

"You met Riley?" Nate blinked. For some reason her words pushed him off center. "Where?"

Ally turned back, grabbing a towel to dry off her hands. "At the beach. It was last Wednesday, I think. I was on my lunchtime run."

Wednesday. That was the day he'd brought her home sick, and left her in her bedroom while he ran back to the coffee shop to meet with the building inspector. He frowned. "She told me she wasn't feeling well."

Ally grimaced. "Ouch. And I just ratted her out. So much for the sisterhood."

Nate sighed. "Don't worry. She's done much worse."

Ally wrinkled her nose. "Is it really that bad?" Her eyes

were full of understanding. "If it makes you feel any better, I was a pretty painful teenager. I'm surprised my dad stuck around as long as he did. I made his life a misery."

"You know what? That does make me feel a bit better."

Ally raised an eyebrow. "Hopefully things will improve soon. Is she any better for her mom?"

"Her mom's not around anymore." Nate's voice dropped low. "She died earlier this year. That's one of the reasons we came down here. To try and make a new start." *Another one.* Which right now didn't seem to be going any better than the last.

Ally's voice was soft. "I'm so sorry. I swear I say stuff before I think it through sometimes." She reached out and touched the top of his hand with her own. The shock of the contact made him feel jittery. "No wonder things are so tough for you both."

Her hand felt warm and soft against his. He swallowed hard, trying to ignore the strange electric sensation shooting up his arm. He slowly pulled his own hand away, not sure whether or not he was relieved at breaking their contact.

He cleared his throat to try and get rid of the lump that was forming there. "Okay, then," he said, trying to keep his voice even as he reached for a stainless steel jug. "Let's try out a latte."

6

"Have you got everything?" Nate asked, as Riley stomped down the hallway with her bag slung over her shoulder. She gave him a look that told him all he needed to know. *Yes*, she had everything, and *no* she didn't appreciate him asking.

He took a deep breath. "I want you to come to the coffee shop after school," he told her.

She frowned. "Why? You know I hate it there."

"Because I want you where I can see you. Not hanging around at the beach or wherever else you've been for the past few days."

She let out a huff. It was big enough for her shoulders to drop forward until her posture resembled that of a Neanderthal. "That's so unfair. I have an assignment to do. I'll come home and do it."

"You can do your assignment at the coffee shop. I'll save you a table."

"Is this about last week? I only went to the beach for a moment. I was sick, remember? I needed fresh air."

"You could have gotten fresh air by sitting on the deck,"

Nate pointed out.

"But it's not salty air, is it? Salty air is what I needed. All those kings and queens of England used to head to the beach whenever they felt ill. I saw it on the history channel."

He still hadn't gotten used to her having an answer for everything. He remembered the days when her eyes would widen as he told her how the earth revolved around the sun, or that stars were always out but you could only see them at night. Now she was so smart – smarter than he ever was at her age – and she liked to use it against him whenever she could.

"Well I don't see a crown on your head, so I'll see you at the coffee shop at three." He raised an eyebrow. "I'll make you a hot chocolate with all the trimmings."

And there was the eye-roll, right on time. "I hate hot chocolate. And anyway, it's like a hundred degrees out there, who wants hot chocolate when you can barely breathe?"

Nate bit his tongue even though it had only just got up to seventy degrees. Sometimes it wasn't worth fighting back.

"Three o'clock," he repeated.

Another huff and she was out of the door. Nate grabbed his bag and his car keys and followed right after her, heading for his Lexus.

"Hope the opening day goes well, Dad," he said to himself, muttering as he unlocked the car. He was talking to himself again. *Great.* His descent into madness was almost complete.

"Is everybody ready?" Nate asked as he walked over to the door. Ally looked over at the team she'd spent the past few days training. Jeff was standing in the doorway to the kitchen, where the ovens were on full blast. She'd been surprised to learn that all the food was made on site at Déjà Brew, rather than being delivered every morning like so many other coffee shops. But then she was beginning to see how much attention to detail Nate put into his business. His success seemed well-earned.

In the days since he'd trained her on the coffee machine, he'd been friendly but reserved, and she'd taken his lead. It was better that way. She really didn't need to be having feelings for the man who'd taken her beloved Beach Café away. It was hard enough that she was working here for him. Better to keep as much distance between them as possible, even if it was only in her head.

"We're ready." Ally nodded at him. They were expecting an influx of customers as soon as he opened the door, and she had four baristas hovering by the espresso machine ready to pick up the orders.

The opening day was the talk of Angel Sands, mostly thanks to the flyers that had been delivered everywhere, promising free drinks to the first two hundred customers.

A huge line had already formed outside Déjà Brew by the time Nate pulled the door wide open. He stepped back and the first customers swarmed in, rushing across the walnut floor to be the first at the register.

"What can I get you?" Ally asked, smiling at Frank Megassey. Of course he'd be the very first customer.

"A coffee?"

"Sure. What kind? They're all up there on the board behind me." She turned and pointed to the huge wooden board fixed to the back wall. "Would you like a latte, a cappuccino, or maybe a macchiato? That's got chocolate syrup in it."

Frank's eyes widened. "Um, just a coffee will be fine. With a little milk."

Not wanting to push it, Ally nodded and called over to

the barista. "One medium Americano with room and hot milk please. In the name of Frank."

Frank looked at her expectantly, not moving. Ally smiled at him. "If you head over to the collection area at the end of the counter, Brad will make your coffee right up."

He frowned. "You're not going to make it for me?" he asked her. "You always make it the way I like it. Just a little milk, and then you sneak the sugar in while Mrs. Megassey isn't looking."

The line of people behind him was getting bigger. And they were getting restless. "No, Frank," she said, trying not to smile too much. "It's like when somebody orders something big from your store. They pay at the register and you pick it up from around the back."

"Is everything okay?" Nate asked, walking up beside Frank.

"Ally just said I have to pick my coffee up at the back," Frank told him. "Isn't that a strange way of doing things?"

Nate caught her eye, his brow rising up. She bit her lip because the urge to laugh was growing. "I was explaining to Frank that you pay here and go down the counter to pick up your drink," she told him. "A bit like at the hardware store."

"Come with me," Nate said, inclining his head. "I'll show you where to pick it up."

"And he'll show you where we keep our stash of sugar, too," Ally said, leaning forward to whisper. "Nobody will see, I promise."

The morning flew past. Even after they'd served the two hundred free drinks, customers kept spilling in. All of them had managed to mess a few orders up, but everybody was in such good spirits it really didn't seem to matter. Ally couldn't remember the last time the place had been so full of loud chatter and deep laughter. And she was pleased, she really was, but there was a little bit of her deep inside that felt some sadness, too. No matter how hard she'd tried, she hadn't been able to keep the café going the way it always had.

And that failure hurt.

Well, suck it up, buttercup. Because this was how it was going to be. There was no going back to the old days. And why would she want to? The truth was she was going to be better off all round working as an employee of Déjà Brew than spending all her savings – and all the hours God gave her – trying to keep a failing café afloat.

"Has everybody had their break?" Nate asked her, as the afternoon stretched on. The traffic was still steady, but they were finally able to take a breath between orders.

"Yep. Alex and Brad finish in an hour, so I've arranged for Christie to cover us until close."

"How about you?" Nate asked her. "Have you had your break?"

"Have you had yours?" she countered, grinning. "Anyway, what would I do if I took a break? Sit and read a book?" She widened her eyes to show him just how crazy that thought was. "I'm better off keeping busy in here."

The door flew open and Riley walked in, stopping dead in the middle of the floor as she looked around. She caught Nate's eye and pointed to herself. "I'm here as commanded, sir." Then she took a bow – a real-life, deep one. Ally had to bite her lip not to laugh as the girl did a little flourish with her hands.

"How was school?" Nate asked, lifting an eyebrow at her antics. Ally watched the two of them with interest. Though she'd met them both, it was the first time she'd seen them together. Had people watched her and her dad in the same way back when she'd spent most of her teenage years here? For a moment she could picture them, Ally's head down as she squinted at her indecipherable math homework, her dad leaning over the counter trying to help her.

She swallowed hard and pushed those memories out of her head.

"It sucked." Riley put her bag on an empty table and pulled out her books. "A sucky day and now a sucky afternoon. I'm just loving it here in California. I'm so pleased we came." Her voice oozed with sarcasm. The cherry on the cake was her pretend valley-girl accent.

Nate opened his mouth to reply, but right then the door opened again and a whole load of high school kids entered the shop. They oohed and aahed at the décor, then squealed as they looked at the cakes and cookies nestling in the glass cases.

"Oh god, this is amazing," one of them said. "So much better than the café. Remember how embarrassingly bad that was? Thank God somebody put it out of its misery."

"Yeah. I swear they made their hot chocolates out of the dirty dishwater."

Ally felt herself flush. She looked down at her hands, not wanting to catch their eyes – or Nate's. She didn't want them to see her reaction, or the way her eyes had watered at the criticism. She swallowed hard, and grabbed a cloth. "I'll just go and clean some tables," she muttered, leaving the other baristas to serve the teenagers.

There really wasn't much to clean. Most drinks were served in paper cups that the customers disposed of on their way out. Gone was the need to stack up plates with one hand while wiping with the other. Now she sprayed and polished before moving on to the next table. From the corner of her eye she noticed Riley sit down at a table in the far corner, throwing her bag on a seat while Nate went back behind the counter. She scrubbed at the table top harder, trying to ignore the frown on Nate's face.

"How's it going?" she asked Riley when she reached her table. The girl had spread out her work and was leaning over it, her hair flopping over her face. It took a minute for Ally to realize she was wearing earphones that meant she couldn't hear a thing. Still, she must have sensed something because she looked up with a start, pulling one of the buds out.

"Um, did you say something?" Riley asked.

"I was just asking how it's going," Ally said, giving her a smile. Yes, she was bolshie as hell, but Ally couldn't help but feel some sympathy for her, especially now that she knew her mom had died only a few months before. "Would you like a drink?"

Riley eyed up the swarm of high school girls who were giggling with Brad as he took their orders. "As long as I don't have to go up there."

"I'll bring it over," Ally said. "Tell me what you want and I'll go get it."

Three minutes later she carried two cups of iced latte to Riley's table. She passed one to the girl. "You mind if I sit with you for a minute?" she asked.

Riley glanced over at the counter. "You sure my dad won't yell at you for slacking off?" she asked. "Because he can shout really loud when he wants to."

Ally raised her brow. "I'm due a break." She didn't bother to tell her she rarely took one.

Riley shrugged, so Ally sat down, taking a sip of her icy drink. She glanced at the book Riley was working from. "Algebra?" she asked, her voice sympathetic. "I swear it was invented by some evil genius to drive me crazy."

"It's not so bad," Riley said. "Better than Spanish anyway."

"I was bad at that, too," Ally confessed. She'd been pretty bad at all subjects except for physical education. "We had this teacher, Senora Palmer, and every time I tried to speak she'd scream 'yo no entiendo' to me. Sometimes when I fall asleep I can still hear it." Ally grimaced.

"She's still there. And still screaming it."

"Shut up!" Ally grinned. "She was old when I was at school and that was over ten years ago."

"Maybe she's one of those vampires that never ages a day," Riley said drily. "All I know is she can't hear any of us and she thinks it's our fault."

"Some things never change." Ally took another mouthful of drink. "How are you settling in otherwise? Your dad said you moved down from Seattle. Do you miss it?"

"Seattle? No. I miss home, but that was never Seattle."

Ally hesitated for a moment. Should she say something about Riley's mom? She could remember how intense everything felt when she was a teenager. How she hated people offering sympathy about her mother when they hadn't even known her. No, best to wait for Riley to bring it up.

"Well this isn't such a bad place once you get used to it. There's the beach for a start, plus the mountains. If you enjoy being outside there's always something to do."

"Did my dad ask you to tell me that?" Riley inquired, her expression suspicious.

"No." The truth was, Ally was enjoying this conversation. Talking about Riley's problems was a great way to distract her from her own.

"Yeah, well I'm not exactly the outdoorsy type," Riley told her, leaning back in her chair and folding her arms in front of her.

"You looked pretty outdoorsy on the beach the other day." Ally leaned forward. "Especially when you fell over."

"You fell over first."

Ally grinned. "Yep. And it was the most fun I've had in a while."

"You should get out more."

"I probably should. But I've got this new boss and I hear he's a dragon."

"Touché." Riley nodded, her eyes serious.

The teenage girls who'd been standing by the register moved down the counter to pick up their drinks. Ally heard their laughter get louder as they approached. Riley slumped down in her chair, as though she was trying to avoid them.

Ally remembered how that felt, too. Trying not to be the center of the mean girls' attention. On a whim, she grabbed a piece of paper from the pocket in her apron, and scribbled on it with a pencil. Leaning forward, she passed it to Riley.

"What's this?" Riley asked.

"It's my number. You're new in town and you probably don't know many people yet. But if you ever need some help, or someone to talk to you, please call me."

"Why? I hardly know you."

But I know you, Ally thought. *Or at least I know who I used to be at your age.* "My name's Ally," she said. "I've lived in Angel Sands since birth. I've worked here since I was fourteen and I hate beets. There, now you know me."

Riley looked at her as though she was crazy, but slid the piece of paper into her pocket anyway.

"You'd better get back to work," she said, raising her eyebrow as she looked over Ally's shoulder. "Before my dad cracks the whip."

Ally turned to see what Riley was staring at, and sure enough, Nate was watching them both from where he stood at the counter. Ally couldn't quite fathom the expression on his face.

"Yeah I had," Ally agreed, standing up and grabbing what was left her drink. "But I meant what I said. Call me if you need a friend. Day or night."

"Yo no entiendo," Riley said, offering her a ghost of a smile.

"Your Spanish is better than your spinning," Ally said, shooting her a grin. And for the first time, Riley smiled back.

7

"Hey big brother. How's it going?" Nate's sister, Kirsten asked. Nate balanced his phone between his shoulder and his ear and glanced at his watch. It was almost seven in the morning – which made it ten in Boston, where Kirsten was studying for her law degree. "Is the new addition to your empire looking good?"

He smiled and leaned on the counter. The coffee shop was due to open in twenty minutes. From the corner of his eye, he could see an old tattered box one of the subcontractors found at the back of the kitchen in one of the cupboards they hadn't remodeled. He'd put it to the side and forgotten about it until now. He'd been about to throw it away when a photograph had fallen out and he'd recognized those familiar blue eyes staring back at him.

"It's early days, but it's going well so far."

"And how about you?" Kirsten asked. "Are you enjoying the Californian lifestyle? Have you taken up surfing yet?"

"Not quite. I'm too busy working in the coffee shop for that."

"I thought you had a manager. Weren't you planning on

working from home as much as you could?" Kirsten sounded confused. "You know, to spend more time with Riley?"

"Yeah, but I'm helping out too. Plus Riley seems to like it here." After that first day of frowning from the moment she'd walked through the door, Riley had stopped complaining about having to come to Déjà Brew every day after school. In fact, she seemed to be enjoying it.

And she'd been spending a lot of time with Ally, he'd noticed.

Nate liked it here, too. He enjoyed sitting at a corner table with his laptop. Liked the atmosphere, the sound of the waves as they crashed against the shore.

And, yeah, he might have liked watching a certain manageress as she served the customers.

"Don't the staff find it intimidating having you there all the time?" Kirsten asked him.

Nate frowned. "Why would they?"

"Because you *own* the company. They must feel like they have to be constantly on their best behavior."

"You think so?" He wasn't sure what to make of that. "I really don't think I'm that scary."

He frowned, thinking for a minute. The staff always seemed happy to see him. Brad had called him over when he came in yesterday to show him his new latte art, grinning like crazy when Nate had complimented him on it.

And Ally didn't seem to mind at all that he came in every afternoon. She was all smiles whenever he walked into the shop, and he had to admit he liked that a lot.

Here in Angel Sands he felt like another member of the team. That made him feel welcome. He couldn't remember the last time people had treated him like a friend rather than a boss.

"It depends how grumpy you are with them," Kirsten

teased. "Hopefully not too much. Talking of which, how's Riley settling in?"

"Not too bad," Nate admitted. "I think she only screamed at me four times last week." And that was a massive improvement on the week before. "She's made a few friends at her new school, too." Another reason why he liked dropping into the shop. He'd pretend to be busy behind the counter, but seeing his daughter smile as she spoke to Ally made his heart swell about three sizes bigger.

Riley had the prettiest smile when she remembered to use it. He could barely recall the last time he'd seen it, but now she was cracking it out every day.

"Wow. Maybe California is good for the both of you. There's something about that sea air."

As much as he hated to admit it, there was definitely *something* about Angel Sands. He smiled to himself when he remembered Lorne's words of wisdom back on his first day renovating the shop. What was it he'd said?

Once this place has its hooks in you, you'll never want to leave.

Well he might not have a choice about leaving – he had a business to run after all. But right now he was happy to be here. And happy wasn't something he'd felt in a long time.

It was one of those rare California early mornings when there seemed to be more white cloud than blue sky. The lack of sun had turned the air cool enough for the weather forecasters to be muttering about rain, something that was uncommon enough here in Angel Sands for it to cause an outcry. On her way into work, Ally had noticed that Deenie Russell hadn't put her usual stands of books outside her shop on Main Street, and Lorne had only put a few of his brightly colored surfboards out on the boardwalk, leaving most of them below the tattered awning that hung from his shop.

"Hey!" she called through the door. She eventually located him in the far corner of the shop, scowling at a dispatch note. "You doing okay?"

"As good as it gets when you get to my age," he said, looking up from the sheet of paper he was holding. "They need to make WD40 for humans."

Ally laughed. "I'll bring you a coffee, since it's pretty much the same thing," she offered. "Milk, two sugars, the way you like it."

"No need. I already had me a latte this morning," Lorne replied, grinning. "It was all prettied up. Did you know they can draw a leaf in the foam?"

"Oh." She tried to knock the expression of disappointment from her face. She'd been bringing Lorne coffee ever since she was a teenager, but that didn't mean he had to wait for her to turn up like some kind of coffee fairy. "Is the shop open early?"

"Nope. Still shut. But Nate knows exactly how I like it." Lorne nodded his head approvingly. "He's managed to sweeten us all up with his drinks. Even Frank Megassey's succumbed to him. I saw him accept a cappuccino with extra sprinkles yesterday. All the chocolate and foam clinging to his moustache." Lorne raised his eyebrows. "He should act his age sometimes."

In spite of her long run that morning, she felt her muscles tighten as though they wanted to do it all over again. She took a deep breath, inhaling the salty air as it rose up from the shoreline.

So what if the locals were accepting Déjà Brew? That was a good thing, after all. They'd point customers their way, as well as being customers themselves. Nate was doing the right thing in courting them.

Even if it made her feel a little bit forgotten, along with the old Beach Café.

"Well, if you want another coffee later, give me a shout," she told him, smiling in spite of the tightness in her chest.

"I will. As long as you can make a latte as good as this one." He widened his eyes and took another sip, smacking his lips together with pleasure.

Lorne had gone over to the dark side. Who would have thought it?

Just as he'd told her, the door to the coffee shop was still locked. She pulled out her keys and let herself in, locking it up again until it was time to open in twenty minutes. When she turned around something caught her eye and she tipped her head to the side, her brow dipping as she looked at the counter.

There was an old battered box on there, the corners bashed in, the lid barely able to close thanks to whatever was stuffed inside. She frowned at how familiar it looked. Biting her bottom lip, she took a step forward, wanting to look inside.

"It's your day off."

She turned to see Nate walking through the kitchen door.

"I just had two weeks off," she told him, taking another glance at the box from the corner of her eye. "I thought I should probably make up the time." She was getting used to the way her heart galloped every time she saw her boss.

"Yeah, but that wasn't your choice," he said, that half-smile still crinkling the skin around his eyes. "You're an employee now. You don't have to keep this place running single handed. You can have a life too."

His words hit her like a slap in the face. She blinked, trying not to show her reaction. Maybe she should start wearing a ski mask every day. It had to be easier than forcing her facial muscles into expressions they didn't really feel.

Did he know that she was crushing on him? Oh God, please don't let that be true. Just the thought of it made her want to run again. Run and never stop.

She looked at the box for a third time, and this time Nate followed her gaze. "I found it in the store cupboard," he told her. "I think it must belong to you." He cleared his throat. "If you don't want it I can throw it away, but I thought it'd be best to ask you first."

Ally reached for the lid and pulled it off, looking at the mass of photographs stuffed into the box. She recognized them instantly, though it must have been years since she'd seen them. Her throat tightened as her gaze fell on the top one.

"That's my mom," she said.

"I thought it was you at first."

Ally glanced up at him, wondering if he was joking, but his expression was completely serious. "You think I look like her?"

He looked back down at the photograph. "Yeah. She was very pretty."

Ally wondered if he'd realized what he'd said. She felt her face flush at his compliment.

She lifted the photograph out of the box, holding it up in the light. It was faded, but still clear. Her mom standing outside the Beach Café, wearing a tank and a pair of shorts. You couldn't have placed her by the cut of her clothes alone – that kind of fashion was timeless. But Ally knew it must have been taken at least twenty years ago. Before her mom and dad split up.

Damn it, she was going to cry. And Ally rarely cried. Not when her father left. Not during the time she was trying to keep this place going and it felt like she was pushing huge rocks up a mountain. Crying meant people looked at you and asked questions. It was better to remain impassive.

She dropped her head and took a deep breath. Holding it for a moment until the emotions ebbed away, she looked back up at him.

"Can I have these?"

"Of course." He looked bemused. "They're yours."

She nodded but didn't reply. Didn't trust herself to.

"You should take these home. It's your day off, after all." His voice was gentle, as if he realized the impact of the photos. "You need your rest the same as everybody else."

"We have a late delivery tonight," Ally reminded him. "I should be here for that."

"I have it covered."

"And it's Tuesday. The historical society will be coming at four," she pointed out.

"I know. I'll have Jeff make some extra pastries."

"And don't forget Brad has a doctor's appointment." She frowned. "Are you sure you've got enough staff without me?"

"Go home, Ally." His smile was gentle. She felt a flush of warmth rush through her.

"I will. But call me if you—"

"Home." His voice was firmer this time.

"Okay, okay." If her arms had been free she would have thrown them up in surrender. "I'm going already. You don't have to throw me out of the door."

"I will if I have to," he warned, putting his hand on the small of her back, the pressure of his palm through her shirt sending a shiver up her spine. "Have a good day off and I'll see you tomorrow."

Yes he would. And damn if she wasn't looking forward to it already.

8

Ally shook her head and put the lid back on the photographs, carrying the box to her closet where she lifted it onto a shelf. She'd been sorting through them ever since she'd gotten home from the coffee shop, and her head was full of the memories and emotions they'd captured so perfectly.

Photographs of her mother, her father, of Lorne looking so much younger than she ever remembered him being. Then there were ones of Ally, ranging from when she was a baby cradled in her father's arms, right up to when she was a pre-teen with crooked teeth begging out for orthodontic treatment. They'd brought back memories of things she'd tried long to forget. Christmases spent with both her parents, summers lying on the sand with her mom. For a few hours she hadn't felt so alone any more.

But she was. Out of the three of them, she was the only one left in Angel Sands, and that thought sent a pang straight through her. Until her father had left town she'd still had something – someone – to cling onto. And right now, sitting in her empty condo as an unseasonal rain spattered against her window, she'd never felt more alone.

She laid the picture back on top of the others she'd piled up in the box. She wasn't ready to do anything with them yet – whether to catalogue them or put them in a fancy scrapbook the way she always planned to with photographs but never did. Instead she put the lid back on, hoping she could shut away the emotions she was feeling along with the photos.

She'd just slid the box into a shelf in her living room when her cellphone started to buzz. As she walked over to grab it she checked her watch. Three o'clock. It was unlikely to be her friends – Ember would be working and Brooke would be at college. It was more likely to be Nate asking about the historical society.

But when she picked her phone up the screen showed an out of area number. Ally slid her finger to accept the call.

"Hello?" she asked, still a little unsure as to who was calling, but thinking it might be Riley since the area code was the same as Nate's. Yep, she'd given the girl her number, but Riley had made no bones about the fact she wasn't intending to use it.

She heard a muffled voice, followed by some others.

"Riley, is that you?" Ally asked, raising her voice.

There was a laugh and some stomping, before the voices became a bit clearer. Wherever it was, wherever Riley was, she must have found some better reception.

"... it'll be fine. It's not that far down." Though the voices were clearer, they still sounded far away. It was only when she heard the reply – just as loud as Riley's – that Ally realized she'd been butt dialed.

"It's not that scary," a voice said.

"Riley?" Ally called a little louder, trying to make herself heard. But still no reply. Just more muttering and a shout of laughter that reminded her so vividly of being a teenager. She smiled and went to end the call when she heard something that chilled her blood.

"Are you sure it's safe to jump? The cliff is really high."

That was Riley's voice, she was sure of it. Ally sat up straight, her heart in her throat.

"Riley?" Ally shouted, not caring if she embarrassed the girl. "Can you hear me? Don't jump off the cliff."

Nothing.

"Riley? I'm calling your dad right now. Don't do it. Don't jump."

Ally's fingers were trembling as she ended the call and pulled Nate up in her contacts. She pressed 'call' and heard the dial tone repeat twice before his voicemail clicked in.

Shit, shit, shit.

"Nate, it's Ally. Please call me back."

She hit the end button and tried calling Riley, but that clicked to voicemail, too. Ally stood, her heart hammering against her ribcage and looked around her empty apartment, as though she might find a solution there.

Was Riley really going to jump?

Of course she was. And she wouldn't be the first. Ally could remember the kids back in high school doing the same thing – leaping from the cliff just past Silver Cove, where the ocean was deeper as it crashed against the shore. She could remember one of them having his arm in plaster from the tips of his finger right up to his shoulder, too, where he'd clipped the edge of some rocks as he'd plummeted into the water.

Her heart hammering against her chest, Ally ran into the hallway and pulled on her running shoes, nearly falling to one side as she got them over her heel. Grabbing her keys, she ran as fast as she could down the stairs to the parking lot, jumping into her car and starting it up.

It took five minutes to drive from her condo to the cliffs,

but each minute felt like it was stretched so thin it was almost breaking. She could feel her breath shorten as the adrenaline rushed through her veins.

Don't jump, Riley. Please.

There was no parking lot at the cliffs, but she could see a collection of cars parked at the edge of the road, and she pulled in behind them. In the distance, at the edge of the cliff, she could see ten or fifteen figures, all clustered together and pointing at the ocean below.

The rain hadn't eased off any since it had begun earlier that day, and the clouds had colored the ocean a foreboding dark grey. Ally felt the nausea rise up in her stomach as she saw the group step back, leaving a lone figure standing at the edge.

"Riley!" Ally called out, but the rain and wind swallowed her words. The girl wouldn't have heard her anyway. The group of teenagers were too loud, and she was too far away.

There was nothing for it but to run.

The ground was wet beneath her shoes, the grass slippery from the rain. Her running shoes skidded against the earth as she tried to speed up her gait, still calling at Riley not to jump.

One of the girls noticed her, and elbowed another who turned around to look. They shouted at Riley, who was right at the edge of the cliff, peering over with her dark hair falling around her face.

Riley slowly turned to look at Ally, her eyes wide with shock. Ally was so close now – only twenty feet away, and she opened her mouth to shout again, certain that this time Riley would hear her.

But it was Riley who shouted first. "Look out!"

Ally had no idea what she meant. Not until her foot hit hard rock instead of soft, wet grass, and she flew up into the air, weightless for a moment, before she came crashing down, her head hitting a rock, and her foot bending beneath her as her ankle gave a sickening crunch.

For a second, Ally felt nothing at all. But a heartbeat later the pain rushed in, shooting like knives from her ankle, and throbbing like a bitch on her head. Her breath felt too shallow, like it was caught in her throat and unable to make it to her lungs. She needed to sit up, to get up, but her muscles wouldn't move at all. It was as though she was pinned to the ground.

"She's bleeding from her head," someone said, leaning over her.

"Jesus, look at her foot. It shouldn't be at that angle."

The voices were muffled, as though she was listening to a butt dial all over again, but she could barely concentrate on what they were saying. The pain was too acute, too overwhelming. She had to grit her teeth together not to scream.

"Oh my God. Are you okay?" Riley asked, crouching down next to her. "Do you think you can get up?"

Ally couldn't reply. She had no breath left in her lungs. It hurt too much to even open her eyes.

"Should we call an ambulance?" one of the girls said.

Riley reached out to touch Ally's face. "I'm so sorry," she said, swallowing down a sob. "This is all my fault."

"It hurts," Ally managed to get out.

"Dude, that ankle looks pretty bad," one of the guys standing by Ally's feet said.

Yeah, it felt pretty bad, too, she wanted to say. But then another pulse of pain shot up from her foot and she let out a low groan.

"Okay, I'm gonna call 911," Riley said, patting Ally's hair as though she was a little girl. "And the rest of you might want to get out of here, because after that I'm calling my dad and he's definitely gonna kill me."

Nate rushed toward the hospital desk, breathless from running from the car to the building. "I'm looking for my daughter, Riley Crawford," he said to the nurse behind the glass. "I'm her dad."

"Riley Crawford," the nurse murmured, tapping something into her computer. "No, we don't have a Riley Crawford here."

"She's not been admitted," he told her, finally catching his breath. "She came in with a friend. She's sixteen, has long dark hair and a pale face." He looked around the waiting room, trying to see if he could see her.

"Is that her?" the nurse asked, pointing over his shoulder. He followed her gesture, and saw Riley sitting on a chair in the far corner, her legs pulled up to her chest as though she was trying to make herself as small as possible. "She came in about an hour ago," the nurse told him. "Her friend has been taken back for examination."

Nate nodded at the nurse before turning and covering the distance to his daughter. Her eyes were rimmed with red, her expression crumpled.

"Oh, Dad." She launched herself into his arms. Nate held her tight, his body slumping with relief. After everything she'd been through he couldn't bear to see her hurt. She might have driven him crazy on a good day, but she was his daughter, and he'd do anything to protect her.

"You're okay?" he asked her, her hair muffling his voice. "Not hurt?"

"I'm fine."

"And your friend? What happened to her?"

Riley looked up at him, and there was something different in her watery eyes. A look of fear. "It's not a friend exactly..." she muttered. "It's Ally."

Nate blinked. It took a second or two for him to connect the dots "*Ally Sutton*? From the coffee shop?" How on earth was she involved?

Riley nodded mutely.

"What happened to her? Why's she here?" Nate asked, every muscle in his body tensing. "Is she okay?"

"I don't know," Riley wailed, her words tumbling over each other. "She looked really hurt. She was bleeding from her head and her ankle was all swollen and I've no idea how she's doing. Nobody will tell me."

"How did she get hurt? Was it a car accident? Did you see it happen?"

Riley shook her head. "She was running and tripped on a rock."

Jesus. Nate closed his eyes for a moment, then opened them again because he could picture her slamming against the sharp, jagged stone, and could almost feel how painful it was. She had to have hit it damn hard to have the injuries Riley described.

"Where?" he asked her. "At the beach?"

As soon as he asked, he knew there was more to the story than his daughter was telling him. He only had to look at the guilty expression on her face. "Riley?" he asked, his voice a little rougher now. "What happened?"

"I'll tell you," she said, "But you have to promise not to kill me." She looked around. "Because I have about a hundred witnesses here."

"Miss Sutton?"

Ally slowly opened her eyes. It took a couple of attempts because they were stuck together with gunk. "What?" she said, frowning as she looked around. Oh yeah, she was in the hospital, with a foot that hurt like hell…

Except it didn't any more. Well that was interesting.

A woman was leaning over her, dressed in green scrubs. "I'm Doctor Southern," she said. "How are your pain levels on a scale of 1 to 10?"

Ally thought for a moment. Yeah, the excruciating pain in her leg had gone, but she could feel her whole body throb with a dull ache. "Um, two or three."

"That's good. We're pumping some pretty heavy painkillers into you right now, so I'm glad to hear they're working. As you can probably feel, we've put your leg in a temporary cast. The x-rays show a clean break in your ankle. I'm hoping you won't need surgical intervention, but we won't know until the swelling goes down and we give you a CAT scan."

"I had an x-ray?" Ally asked, frowning. "Was I unconscious?"

Doctor Southern smiled. "Not unconscious, but you were a little out of it. It'll probably come back to you slowly." She picked up the white pad at the end of Ally's bed and scribbled something on it. "We also had to put a couple of stitches in your head. There's no permanent damage there, but there's always the danger of concussion. Do you have somebody who can sit with you tonight?"

"You're releasing me?" Well that wasn't so bad. At least she wouldn't have to stay here any longer. Ally couldn't wait to get back home.

"Yes, if you have someone to take care of you. Then you can come back tomorrow for us to fix you up."

She considered lying. Inventing a friend or a family member who wouldn't mind dropping everything and sitting by her bed all night to make sure she was breathing.

But what if she actually stopped breathing and nobody was there?

"I live alone," she said. "And everybody I know works. I couldn't ask them to do that."

The doctor looked way too sympathetic for Ally's comfort. "It's not like I don't have any friends," Ally added. "I'm not a loser or anything. I'm just very independent."

"I'd like to keep you overnight then, just to be safe," the doctor said. "But you're really going to need somebody to support you when you go home. You could be in a cast for up to twelve weeks, and using crutches, too. It takes some time to get used to the decreased mobility."

"Twelve weeks," Ally repeated, her voice faint.

"It might be less. We'll know more when the swelling goes down." She hooked the clipboard back in place. "Now, try to get some rest and I'll arrange for you to stay the night. Oh, and you have a couple of friends asking about you. Is it okay if I let them know how you're doing?"

"Sure," Ally agreed, letting her head fall back on the pillow. She really did feel drowsy. Maybe it was something to do with the painkillers. Whatever it was, her eyelids were fluttering before Doctor Southern made it out of the door.

And as she heard the creak of the hinges and the door close behind the doctor, the last thought that made its way through Ally's conscious mind made her want to shiver.

She wasn't going to be able to do any running at all for the next three months, right when she needed the distraction the most.

❧ 9 ❧

"Oh sweetie, you look awful. How are you feeling?" Brooke sat down in the chair next to Ally's hospital bed, wincing as she took everything in. "I can't believe you did all this just from tripping over a rock. It must have been so painful."

"It wasn't a lot of fun," Ally said, her voice croaky. She took a sip of water from the cup next to her bed. "But the painkillers are great. I don't feel a thing right now."

"Only you would go out running in the rain," Ember said. She'd taken the chair on the other side of Ally. Her fiancé, Lucas, was sitting at the end of the bed, and gave Ally a reassuring smile when she looked over at him.

"I wasn't doing it for fun," Ally pointed out. "I was trying to stop Riley from jumping off the cliff."

Lucas sat straight up at that. Always the firefighter, he was alert at the first sign of danger. "It's okay, Lucas," Ally told him. "She didn't jump."

"I'll never get why kids do stuff like that," he said, shaking his head. "As if there aren't enough dangers around already, they have to invent some more."

"As I recall, you liked a little bit of danger yourself when you were younger," Ember pointed out, her eyes soft as she smiled at him. "Or at least, that's what I've heard. There were always more injuries on the sports field than anywhere else at school. Didn't you break your arm once?"

"Yeah, but that was football. It's different."

"Of course it is."

"Hey, does anybody want coffee?" Lucas asked, standing up and stretching his arms. "I'll head over to the café and pick some up before I get myself into trouble."

Ember and Brooke gave him their order, and he left in a hurry, as though he was allergic to hospital rooms and legs in casts.

"Okay, so now that he's gone, tell us all the gory details," Ember said, leaning forward. "And don't leave anything out."

It took Ally ten minutes to tell them the story of Riley and the cliff – mostly thanks to their questions about who Riley was, why she had Ally's number, and why Ally had run as soon as she'd called.

"So she's your boss' daughter?" Brooke asked. "That's the only connection?"

"I felt sorry for her," Ally said, feeling a little defensive. "She's new in town and she lost her mom earlier this year. Now her dad's spending night and day running a coffee shop while she has to come to terms with everything."

"Sounds familiar," Ember said, raising her eyebrows. "No wonder you feel sorry for her. You know exactly what she's going through." She leaned her head to the side. "What's her dad like?"

"He's okay." Ally's cheeks heated up too much to escape the notice of her two best friends. She quickly added, "For an older guy and a boss."

"Why are you blushing?" Ember asked. She turned to Brooke. "She's totally blushing, right?"

"Mmhmm." Brooke nodded. "As red as they come."

"It's hot in here," Ally complained. "That's why. It's warmer in here than it is at the beach." She pulled at the collar of her gown and looked up at her friends. "Aren't you hot?"

"Nope." Ember shook her head. "Let's take it back a bit. So Riley's dad is nice for an older guy." There was a glint in Ember's eye. "And he makes you get all hot and bothered."

Brooke rubbed her palms together. "I knew I did the right thing leaving Nick with my parents," she said. She and Ember looked as though they were having way too much fun for Ally's liking.

They were both looking right at her, their eyes wide, and their lips curled up while they waited for her to say something.

"What?" she finally responded.

"He's hot, right?" Ember asked.

Ally shrugged, trying to look cool, which was almost impossible in this heat. "I've no idea. He's my boss." She pulled at the gown she was wearing, dragging the lines that were attached to the top of her hand. "I can't believe they've put the heat on in here. So we had a bit of rain. It's hardly arctic conditions out there."

"The heat isn't on," Ember told her, giving her a knowing smile.

"Are you enjoying this?" Ally asked her, grimacing like a child.

"Yep. The hunter is finally being hunted. Remember how much hell you gave me when I first started seeing Lucas?"

"Ugh." Ally lay back and closed her eyes for a moment. "I'm injured, guys. You're supposed to be nice to me."

"Do you need some more painkillers?" Brooke asked. "Shall I call a nurse?"

Ally shook her head. "No."

But then the door opened, and Ally took a moment to steady herself again. She loved Ember and Brooke like sisters, but sometimes they were way too inquisitive for their own good.

She'd have to remember that the next time she was interrogating them.

"You have some more visitors," a nurse said, popping her head around the door. "You're only supposed to have three at a time, but as long as they don't stay too long I'll look the other way."

She stepped back and opened the door wider to allow Ally's visitors to walk inside. Lorne Daniels shuffled in first, followed by Frank Megassey and his wife. Ember and Brooke immediately stood up, offering their chairs to Lorne and Mrs. Megassey. Frank stood to the side of her, inspecting each machine as though he was planning to sell them in his hardware store.

The room that had seemed so spacious and empty had turned decidedly cozy.

"Heard you got up to some fun on the cliffs," Lorne said, leaning forward to clasp her hand between his. "What have I told you about cliff jumping?"

Ally smiled at him. "You know me, I never did listen to my elders."

"Ain't that the truth," Frank said. He was staring intently at the machine that was liberally dripping painkillers through the tube into Ally's hand. "Remember how much trouble she was as a kid? Her dad was always pulling his hair out."

"Well, this time it was another kid in trouble, not me. I'm blameless, " Ally told him. Her mock petulance made him raise his eyebrows.

"That's what you always used to say. '*It's not my fault, Uncle Lorne. The other kids dared me.*'" He said it in a falsetto tone which made Ember and Brooke crack up.

"Remember that time you camped out alone at the Silver Cove Resort?" Brooke said.

"You're starting in on me, too? I thought you were meant to be on my side." Ally considered pushing the button to let out an extra shot of painkiller. The doctor had told her she had up to one boost an hour.

"I am. I was in awe of you. That place always scared the hell out of me."

"Well, I can confirm there are no ghosts at the Silver Cove Resort," Ally told her. "Just crumbling old buildings and a whole lot of dust."

"Well, you're not gonna be camping anywhere for the next few weeks," Frank said, finally pulling his attention away from all the equipment. "Not going to be doing very much at all until your ankle heals."

Ally took a deep breath. The thought of sitting around for that long made her want to get up and run away.

Except she couldn't. And she wouldn't be able to for a long time.

"The doctor said it's a clean break. Hopefully it will heal up quickly."

"Bones always do when you're young." Sandra, Frank's wife, smiled at Ally. "It's when you get old like us that you have to look out."

"Hey, less of the old," Lorne said, frowning. "I still surf every day."

"Yeah, and I go pole dancing on the weekend," Sandra retorted.

Ally had to bite down on her lip not to giggle. When she looked over at Brooke and Ember, she could tell her friends were having exactly the same problem.

"I got coffee for everybody," Lucas said, walking in. He stopped dead when he saw all the visitors crowding around

Ally's bed. "Except apparently I didn't. Looks like I'm taking another trip to the café."

As if to add to the chaos, the nurse opened the door again. Her eyes were wide. "Um, you have some more visitors," she said. "Though, I have no idea where they're going to fit." She shook her head and frowned. "I'm sure the doctor said something about you having to stay here because you had no family."

The nurse backed out slowly as Riley and Nate walked in. Riley was carrying a huge bunch of flowers – pretty roses and lilies that almost obscured her face. She looked with wide eyes at everybody crowding around Ally's bed, her face turning white.

"You know what?" Ember said loudly, using the same tone Ally imagined she always used with her elementary class. "Why don't we all go to the café? Brooke, Lucas?" she said, smiling at them. "And if you come with us we'll buy you coffee too, Mr. Daniels. And Mr. and Mrs. Megassey."

"But we just got here," Frank complained.

"That's okay. We'll have a drink and then we can pop back in on our way out," Brooke said, catching on to Ember's plan. From the way she was staring at Frank and Lorne, she wasn't taking no for an answer.

Ally looked over at Riley who seemed to be cowering into her dad. Then she looked up, her eyes connecting with his, and he gave her a smile. One that she couldn't help but return.

She'd noticed that his smiles always had that effect on her.

As soon as the others left, Riley ran toward Ally, flinging the flowers on the chair beside the bed. "How are you?" she said, still sounding scared. "Does it hurt?" She paused for a moment, mashing her lips together before she added in a quavering voice, "I'm sorry you broke your ankle. It's all my fault."

Ally reached out for her hand. "It's not your fault," she told her. "The rain needs to take some of the blame, and the rock. And a stupid woman who wasn't looking where she was running."

"But you wouldn't have been there if I wasn't."

"True. But I'm glad I was."

"So am I," Nate said, walking forward. He took the flowers Riley had left on the chair and placed them in an empty vase, carrying it over to the sink in the corner of Ally's hospital room. "Thank God you were. Even if it means Riley's grounded for life."

"I don't ever want to go out again, anyway," Riley said, slumping down on the chair and crossing her arms over her chest. "This place is way more dangerous than Seattle."

Ally gave her a sympathetic look. "Angel Sands is the safest place I know. Just as long as you don't hurl yourself into the ocean."

"Yeah, well I'm not planning on doing that any time soon, either." Riley grimaced. "Not that anybody's talking to me. Dad called all my friends' parents and now everybody's grounded."

"I thought you didn't have any friends," Nate said, his voice light.

"Hmmph." Riley picked up a magazine that Brooke had left for Ally and started to thumb through it. Nate sat down in the chair on the other side of her.

"The doctor said you'll be out of here tomorrow, so that's good."

"It is. One night in the hospital is enough." Ally sighed. "I'm not sure I'll be making it into work this week, though. Not until I get the hang of walking with crutches."

"You won't be working at all," Nate said, raising an eyebrow. "You can't come back until the doctor gives you the all clear."

Ally tried to sit up taller, but her damn leg wasn't playing ball. She ended up sliding to the left like she'd been drinking too much. Nate reached out to steady her, his hands gentle against her bare arms.

And if she'd thought it was warm in here before, now it was feeling tropical.

"You need some help getting comfortable?" he asked her.

"I just need another pillow," she said, trying to ignore the way her heart started to speed. Surely it couldn't be good for her, not with the cocktail of drugs that were already pumping through her veins. What happened if they got delivered too fast? Would she explode?

Nate gently pulled her forward and plumped a pillow up behind her, then helped her scoot back a bit until she was fully sitting up. "I had to do this for Riley when she was in the hospital having her tonsils removed," he told her as he moved his hands from her arms. Her exposed skin felt suddenly cold.

Ally knew she needed to stop reading too much into things. It was obvious that she felt something toward Nate, but even more obvious that it was all mixed up in her father's leaving and the sudden loss of the café. In spite of their frequent spats, there was a connection between Nate and Riley that made Ally's heart ache. It made her feel wistful and achy and a little bit envious.

Whatever weird kind of daddy complex she was feeling needed to take a hike right now.

"I need to work," she told him, trying to push all those crazy feelings out of her brain. "I have a mortgage to pay. Bills. And we both know I'm not owed any more paid time off."

"You'll be paid your full wages while you're off," Nate told her, his voice firm. "Boss' orders."

"I can't accept your charity," she told him, shaking her head. "I've always paid my own way."

"You think this is charity?" Nate asked. "As far as I'm concerned, it's all business. First of all, you'd have every right to sue me, as Riley's guardian, for lost wages which would cost me a hell of a lot of money in lawyer's fees. And secondly, what do you think it would do for business if everybody heard you were on unpaid sick leave? You think Lorne would send any more of his surf buddies my way? Or that Frank would put fliers up next to his register to tempt his customers? How about Deenie at the bookshop? She's your best friend's mother-in-law, right? I'm pretty sure she'd run me out of town if she thought you were being treated badly."

"So you're not doing it out of kindness?"

Nate blinked a couple of times. "No, not at all."

"You clearly don't know him if you think he does anything out of kindness," Riley said from behind her magazine. There was no malice in her voice. "Just let him pay."

"Don't worry, I'll be taking some of it out of Riley's allowance. Since she's the one responsible for all of this." He shot his daughter a look that she had no chance of seeing behind the magazine.

"I get an allowance?" Riley retorted. "Could have fooled me. You stopped it after I got arrested in Seattle."

Ally laughed. She couldn't help it. The two of them were so damn cute. They reminded her so much of the good times she'd had with her dad. And yes, there had been good times. Nate shook his head and started to laugh, too, the corners of his eyes wrinkling up in the most devastating way.

"It's not funny," Riley said, pulling the magazine down. Her lips were twitching like crazy. "Okay, it *kinda* is," she said, finally letting her smile shine through. "But it's true, Dad. I have no money at all."

"You could take some of my shifts," Ally suggested. "If

you wanted to contribute, too."

"But I have school."

"Not on the weekends," Nate said, raising his eyebrows at Ally. "I like it. It's natural justice. You incapacitated one of my employees, so now you have to take her place."

"Come on, let's not get hasty," Riley said, looking from Ally to her dad. "I can't make coffee to save my life. I'll be more of a liability than help. Plus, I have a lot of homework to do. You don't want me failing any classes."

"Do it," Ally urged. "One day you'll look back at this time and realize it was one of the best parts of your life. You'll get to spend time with your dad, you'll meet new people. And some of the others go surfing after the shop closes on Saturdays. Who knows, you might even want to go, too."

She could sense Nate's stare. Could almost see it from the corner of her eye. But she didn't dare turn her head to see what his expression was.

"Visiting hours are almost up," the nurse called out from the doorway. Ally turned to look at her, shocked. She hadn't even heard the door open.

"We should go," Nate told her. "Let you get some rest." He stood up and stretched his arms, the action lifting his t-shirt high enough for her to get the tiniest glimpse of toned abs. He tucked it back in again, ruining the view completely. "Come on, Ri." He leaned down and squeezed Ally's hand. "I'll see you tomorrow," he said, his breath warm against her skin.

"*Tomorrow?*"

"Yeah. We're your designated transport home. The doctor's going to call me once you've been discharged."

He was? Okay, then. If she wasn't certain to look like a complete fool trying to navigate herself out of the hospital with her leg in a cast and her body relying on crutches, she might have looked forward to that.

✿ 10 ✿

Nate pulled his dark blue Lexus into the lot behind Ally's condo building, taking a right so he could park as close as possible to the entranceway. It was a small complex, four white stone buildings clustered around a central grassy area. It was shabby, too, with paint peeling off the exterior, and black graffiti scribbled on the signs that warned residents not to play ball games there.

"Okay," he said, when he'd pulled up beside the curb. "Stay there. I'll run around and help you out."

Ally nodded, but didn't say a word. She'd been quiet ever since he and Riley had arrived at the hospital to pick her up that afternoon. The doctor had warned that she'd be in more pain today than yesterday since they'd taken her off the intravenous painkillers. Every now and then, he'd see her grind her teeth together as if to try and wait the pain out.

Grabbing the crutches the hospital had provided her from his trunk, he walked around and opened her door. Riley was hovering behind him, as though she wanted to help but had no idea what to do.

"Ri," he said, giving her a smile. "Can you hold these while I help Ally get out?"

Riley nodded and took the crutches from his grasp, standing back to give him some room. He scooted down next to Ally. "I'm going to help you swing your legs out first," he told her.

"I think I can do it." She frowned, trying to lift her cast-covered ankle. She winced and fell back in her seat, muttering something he couldn't quite hear.

"Let me." He gently slid his arms beneath her legs and lifted them an inch or two from the seat. She was wearing a pair of cut-off baggy sweats, and one of them rode up as he twisted her, leaving his palm holding her warm, tan thigh. He could feel the softness of her skin contrasted against the suppleness of her muscles. Taking a deep breath in, he pulled her until her feet were over the lip of the car and resting on the sidewalk.

"You okay?" he asked.

"Yeah." She nodded. "A bit embarrassed, but fine."

"There's no need to be embarrassed." He looked into her eyes, so close to his. "I'm going to help you up, after that you can take over. Can you put your hands on my shoulders?"

She reached out and did as instructed. Then Nate wrapped his palms around her waist. "Lean forward. Put your weight on me."

He slowly began to lift her upright, taking care not to cause any more pain to her leg. She was light in spite of all the muscles she'd developed from running. When she was finally up, he inclined his head at Riley, who slid the crutches under Ally's arms. Still holding her, he took a step back, encouraging her to put her weight on them.

Ally began to shake. "Don't let go."

"I won't. Not until you're ready."

"They made me practice with them this morning, but it was easier then."

"It always is. Okay, I'm going to take another step back. Try to move forward. I promise I'll keep hold of you."

She nodded, her face tight with concentration. He could feel her transfer her weight from him to the crutches, then watched as she shunted them forward. Inhaling sharply, she gritted her teeth together and lifted her body until she was moving toward him.

"You did it." Nate gave her what he hoped was an encouraging nod. "You want to try without me holding you?"

"Not really, but I'll do it anyway."

He released his hold on her waist and stepped to the side, only an arm's reach away if something went wrong. Ally balanced on her good foot, holding the one in the cast a couple of inches from the ground. Within seconds, she was moving forward, Nate and Riley right behind her as she made her way to the building.

Riley ran ahead to open the door. Ally maneuvered herself inside until her foot was on the tiled floor. "I think I've got the hang of this. Maybe it won't be so bad after all."

"I wouldn't count on it," Riley said. "Unless your unit's on this floor." She was pointing to a sign in front of the elevator.

Out of order.

Ally's face turned pale. She looked over at the stairwell, swallowing hard as her eyes scanned up it.

"I'm on the fifth floor." Her voice was so quiet he had to lean in to hear her.

"Is there another way to get there?" he asked. "Can you use an elevator in one of the other buildings?"

"They're not connected. I guess I'm going to have to try the stairs."

"We can help you up there," Riley said. "Can't we, Dad?" she asked eagerly.

They both turned to look at Nate. "Yeah, we can help you up. But what happens when you need to come down again?"

Riley frowned and looked up at her dad. "You've got a point. I hadn't thought of that."

"Is there a superintendent around here?" Nate asked Ally.

"Yeah. Let me call him and find out what's going on." She tried to pull her arm out of her crutch to grab her bag, but the effort made her fall to the side. Nate reached out to steady her, then kept his arm around her waist as she made the call.

"Mr. Stephens, it's Ally from 509. I see the elevator isn't working. Do you know how long it will be until it's fixed?"

Even though he was close, Nate couldn't hear the reply. He got the gist of it though, from the way Ally's breath caught in her throat.

"Two weeks? Where's the part coming from? Mars?"

"Two weeks?" Riley mouthed at him. Nate shrugged at her.

"And there's nothing you can do until then?" Ally asked, pausing for his reply. "No, I understand that it's an old elevator. Thanks, anyway." She disconnected and looked up at Nate and Riley. "There's nothing I can do. I'm going to have to learn to use the stairs on these things," she told them, sliding her phone back into her pocket.

"The chances of you making it up five flights of stairs without breaking another bone is pretty slim," Nate told her.

"Well, unless I'm going to camp out in the lobby I don't think I have a choice."

"Dad," Riley said, tugging at his arm. "*We* don't have any stairs. Apart from the ones that lead up to the front door, and they're wide."

Riley's face was bright with excitement. Nate knew exactly what she was trying to say, but he needed to think it through for a moment. It was one thing helping Ally up to her apartment, but having her at home with them, living in their house, sleeping in one of their bedrooms? Well, that was something completely different.

The thought of it made his skin heat up.

And yet what choice was there? He couldn't leave her here stranded. Not when it was their fault she was in this situation in the first place. Even if it hadn't been their fault, she was still an employee. And he took care of his staff, always.

"You can come home with us," he said, not wanting to think it through any more. He could handle it, couldn't he? He was a grown-up and he had self-control. Yes, she was pretty, and yes, in another lifetime he might have been attracted to her, but right now she was just somebody in need.

Somebody he could help.

And that was all there was to it.

"I'm sorry? What?" Ally lifted her head to look at him. For a second she stared at him with her mouth wide open.

"We have a spare room, plus everything's on the same level. And you'll have the added bonus of having me and Riley there in case you need anything you can't get."

"But my things..." Ally shook her head. "I can't even get up there to pack them."

"Do you have a friend you can give a list to?" he asked her. "I'd do it, but I'm notoriously bad at packing."

"He is," Riley agreed, smiling. "That's why he always pays the professionals."

"Yeah, I guess," Ally said. "My friends Ember and Brooke would do it." She swallowed hard. "But you don't even know me, not really. I'm sure I could find somewhere else to stay."

"Like where?"

She paused for a moment. Ember and Lucas's house could barely fit the two of them in it. Brooke lived in the small pool house attached to her parent's estate – no room for more than her and Nick. That left maybe Lorne and his wife, who lived in a one-bed cottage that would be more than cozy if Ally moved in. "Um, I'm not sure," she admitted. "I'd need to call around."

"You don't need to do that. We have plenty of room. You'll have your own bedroom and bathroom, and all the privacy you need." He inclined his head at the car she'd climbed out of only minutes before. "Let's go back to the car and head to our place, and you can ask your friends to pick some clothes up for you." He helped her slide her arm back onto the crutches. "It's the best solution."

As Nate drove them back to his house her ankle throbbed like crazy. Every now and then, when the car hit a bump in the road, a sharp pulse of pain would shoot up her leg, making her wince in her efforts not to cry out. It didn't help that her heart was clamoring against her ribs like a crazed animal, either.

Nate pulled the Lexus up to a pair of black gates and hit the remote control that was attached to the dashboard. As they slowly opened, he edged the car in, speeding up as they made it to the driveway.

Like so many of the houses in this part of town, Nate's home was a sprawling ranch-style building, the low white frontage bigger than the footprint of her condo building. Beyond the palms that had been planted to give the building some shade she could see the yellow sand that led to the azure ocean, which had chosen to be still today.

It looked glorious, and so much easier to navigate than

her own building. And yet the idea of spending two weeks there with Nate, and Riley, was making her anxious. Her muscles were urging her to run in spite of the heavy cast on her leg.

Nate turned off the engine and climbed out, walking around the car to help her. With his support, she managed to make her way to the bottom step on crutches. There were only six of them – wide white flagstone stairs that led up to the oak front door – but the thought of trying to get up them made her feel exhausted before she'd even started.

"Why don't you practice the steps tomorrow?" Nate suggested, as though he could read her mind. "It's been a long day and you're looking pretty tired."

"How's she going to get up to the house if she doesn't use her crutches?" Riley asked. Nate pointed at himself with a finger, and she let out a little "oh."

"Can you take the crutches?" he asked his daughter. Then he turned to Ally. "Are you okay with me lifting you up there?"

Was she okay? No, not really. None of this was okay. Ally felt like one of those fish that jumped out of the sea, flapping uselessly on the sand until somebody put them out of their misery. She was so unused to accepting help from other people. Add to that the crazy attraction she felt toward Nate every time he looked at her and she was pretty much done for.

"That's fine," she managed, though it felt anything but.

A second later he was sliding his hand under her thighs, his palm soft as it brushed against her skin. His other arm hooked around her back as he lifted her easily, pulling her body against his chest to keep her steady.

"Put your arms around my neck," he instructed, his voice soft.

She did as she was told, looping her hands around him, feeling the ridges of his shoulder muscles. She tipped her head to look at him, and he was staring right back at her, his gaze intense.

Her stomach contracted. She'd never been this close to him before. She took a deep breath in, but it only made things worse as she inhaled his warm scent.

He carried her carefully, as though she was some kind of precious cargo. And not once was she afraid he might drop her. His hold was strong and sure, comforting, even. She closed her eyes for a second to try and savor the moment. She wanted to commit it to memory – the warmth of his skin beneath her hands, the feel of his chest against her cheek – and maybe that would be enough to get her through the next few days.

"Ally? We're here. I'm going to put you down now. There are no stairs inside the house." If he'd thought she was crazy for closing her eyes as he carried her, he gave her no indication.

"Shall we give her the tour?" Riley asked, passing the crutches back to Ally.

"I don't know. How are you feeling? Do you need some rest?" Nate asked, studying her. "We can show you around later if you prefer?"

She gave him a small smile. "I'm feeling pretty beat. Plus, I think it's time to take some more painkillers."

"We can show you to your room, then," Riley said, grinning. "Or if you prefer you can go in the living room. There's a TV there, and a footstool. And dad makes a mean batch of popcorn."

"The living room sounds good."

She followed them, the sound of her crutches echoing through the hallway as they hit the flagstone floor. As she walked into the vast living room, Nate helped her over to the sofa, gently lowering her until her bottom hit the cushion. Riley slid the footstool she'd talked about beneath Ally's leg cast. Ally turned to look out of the huge wall of glass that led to the small backyard and the beach beyond. The sun was shining in the sky, the surf calm and gentle. After yesterday's storm it was a beautiful day. The sort of day she could run down the beach until her lungs couldn't work any more.

She sighed. How the hell was she going to manage to go without exercising? It was the one thing that kept her sane. And right now she needed to keep her thoughts under control more than ever. She was going to be cooped up in this house with Nate and Riley for at least two weeks.

The thought both alarmed and excited her.

"I need to do some homework," Riley said, giving them both a wave as she left the room. "Catch you later, mashed po-tay-ta."

"Homework." Nate smirked. "That's her code word for spending the rest of the night on Snapchat and Netflix," he told Ally. "In case you were wondering."

She laughed. "I'm glad social media wasn't such a big thing when I was a teenager. At least nobody got to share photographs of all the stupid things I did."

"I can't imagine you doing stupid things."

"Can't you?" she asked him. "Things like running on wet grass and tripping over a huge rock I hadn't even seen." Her eyes widened. "Hey, they didn't get a photo of that, did they?"

Nate grinned. "Not that I've heard. Though I'd probably pay good money to see it."

"Thanks."

Her eyes were drawn to the beach again. Somebody was running along the shoreline with a dog. She shifted in her seat to try and get comfortable.

"You really hate sitting still, don't you?" Nate asked.

"It's not my favorite thing," she admitted, surprised that he'd noticed. "I like getting things done, I always have. I prefer to be on the move instead of sitting around doing nothing." She shrugged. "But I'll be okay. I'll read a book or something."

He inclined his head at the bookshelves that lined the far wall. "Help yourself. And there are movies on demand on the television." He handed her the remote, his fingertips brushing against hers. "Anything you want we can order in."

"I'll be fine," she said again, embarrassed that he'd even noticed her discomfort. He was being so nice to her, and it was taking some time to get used to.

He tipped his head to the side, looking at her as though he was trying to work her out.

"Well at least let me get your pain meds and a drink." He slowly ran his thumb along his jaw. "And then I should do some work. That's if you're okay here. You can holler if you need anything, if I don't hear you Riley will."

Embarrassment washed over her again. "Of course. I must have really messed up your day. Go and do whatever you need to do." She picked up the remote and aimed it at the television, trying to look busy.

"If you're sure..."

She looked up at him, smiling. "Go."

He nodded as the screen lit up and the sound cut through whatever was happening between them. "I'll check on you in a bit."

"Sure thing."

She watched as he left, then switched the television off again. She barely watched the thing anyway. Between work and running and seeing her friends, there was little time to keep up with a series.

Yeah, well. You may need to rethink that, sweetheart.

Strange how the voice in her head seemed to sound just like *him*.

But maybe it was right. Two weeks in close proximity with Nate Crawford. With no work to do, and no ability to run off her feelings.

She was either in seventh heaven or the seventh circle of hell. Right now, she couldn't tell the difference.

❧ 11 ❧

Could a day really feel this long? Ally stared out of the window at the beach beyond the house, watching the rhythm of the waves as they broke against the shore. The tide was out, leaving an expanse of golden sand, and she curled her toes at the sight of it.

Or one set of them, anyway. The others were too constrained by the plaster.

She tried to keep herself busy, pulling down a book from Nate's extensive collection, settling down in the corner of the sofa, and opening it up, hoping it would use up some time. But her mind was too active, her body too fidgety, and every time she finished a paragraph her thoughts would wander. She'd think about the café and what everybody was doing there right now.

What Nate was doing, in particular.

Ugh.

The television wasn't much better. She'd never watched daytime TV before, but it was full of grown women arguing with each other as their rich husbands ignored them – and those were just the reality shows.

She made a really terrible patient, that much was for sure. It was a good thing Nate and Riley weren't here to see her embarrass herself. Maybe if she got the restlessness out of her system now, they wouldn't notice.

But her body had other ideas. After Nate called her at lunchtime to check that everything was okay, she let her head fall back on the leather cushion of the sofa and felt her eyes fall down like curtains on a play. The next thing she knew the door was slamming and she heard Nate and Riley talking as they walked up the hallway, their footsteps loud as they reached the living room.

"Hey, Ally," Riley called out through the open doorway. "How was your day? Did you have fun?"

Ally smiled. "Yeah. I did some reading and watched some TV." Lie, lie, and lie.

Riley sighed. "Sounds like heaven. I wish I could break my ankle and stay home from school."

Ally couldn't help but laugh at her wistful expression. It was so nice to have people home with her. She'd never tell them how lonely she'd been while they were both out at school and work, though. It would be her secret.

"I gotta go and finish my homework. I'll see you at dinner, okay?"

"Sure."

Behind her, Nate raised his eyebrows. Ally remembered what he'd said yesterday about homework being a code word and grinned again.

He smirked back at her and yep, her heart stuttered. Just a little.

"How are you feeling?" he asked her, walking in. It was only then that she saw the huge box he was carrying. "Did you get any rest?"

"A little."

He put down the box and opened up the lid, sliding some

white Styrofoam out. "I got you something on the way home," he told her. As he removed the foam, she saw exactly what he'd bought. "I thought it might help."

"A game console?" she asked as he put the white box on the floor.

"Yep. It works for teenage boys who have more energy than they know what to do with." He pulled the leads out, connecting them up. "Well, that and other things, but I figured we're keeping this family friendly, so the console will have to do." He gave her a wink.

She couldn't help but laugh. "I don't think I've been compared to a teenage boy before. What is it, the low voice or the bad attitude?"

Nate plugged the console in. "I've never met anybody less like a teenage boy," he told her. "But the energy thing is a shared problem." He pulled open the shopping bag he'd brought in, and took out some games. "I asked the guy at the counter for his recommendations. He says that Echoes of War is the best thing to get rid of any excess energy."

"Echoes of War," Ally repeated. "It sounds dangerous."

"There's lots of running which should be right up your street. I'm not so sure about the blood and gore."

She glanced down at her leg. "Apparently, I'm good at that, too."

Nate switched on the television and sat next to her. He handed her one of the controllers, keeping the other in his hands, and waited for the console to boot up.

"I should give you some money for this," Ally said. "I can't believe you went out and bought this for me."

"It's fine. I've been looking for an excuse to get one of these for ages. I just haven't had the time to think about it."

Half an hour later and they'd both worked out how to use the controllers. On the screen, their soldiers were kneeling behind some barrels, trying to snipe at their enemies. "You're a terrible shot," Ally said as she managed to hit another mercenary. "You want me to do all the work?"

"I'm just being polite," Nate replied, squinting his eyes as he took another shot. "I'd hate to beat you on your first try. I'm a gentleman."

"You unpacked the console," Riley said, wandering into the den. She slumped next to Nate on the sofa. "Who's winning?"

"Your dad," Ally said, at exactly the same time Nate said, "Ally is." The two of them looked at each other and started to laugh.

"Look out," Ally said, bringing her eyes back to the screen. "Too late. You just got shot."

Red covered half the screen as Nate's soldier died.

"Don't worry," she told him. "I'll make sure you have a decent burial."

Riley shook her head. "You two are weird. And it's dinner time. Aren't you hungry?"

"Not really, " Ally said. "When you're trying to save the world there's no time to think about your stomach."

"Good job you have us to do the thinking for you." Nate put his controller down on the arm of the sofa. "I guess I'll call for some take out. Is there anything in particular you'd like?"

Ally shrugged. "I'll eat anything. But you have to let me pay for this one."

One look from him was enough to shut her up.

"You'd better get back to the game before you die too," he suggested. "You still owe me that decent burial, remember?"

It was dark when Ally opened her eyes. Silent, too. Her heart skipped with panic as she looked around the unfamiliar room, her breath catching in her throat until she remembered where she was.

And why.

She looked down at the cast covering her leg from beneath her calf to the tip of her foot. Only her toes were visible. She wiggled them to make sure they were still working.

Ouch. Maybe that wasn't such a good idea.

"You're awake." Nate walked into the room. Though he was still wearing his dress shirt, he'd rolled the sleeves up and unfastened a few buttons. He rocked the business casual look.

"Sorry, I must have dozed off again. It's getting to be a habit. How long was I out?"

He checked his watch, the glass glinting against the light of the moon. "It's almost ten, so I guess a couple of hours? I've been in the office working." He glanced into the hallway. "Your friend Brooke called for you, but she didn't want me to wake you up. She said she'd come visit you tomorrow morning if you're up to it."

"Thank you." A yawn came out of nowhere, stretching her jaw muscles. She covered her mouth with alarm.

Nate laughed. "You should head for bed."

Ally wrinkled her nose. "I should, but I still haven't unpacked." Last night she'd just grabbed her toiletry bag and pajamas out of the suitcase Ember had brought over. But it would be so much easier if she took everything out of the bag so she could see what she had. Even getting dressed was like planning a military operation.

"I can help if you need it. I've finished work for the night."

She smiled at him. On top of those good looks he really was a nice person. Much too nice for her. "That sounds like a good plan."

They walked into the oversized guest room, Ally being

careful not to let her crutches get caught in the beautifully woven rug that half-covered the polished wooden floor. The walls were painted a warm blue that reminded her of the ocean.

Not that she needed reminding – the glass doors at the far end of the room looked out onto the beach and beyond. When she'd woken up this morning she had laid there a while and stared out, wondering what it would be like to wake up to that view every day.

Nate must have followed her gaze. "Riley and I have the same view. They built it to maximize the location. There's something awe inspiring about seeing the ocean right as you wake up."

"Do you sleep with the curtains open?" she asked before thinking it through. "Ugh, you don't have to answer that. I'm way too nosy for my own good."

He gave a soft chuckle. "Yeah, I do," he said, nodding. "And not just because I'm too lazy to close them, either."

She turned to look at him, trying to keep her voice steady, even though she was feeling overwhelmed all over again. "I really do appreciate you letting me stay here," she told him. "I'm not the easiest person to live with. So, thank you."

"You're the easiest person in the world to take care of," he told her. "And it's my pleasure. We want you to be here."

Her whole body felt light at his words. Even her leg with that damn cast on. When was the last time somebody said something like that to her? "I'm happy to be here, too."

"Then let's get you unpacked and settled in." He led her over to the bed, helping her sit down on the edge, then he leaned her crutches against the wall. "I was thinking we should only put things in the top drawers of the dresser. That way you'll be able to reach them while you're supported on your crutches."

"That sounds good."

Ally watched as he unzipped her case, then pushed it across the mattress toward her. "Would you rather Riley helped you with this?" he asked her. "I can call her if it makes you more comfortable."

"No, it's good. Stay." She reached for his wrist, curling her fingers around it without thinking. She wasn't sure who was more surprised. She opened her lips, but she couldn't think of a word to say. Nate was silent, too, unmoving, but he didn't look angry at her touch. The shock on his face melted into something very different. Something that made his skin flush and his eyes narrow.

"Ally..."

He reached out with his free hand and traced a soft line from her cheekbone to her jaw. His eyes were dark as they stared intently into hers.

"Where are you guys?" Riley called from the hallway. Nate immediately pulled back. Ally barely had enough time to breathe in some much needed oxygen before Riley came into her room. She tucked a stray piece of hair behind her ear, hoping to God she looked more composed than she felt, and turned to smile at the girl.

"Your dad was just helping me get unpacked."

"You drew the short straw, huh?" Riley said. "Remember what I told you about his packing? He's just as bad at unpacking, too. Look in his room if you don't believe me. There's still at least six sealed boxes in there."

"Winter clothes," he said, his voice rough. "I don't think I need them right now."

"Yeah, well." Riley shrugged and walked over to the bed. "You want my help?" she asked Ally as she sat down next to her. "At least this way you might be able to find everything again."

"I'll... ah... leave you to it," Nate said. He was hovering by the door, his hands stuffed in his pockets. "If your friends want to visit you here tomorrow, that's fine. I'm planning on being at the shop for most of the morning. Riley's coming with me."

"I am?"

"Yeah. I'm a staff member short, thanks to you." He was looking in their direction, but seemed to be avoiding Ally's gaze. Maybe that was a good thing. She didn't trust herself to keep a poker face. "You could probably both do with an early night. I know I could. I'm going to hit the sack."

"Thanks for your help," Ally said. "And for... everything, really."

"Any time." He gave a nod, hesitating for a second before he turned and walked out the door.

"Sorry about my dad," Riley said. "He really needs to learn some people skills."

Ally smiled at her, but inside she could still feel that aching hole. "Maybe we could all do with learning some of those," she said.

Wasn't that the truth? Because right now she had no idea how she was going to be able to stay here for two weeks without embarrassing herself one way or another.

❧ 12 ❧

"There you go." Ember walked out of the house and set three coffee mugs down on the wooden table. "Three lattes, I think. Or at least that's what the coffee machine said when I pressed the button." She turned to Brooke who was sitting on an Adirondack chair, facing out to the ocean. "Have you ever seen a machine like that before? I was almost too scared to touch it."

Brooke grinned. "At least it's not like the one at Ally's coffee shop," she said. "It looks like you need to have a pilot's license to use it."

"It's not my shop," Ally pointed out, swallowing hard. "Not any more."

It was right after ten on Saturday morning, and the three of them were sitting on the deck outside Nate and Riley's huge living room. The floor-to-ceiling glass doors had been pulled back so that the wooden floor of the interior flowed seamlessly onto the deck. There was a small, grassed area in front of the deck bordered by low-level shrubs which were in full bloom, the dark green of the leaves almost obscured by the pink-and-white petals. Beyond the shrubs were steps leading down to the sand. At this end of the beach – away from the bustling center of Angel Sands – there was nobody there.

It was the three of them and the ocean.

"God, it's lovely here." Ember sighed, looking out at the white-tipped waves. "Do you think if I kicked the wall hard enough your boss would let me stay here too?"

"Talking of lovely," Brooke said. "I had a good talk with Nate on the phone the other day." She raised her eyebrows. "He's great. You lucked out getting him for a boss."

Ally let out a sigh, and it was much heavier than she intended.

"He was really worried about you," Brooke continued. "He asked me what your favorite food was, and whether you were a morning or a night person." She turned to Ember and smiled. "Did you know he bought her a video game console to keep her busy?"

"Wow. Let's hope you never have to move out." Ember wiggled her eyebrows.

Ally leaned forward to try and scratch her leg above where the plaster was covering it. It was constantly itchy.

"He's really good looking too. For an older guy." Ember turned to Ally. "Just how old is he, anyway?"

"I don't know." Ally's brow crinkled. "That's not the sort of thing you ask somebody."

"He has a sixteen-year-old daughter. He has to be forty, right?" Brooke said. "Not that he looks much over thirty-five. Either way he's hot."

"He's my boss," Ally pointed out. She wanted this conversation to end now. Everything felt so jumbled up. She couldn't live in her apartment, she couldn't run. She couldn't even work. And now her friends were talking about the one guy she was trying not to think about.

"Doesn't mean you can't look."

"Or touch," Ember added, grinning.

"Can we change the subject, please?" Ally snapped. Seeing her friend's shocked expressions she immediately felt bad. "Sorry, I'm just a bit..." she trailed off, trying to find the right word. "Confused."

"Confused?" Brooke echoed. "What about?"

Ally inhaled deeply, staring ahead at the ocean as it gently lapped against the shore. Her chest tightened at the thought of admitting her feelings out loud. As long as she kept them buried they weren't real. But out in the open...

They could hurt her like a knife.

"Are you okay?" Ember asked softly. "You've got the strangest expression on your face."

Another deep breath, this one so big it almost hurt her chest. Ember and Brooke were staring at her with pinched brows. They were her best friends. They'd kept each others' secrets since kindergarten.

She could trust them, she knew that.

"I like him," Ally said. "I like my boss." And it was as simple and as complicated as that.

"Ohhhhh." Brooke dragged the simple word out for a few syllables.

Ember gave her a sympathetic smile. "I could have told you that when we were in the hospital. In fact, I did tell you that if I remember correctly."

"Telling is one thing," Brooke said gently. "Realizing it for yourself is a whole other pack of cards." She turned to look at Ally. "Does he know how you feel?"

"No." Ally shook her head rapidly. "And I want to keep it that way. It's just a stupid crush. I'd hate for him to find out."

"Maybe you should relax and see where this goes. You never know, he might feel the same way as you do." Ember shrugged.

Ally thought about last night and how he'd traced her

cheek with his finger. Had that meant something? She wasn't sure. All she knew was that he hadn't done it again and yet she could feel the heat of his touch for hours.

"There's nowhere good for this thing to go," she told them. "He's my boss, and we all know what they say about doing the deed where you eat. It's asking for trouble." She gave a little shudder. "But more importantly there's Riley. She's so vulnerable right now. She thinks I'm her friend, and what kind of friend goes behind your back and starts something up with your dad?"

"A bad friend?" Brooke suggested. Her voice was low, as though she really didn't want to say it.

"Exactly." Ally pressed her lips together, thinking about it. "Remember how I hated Marnie?" she asked them, reminding them of her dad's ex-girlfriend. "And she hated me, too. It was awful and I could never do that to Riley."

"You're nothing like Marnie. She was just... ugh." Ember shuddered. "And she was way too young to understand what you were going through. Let's face it, she thought she'd signed up to live happily ever after with your dad, and then..." she trailed off. "You came along."

"And brought all my baggage with me." Ally hated thinking about those terrible days after her mom died. She could still remember the pain and the anger. All those arguments between her dad and Marnie when he told his girlfriend that his teenage daughter would be moving in with them. "And I could never do that to anybody else. Especially not Riley. She's so hurt and lost, but underneath all that she's a good kid. She deserves all her father's attention."

Brooke was holding Ally's hand and she squeezed it gently. "But you're not Marnie. Don't you see? More than anybody you understand what Riley's going through. You could be good for her, for both of them. If you'd just let yourself go."

"I wish it was that easy," Ally said.

"It *is* that easy. What's stopping you?" Ember finished her coffee and put the cup on the table in front of them.

"The same thing that stopped you when you fell for Lucas, I expect," Brooke said to Ember. "Fear."

"I'm not afraid," Ally protested, her brows knitting together. "What makes you say that? I've dated, I've had boyfriends. I'm not afraid of being with somebody."

"When was the last time you had a serious relationship?" Brooke asked. She was always so gentle, and yet her words cut deep.

"I don't know." Ally bit her lip. "It's been a while. Angel Sands is very short on good looking guys." She glanced over at Ember. "Even you had to widen your search if I recall."

"It's not the good looking guys that's the problem," Brooke told her. "It's the fact you didn't feel very much for them."

As much as Ally hated to admit it, she was right. Casual dating was easy when your heart wasn't on the line. If you didn't care if they led to another date or not. When you weren't spending your time constantly checking your messages to see if they were thinking of you.

But there was nothing casual about the way she felt toward Nate. Seeing him every day made her leg muscles quiver with the need to run it off. It made her chest ache in a way she couldn't ever remember feeling.

"I'm scared," she admitted, her voice small. "So scared of getting hurt. Scared I'll mess this up the way I mess everything up and I'll end up at rock bottom again." Her voice wobbled with emotion, and tears stung at her eyes.

"Oh, sweetie." Brooke scooted off her chair and knelt in front of Ally's, enveloping her in a hug. "Of course you're scared. You've been through so much. But if you let fear stop you from doing anything you'll never let yourself be open to happiness."

"She's right," Ember said, her voice thick as though she was crying, too. "I should know. I was scared of telling Lucas how I felt. Imagine if I hadn't. We wouldn't be living together now."

Ally wiped her tears away, not wanting to stain Brooke's blouse. It felt strange to be this honest about her emotions. She'd spent more than a decade covering them up, not wanting people to see how she was really hurting inside. She never wanted to burden them with her fears.

Brooke leaned back, flipping her blonde hair over her shoulder before cupping Ally's wet face with the palm of her hands. "You're a catch," she told her. "You're beautiful, you're funny, and you work harder than anybody I know. And even though you don't like us to see it, we know how much you care. So does Riley, and she knows you won't do anything to hurt her."

"Of course you won't," Ember agreed. "It would be like hurting yourself. She'd be lucky to have somebody like you dating her dad."

"I think we might be going too far here," Ally said, her voice gritty with tears. "I have no idea how he feels about me."

"Well the main thing right now is to decide what *you* feel," Brooke said, smiling at her. "It's the only thing you have control over."

"You're right. How did you get so wise?" Ally asked her, allowing her lips to curl up in a watery smile.

"At prenatal classes." Brooke shrugged. "They take you aside and tell you all the secrets of the universe." She folded her arms in front of her. "If you'd both just listen to me more often, you'd be a lot happier."

Ally laughed again, and it felt good. She felt lighter, too, despite the cast on her leg. As though she could breathe easily again without worrying that her chest was going to explode. Maybe Brooke was right.

She had no idea how Nate really felt about her. Whether that touch the other night meant anything at all. But maybe, just maybe, if she tried to relax and enjoy the ride, good things could happen too.

And if that didn't work? Well at least she could blame Brooke and her damn prenatal classes.

❧ 13 ❧

Lifting her head from the pillow, Ally checked her watch. It was only 9 p.m., but fatigue was already weighing her down. The past few evenings she'd been like this – lethargic and slow after dinner, and then at midnight it was as though somebody had turned a switch on inside her and flooded her with lights. She'd sleep fitfully through the night, all ready to be tired again the next evening.

Maybe it had been a good thing Nate had been working late since Monday. Something to do with a quarterly business meeting with the bank, or so he'd told her as he ran out of the door early that morning, muttering something about needing to check some spreadsheets. By the time he'd gotten home in the evenings, she'd inevitably been in bed, and he'd wished her goodnight from the doorway – never once venturing into her bedroom.

Ally didn't mind. She'd felt calmer ever since she'd talked with Ember and Brooke. There was no fight going on inside her anymore and it was liberating. Whatever happened with Nate happened. But she wasn't going to resist the pull to him anymore.

"Hey." Riley walked into her bedroom. "I'm bored. Want me to paint your toenails?" She lifted a bag full of brightly colored polishes.

Ally wiggled her toes. The movement didn't hurt anymore. "How did you guess they needed painting?" she asked. "Is it something to do with all the chipped color on there?"

Riley shrugged. "Nope. I heard you complaining about your pedicure on the phone."

Ah yes, she'd spoken to Ember earlier and moaned about not being able to make her feet look pretty. Thank God she hadn't spoken about anything more personal. She made a note to herself – Riley had the hearing of an elephant. Or were they the ones with good memories? Ally wasn't sure. All she knew was they had huge ears.

"So, what's your favorite color?" Riley asked, pulling some bottles out. "I love black, but there's this bright pink if you want to be girly." She held up a pale taupe. "Or if you prefer neutral, I have this one. This was my mom's favorite."

She said it lightly, but Ally could detect the emotion in Riley's voice. "Your mom had good taste."

"Yeah, well." Riley shrugged. "I'd guess you're more of a pink kind of lady."

Ally nodded. She really didn't mind what color Riley used, but she was wary of saying the wrong thing. "You choose," she said. "I'll go with whatever you think is best."

"Pink it is." Riley pulled out a bottle of remover, shaking it before pressing it against a cotton pad. She rubbed the cotton against Ally's big toenail. "You want me to trim them, too? I used to do Mom's when..." she trailed off and looked away for a moment, before glancing back at Ally. "She said I did a good job."

"That'd be great."

"If you like your toenails, maybe I'll do your hands tomorrow."

Ally smiled. "That would be nice."

Riley finished removing the polish and threw the cotton pads in the trash. Then she got to work with a nail file, shaping Ally's toenails into soft squares with a rounded edge.

"How's school?" Ally asked, as Riley massaged some foot cream into her skin.

"It's okay." Riley shrugged. "A couple of the girls I was at the cliff with apologized to me about trying to make me jump. Laura and Alice. They even asked me to sit with them at lunch."

"They did? That's great."

"It was just lunch." Riley shrugged. But the corner of her lip pulled up into a half smile. "They also asked me if I'd go to the movies with them on Saturday night."

"Ooh. What are you going to see?"

"Probably nothing. Dad grounded me after you broke your ankle. I'm pretty sure he won't let me go."

"Oh." Ally mashed her lips together. "That's a shame."

"I probably deserve worse." Riley shrugged, but Ally could tell she was disappointed. "Anyway, I'm going to put a base coat on first, so this pink doesn't stain your nails." She pulled the bottle open and painted the clear polish on each of Ally's toenails. "You have really pretty feet." Riley frowned. "Well, foot. I can't see the other one very much."

"It's almost the same as this one," Ally said, wiggling the toes on her unharmed foot. "Except in mirror image."

"Well, duh!"

The front door slammed, making both of them jump, and the shock made Riley's hand brush the nail polish onto Ally's big toe. "Frick. It's lucky I'm still on the clear polish," she said, raising her eyebrows. "Otherwise you'd have pink feet right now."

"Anybody home?" Nate called out. Ally tried to ignore her body's response to his deep, warm voice.

"We're in Ally's room," Riley replied. A second later, he was standing in the doorway, a bemused expression on his face as he looked from Ally to his daughter. "Everything okay?" he asked.

"Fine. We cooked spaghetti," Riley said. "There's a plate in the refrigerator for you."

"Oh right." He blinked a couple of times. "Thanks." He ran his thumb across his chin. From where she was sitting, Ally could see the shadow of beard growth that had come in since his morning shave. "I was going to order takeout."

"No need. I asked Ally to show me how to make it, and now I know." Riley grinned at her dad. "I can make it for you whenever you want."

Nate turned to look at Ally. "What have you done with my real daughter?" he teased.

Riley groaned. "Dad."

"I should work late more often," Nate continued, ignoring her. "If it means I get to come home to this."

"It's just dinner," Riley told him.

But Ally knew that wasn't what he was talking about. She could tell from the expression on his face. The stubborn, gruff daughter had lightened up, for as long as teenage hormones permitted.

As if the universe was listening to Ally's thoughts, Riley's phone started to ring. She pulled it out of her pocket, her eyes widening when she looked at the screen.

"Hi, Laura. Just a minute, let me take this in my room." She walked over to Nate. "You're up," she said, putting the bottle of pink polish she'd been holding into his hands. "Two coats and a topcoat, okay? And don't let her move until it's dry." Without waiting for a reply she put the phone to her ear again, resuming her conversation with Laura. "Yeah, that assignment was tough. I managed to find all the answers though. Which one are you having trouble with?" Her voice faded as she walked down the hallway, then disappeared altogether after she slammed her bedroom door shut.

Ally bit down a smile and looked at Nate, who was still hovering in the doorway.

"It's okay. You don't have to paint my nails. I can probably manage if I bend over enough."

He looked at the bottle Riley had shoved in his hands. "It's a nice color."

"Riley chose it."

He took a step inside then hesitated, looking over at Ally. "Is it okay if I come in?" he asked.

"Of course it is. It's your house."

"But it's your room."

His words made her feel warm. As though she finally belonged somewhere.

"Come in. It's nice to have the company."

He walked up to the bed, and looked down at her feet. "Let's do this thing," he said, sitting down in the space his daughter had vacated. "I don't want to incur the wrath of Riley."

"Do you even know how to paint nails?" Ally asked, trying to keep her voice even. It felt so intimate, having him here in the room when she was wearing only a tank and sleep shorts. God only knew how much more intimate it would feel once he touched her.

And if he painted her toes, he'd definitely have to touch her.

She wasn't sure how she felt about that.

"I used to paint Riley's when she was a little girl," Nate admitted. "She'd insist on having beauty nights when she stayed over."

"Did you let her paint yours?" Ally asked.

Nate shook the bottle and unscrewed the lid. "I'm gonna plead the fifth on that one." He reached out for her good foot, sliding his palm beneath her sole. She held her breath for a moment as he gently pulled it toward him, resting her heel on his leg. "You have soft feet for a runner," he told her.

"I try to take care of them," she said, attempting to ignore the way his leg felt under her foot. Warm and muscled. "Apart from going head first over rocks that is."

He gave a little laugh. She liked the way it sounded. "Could have happened to anybody," he said.

"Nope. I'm pretty sure it's just me."

He angled her foot toward him, and pulled the brush out of the bottle, wiping the excess on the edge. He frowned with concentration as he painted her nail with three strokes.

"You *do* know what you're doing," she said, surprised at his deftness. "Most guys I know would have covered half my skin as well as my nail."

"I'm a man of many talents." He finished painting the rest of the nails on her good foot and eased it off his leg, pointing it upright so the polish didn't smudge. "So how was your day?" he asked her. "Get up to anything good?"

"Oh, I managed to kill two hundred evil soldiers, save thirty children and their orphanage, and then I had a little nap."

"All that with a broken leg. Impressive."

"How about you?"

"I made some coffee." He said it deadpan, but there was a smile at the corner of his eyes that made her heart take a little gallop.

He moved across to her other foot. This time he didn't put it on his thigh. "Tell me if it hurts, okay?"

"It's fine. Riley did the base coat and I didn't feel a thing."

He painted her nails in quick succession, once again avoiding getting any on her skin. "I'll let the first coat dry for a minute before I put the second on." He replaced the lid on the polish. "That's if you want a second coat."

"Of course." She grinned at him. "I expect full service in this salon."

"As long as you're a generous tipper, you'll get all the service I can give."

He touched her good foot again. It was all she could do not to curl her toes in response. He was gentle, yet every time his fingers brushed her skin it sent electricity up her leg.

"What are your plans for tomorrow?" he asked, testing the polish with the pad of his finger to see if it was touch dry. Yeah, he'd definitely done this more than a few times. Was it possible to like him even more?

"Apart from saving the world?" she asked. "I'm not sure."

"Well, if the world can live without you for one day, do you want to join me on a little trip?" He had the same expression he'd worn when he was showing her how to make coffee the day when he first trained her. His eyes were alert, as though he was willing her to say yes.

"What kind of trip?"

"I need to visit a couple of places. There's a store just south of LA that the company took over a few months ago and I want to show my face. Plus I'm looking at buying another beach café and I want to check the town out."

"Another beach café?" Ally repeated. "Should we be worried?"

"Nope. You should be pleased. It's a testament to how well the Angel Sands acquisition is going. It's our first non-city location and it's doing better than we expected." He shrugged. "I wasn't planning on expanding any more this year, but this building is going for a song and it's too good not to take a look." He pulled out the brush and started to put on the second coat of polish. "So what do you think? It might do you some good to have a change of scenery. Plus you're the expert on beach towns. I'd be interested to hear your thoughts."

She tried to ignore the shivers snaking up and down her spine. "Yeah, sounds like a nice change," she said. "I was getting bored of saving the world anyway."

He looked up, his gaze meeting hers, and the smile that was crinkling his eyes spread down to his lips. "Well tomorrow you can save me instead." He'd finished the second coat. Tightening the lid back into the bottle, he reached forward to put it on her bedside table, grabbing the bottle of top coat. His arm brushed hers, sending a fresh pulse of energy through her body.

"Okay," she agreed, taking a deep breath. "It's a deal."

❧ 14 ❧

"You took the roof off the car."

Nate looked up to see Ally standing at the top of the stairs that led down to the driveway. She was wearing a grey skirt that was fitted at the hips and flared out to her mid thighs, complementing her toned, tanned legs that seemed to stretch on forever. She'd teamed it with a simple white t-shirt that skimmed her curves. But it was her hair that drew his eye. In the coffee shop she mostly wore it up in a twisted bun, and for the past few days she'd had it in either a ponytail or braids.

But not today. Today she was wearing it down, golden waves tumbling over her shoulders. Looking at her was like looking into the sun. He was almost certain he was going to get burned.

"It's the right kind of day for it," he said, looking up at the cloudless sky. "Though we might regret it when we're sitting in traffic for an hour in LA. It'll probably turn into an oven."

"Every day's the right day for it." Her eyes twinkled. "You're not in Seattle anymore."

And didn't he know it. You only had to take one look at

Ally to know she wasn't from the Pacific North West. She was a California girl through and through. She looked tan and outdoorsy. It took all the strength he had to pull his eyes away from her.

"Stay there," he said. "I'll come and help you down."

"No need. I've been practicing." With the help of her crutches she made it to the top step. "It's easy when you know how."

He watched as she slowly made it down to the driveway. And yeah, maybe there was a part of him that wanted to carry her. Not because she was some kind of damsel in distress, but because he wanted some contact – *any contact* – with her.

"When did you learn to do that?"

"After I saved the world, I had a thought that I might need to save myself in an emergency. What if I needed to evacuate and you and Riley weren't here?"

He glanced to his left. "You could leave by the back door and come through the gate," he said. "I thought you knew that."

Her face fell, and he immediately felt bad. "Not that you need to now," he added. "And anyway, now that you can navigate steps it should make today a lot easier."

He opened the passenger door and helped her inside, putting her crutches on the backseat. Then he settled himself into the driver's seat and pushed the ignition button to start it up. Almost immediately the stereo came on at full blast and he leaned forward to turn it off.

"Sorry about that. I tend to play my music loud."

She smiled at him. "Me, too."

He put the gear shift into drive and maneuvered the car out of its spot on the driveway, clicking the remote control to open up the gates. He could feel her looking at him.

Eyes on the road, Nate. Not on the pretty lady's face. That way you might both make it home in one piece.

It had seemed like a good idea to invite her to join him when he'd suggested it last night. But right then he'd been a little high on the smell of nail polish, and the feeling of Ally's skin as he held her feet and painted her nails. It had made sense – she was clearly bored at home all day, and the thought of having some company as he drove around California seemed like a bonus. It was always good to have somebody to bounce ideas off, after all.

But he hadn't banked on the effect she'd have on him this close up. He could smell the scent of her floral shampoo as the wind lifted her hair, could see the glow of her skin every time he glanced out of the corner of his eye.

"So what were you listening to?" she asked him. "I didn't hear the song long enough to recognize it."

"Dark Wolf. They're a Seattle band. You probably won't have heard of them."

"No, I haven't. Are they good?"

"Yeah. They play at a club down the road from my place on the lake. They're even better live than they are recorded."

"Can we listen to them?" Ally asked.

He nodded at the center console. "Be my guest."

She flicked the stereo back on and sat back in the seat, tucking her hair behind her back. "I really picked a bad day to wear my hair down," she told him. "I should have thought about the wind."

"You want me to put the roof back up?"

"No. It's too nice to hide the sun. I'll just keep leaning back on it, that way it won't look like a bird's nest by the time we make it to our first stop."

He was glad. If he had to make a choice he'd prefer looking at her hair to having the sun shine down on them, but right now they were both welcome. He felt a sense of joy rush through him – a feeling that today was going to be a good day.

By the time they made it to the outskirts of the city,

they'd listened to the whole album. When it finished, he asked Ally to play something she liked, and she'd pulled out her phone, a small smile on her face as she scrolled through some tracks.

"Since you played me a bit of Seattle, I thought I'd play you some California," she told him. Almost immediately a guitar riff struck up, joined by a deep bass. He recognized it right away. Who wouldn't? It had to be one of the most played songs in the world.

"'Hotel California'?" he asked. "You're an Eagles fan?"

"My dad used to listen to them all the time. I didn't really get a choice. He always said they were the best Californian band he ever heard. And he went to a lot of gigs when he was younger."

She was tapping her fingers against her bare thigh to the rhythm of the song. When it got to the chorus she joined in, singing softly enough that he had to concentrate to hear her over the noise of the highway.

He was almost disappointed when they made it to the first shop and he parked in the lot behind the building. He got out and looked around, taking in the overflowing bins and trash that was scattered on the ground. Frowning, he opened Ally's door and grabbed her crutches to hand to her.

"So this is an incognito visit," he told her. "I want to watch how they do things for a little while before I introduce myself. If they know who I am as soon as I walk in, they'll play up for me and I don't want that."

He glanced over at the trash again.

"Like Undercover Boss?" Ally asked, a smile in her voice. "Won't they recognize you?"

"I wasn't involved in the training or opening of this location. One of my staff members took the lead." He shook his head. "Christ, this place looks terrible."

The trash stank to high heaven. Ally wrinkled her nose as

they walked past it. "This is the first impression a customer gets of the place."

"Exactly." His voice was grim as they walked into the shop. It was half empty even though it was lunchtime and usually the busiest time of the day. "You want to find a seat and I'll go order?" Nate said, gesturing at the vacant tables.

"I should go and order while you sit down," she suggested. "Just in case somebody recognizes you. And anyway, it'll be a good test of how they treat customers who aren't as mobile as others."

He looked at her for a moment. Her smile did things to him he didn't want to think about for too long. "Okay. But you'll need some help to carry the drinks over."

She shrugged. "That's what the staff is there for, right?"

Nate walked over to a table next to the window, looking out onto the road. There was a lot of traffic, or a lot of potential customers, as he classified them. All they had to do was nip into the shop and grab a drink to go – it would take them five minutes. And yet they all drove on by.

He'd chosen this shop to be part of the Déjà Brew chain for a reason. It was in the central business district, surrounded by offices and retail outlets. There was no way he should have been able to grab a table at this time of day, and yet here he was with a choice of them.

The tables were mostly covered in old half-drunk cups and crumb covered napkins that nobody had bothered to clear away after the last customer had left.

He looked over to where Ally was resting on her crutches, her leg stretched out as she waited at the counter. The only staff member he could see was at the other end, either ignoring her or completely oblivious to the fact he actually had a customer.

Nate sighed. Some asses were definitely going to get kicked today.

"What can I get for you?" the barista asked when he finally noticed Ally standing there. She'd been waiting for over two minutes without any acknowledgement. She'd timed it, just in case Nate asked her to report back.

"What have you got?" she asked.

"It's on the board." He gestured up with his thumb, a bored tone to his voice.

She leaned forward, scrutinizing it as though she hadn't looked at the same board in Angel Sands for the past few weeks. "Um, what's a latte?" she asked. Was it wrong she was enjoying this? After years of being on the other side of the counter, being an undercover customer was so much more fun.

The barista looked at her as if she'd asked him to do a little polka on the countertop for her. "It's a coffee," he said, incredulity laced in his voice.

She tipped her head to the side, still smiling. "What kind of coffee?"

"With milk. Steamed milk."

"Do you have soy milk?"

"Yeah, we do." He frowned and muttered to himself. "Somewhere."

"In that case, I'll have one soy latte and a cappuccino. With one percent. And two lemon muffins, please."

He rang it up on the till and took her money, then ambled slowly off to make the coffees. She watched him surreptitiously as he loaded up the filter basket with fresh grounds, then tapped it out before he screwed it into the machine.

So far so good. At least he knew how to make a coffee, even if his customer service needed a little work.

When he'd finished he slid the cups across the counter,

then bagged up a couple of muffins for her. "There you go," he said, turning away.

"Um, can you help me carry these over?" she asked, looking down at her crutches. "I'm a little incapacitated."

"Can't your boyfriend help?"

Oh, it was going to be so much fun when Nate revealed himself. If she wasn't undercover she'd be rubbing her hands together with glee. "He's got terrible balance. He'll end up spilling it all."

The barista gave another huff, but walked around the counter and picked up her cups and hooked the bag of muffins on his fingers. Ally followed him to the table Nate had chosen. It was completely covered in dirty cups and napkins, with nowhere for the barista to put down the coffee.

Nate looked up from his newspaper, his face a picture of innocence. "You'll probably need to clean this table," he said, his voice even. But Ally could see a glint of steel in his eyes.

The barista sighed loudly and put the cups down on the table next to Nate and Ally's, which had slightly more space than theirs. Then he picked up some of the empty cups and ambled over to the trash can. "You know, the customers are supposed to throw their own trash away," he mumbled, coming back to pick up some more. "It's not in my job description."

"I think you'll find it is." Nate glanced at the table – now devoid of cups. "Just like it's in your job description to clean the tables between every customer."

The barista jerked his head back, and looked at Nate for a moment, saying nothing. Then he walked back to the counter, picking up a cloth and a spray bottle, coming back to clean up their table.

Ally sat down, resting her crutches against the window, and reached behind to grab their coffees. She passed the cappuccino to Nate and took a sip of the soy latte.

"How did he do?" Nate asked. The barista glanced at them suspiciously. He was lingering around even though their table was completely clean.

"Good. There was a crema in the espresso glass. Three layers like you taught me. And the latte tastes pretty good for a soy one."

Nate took the lid off his cappuccino and glanced at the foam. "A little too much," he murmured, lifting the cup to his lips. He closed his eyes for a moment, his mouth shut tight. When he opened them, he shrugged. "It's passable."

The barista looked up from where he was wiping the table next to theirs. "Is there something wrong with the coffee?"

"No. Out of everything that's wrong with this place, the coffee's at the bottom of the list." Nate put his cup down and reached his hand out to the man. "My name's Nathan Crawford. I own the Déjà Brew coffee chain."

The man's mouth dropped open. "Oh." He gave a little shudder, then quickly took Nate's hand. "It's good to meet you, sir. Is this one of those TV programs they make?" he asked, looking around the shop. "Where are the cameras? Are they hidden on you?"

Nate raised an eyebrow at Ally. She grinned back and mouthed, "Undercover Boss."

Nate rolled his eyes at her before turning to face the barista. "This isn't a TV show. I'm just doing a check, and if I'm honest, I'm not liking what I'm seeing. He glanced at the barista's nametag. "Alex, where's your manager?"

"Mandy? She's, ah, out in the back. Having a smoke."

"How big is her cigarette?" Nate asked. "We've been here for ten minutes and she hasn't been back." He shook his head. "You know what? Just take me out so I can talk with her." He glanced at Ally. "You gonna be okay here for a while?"

"I got my soy latte," she said, tapping the cup. "And if I get bored I'll pick up some of the trash on the other tables."

"No you won't," Nathan warned. "That's your job, isn't it, Alex?"

"Yes, sir." Alex nodded. "I'll get right on that as soon as I've taken you to Mandy."

"Wish me luck," Nate said quietly.

"Good luck," she whispered as he followed Alex behind the counter, and out through the door that led to the kitchens at the rear.

Not that he needed it. She had a feeling that Nate Crawford ate Déjà Brew managers for breakfast, followed with a nice cup of espresso.

❧ 15 ❦

It was late afternoon by the time they made it to their second stop. San Martino Bay was a hundred miles north of Angel Sands, but had that same small town feel, complete with a boardwalk that ran along the sand and some retail outlets behind it. The building Nate was interested in was empty right now – but before it had shut down it was a seafood restaurant. The walls still held a stench of shellfish as they looked around.

"What do you think?" Nate asked her as he walked around the empty room. "Would you open up an outlet here?"

"It's pretty," Ally said, looking around at the golden sand and the pastel shops that lined the beach. "So yeah, I probably would. But then I never was the best business person. That's why my dad ended up selling to you." She smiled, as though it still smarted a bit.

"Even the best business person can't keep a company going on air. With the cash flow like it was, you were always fighting a losing battle. I'm amazed you kept it going as long as you did."

Her face lit up when he complimented her, making her

eyes glow and her lips curl. Man, was she beautiful. No wonder she'd started to haunt his dreams.

"Well for what it's worth, I think this place has good bones." She made her way over to the window, and looked outside. "The beach is quiet right now, but that's not a surprise on a weekday. I'd want to come back on the weekend and during the tourist season to make sure the footfall was good." She glanced back at him over her shoulder. "How many tourists visit each year?"

"Around two million according to the local business bureau."

"A bit less than Angel Sands. But still sustainable. And the location is great." She turned on her good foot. "Are you thinking of branching out into beach locations, or will this and Angel Sands be your only ones?"

"I wasn't thinking of expanding at all," he answered honestly. "We've had a massive period of growth in the past few years. I wanted to bed everything in before we go through another one. But then this place came up and it's too good an offer to miss. Plus Angel Sands is doing much better than we'd projected, so I'm thinking that we may look at acquiring a few more up and down the Pacific coast."

"That makes sense." Ally nodded. Her brow dipped, as though she was thinking something through. "But you know, these beach cafés have a much different feel to your urban ones. Maybe you should think about branding them a little differently." She bit her lip and stared out at the bay, her brows dipping together in concentration. "I don't know, maybe something like 'Coastal Coffee by Déjà Brew.' You could make them less about grabbing a coffee to go and more about the experience. Make them somewhere people want to visit whenever they're on vacation at the beach."

Nate stared at her, feeling his heart pound against his chest. "Say that again," he asked, his voice graveled.

She shook her head. "Sorry, I was talking without thinking. Ignore me. You know better than anybody else what you're doing."

"No, tell me what you'd call the shops again."

"Coastal Coffee?"

"By Déjà Brew," he murmured, tapping it quickly into the notes on his phone. "Jesus, who told you that you had no head for business? You're a genius."

The glow spread down her neck, pinking up the top of her chest. "I just know beach towns. I've lived in one all my life."

"What would you do differently to the coastal Déjà Brews?" he asked her, staring at her lips. It was taking everything he had not to clear the two strides between them and pull her against him. He wanted to feel them on his mouth, feel her hair as he knotted it in his hands. She was so damn enticing it made his body ache.

"I'd change the menu up. Maybe put more emphasis on meals rather than pastries. And the décor. It might be a bit cheesy, but I'd make it more beach-themed. Let's face it, locals are going to come in to grab a coffee no matter what the place looks like, but tourists want the full experience. And they're usually willing to pay extra for it."

A pulse of excitement shot through him. "Yes they are," he said, slowly nodding his head. "You're right. They're a completely different kind of customer."

"It would be worth doing a little market research before you commit to anything," Ally said, though she was glowing at his approval. "But the way I see it, if Disney can charge eight bucks for a cup of coffee, then Déjà Brew can probably find a way to mine the tourist gold too."

"How come you never went to college?" he asked her. "You're clearly bright enough."

"How do you know I didn't?"

"I've seen your resume, remember?"

She raised her eyebrows. "That's not fair. You're one up on me. I don't know anything about you."

"There's not much to know. What you see is what you get," he told her.

"I don't believe that for a second." The corner of her lip lifted into a smile. "You know, they should give employees their bosses' resumes. We should know who we're working for."

"I'll print you one out when we get home." He couldn't help grinning. He liked that she wanted to know more about him.

"Well, I didn't go to college because I was chickenshit," she said, adjusting her stance as if she was trying to get comfortable.

"You want to sit down? You've been standing for a while."

"Yeah, my leg's getting tired."

He led her out of the store and down to the boardwalk, finding an empty bench seat overlooking the ocean. Helping her down, he took her crutches and sat next to her. There was only an inch or two between them. And it felt like too much and not enough all at the same time.

"So you were saying..." he said, when they were comfortable. "Something about being chickenshit?"

She laughed. "Yeah. I had an offer to go to Sacramento. I accepted it, too. And right until the last moment I really thought I could go there." She was staring into the distance, her face forming a perfect profile. She sighed and it lifted her chest up. Nate tried not to look.

"So what happened?"

"I got scared." She looked down at her hands, turning them palm up. "I'm not great at changes, and I was so afraid that if I went away something would happen to my dad. He tried to get me in the car to drive me up there, but I cried and cried until he got the message. I took a few classes at the community college, but really I spent most of my time working at the café." She turned, her eyes still downcast as she gave him a rueful smile. "So there you go. I'm not exactly setting the world on fire."

"It's never too late."

"I'm twenty-seven years old. And even if I could get an offer, I couldn't afford the tuition. I made my bed when I was a teenager, now I get to lie on it for the rest of my life."

"You sound defeated," he remarked. What the hell had stopped her from reaching her potential? He wanted to dig it out of her.

She looked up. This time her expression was defiant. "No, I'm not," she said, shaking her head. "I've accepted what happened. And I'm happy in Angel Sands. The only time I get embarrassed about my lack of college education is when I have a conversation like this one."

"Would you like me to change the subject?" he asked, even though he didn't want to. There was so much more he wanted to ask.

Her eyes caught his. "I'd like that a lot."

He blew out a mouthful of air. Time to lighten the mood. "Okay, then. Can you tell me why some women shave their eyebrows off and pencil them back in? Because I've always been wondering about that."

This time her laughter was genuine. She tipped her head back, her eyes closing as she giggled out loud. "I've no idea," she said when she got herself under control. "But I'd like to know, too."

"You're beautiful when you laugh." The words escaped his lips without going through his common-sense filter. He wasn't sure he'd have been able to stop himself anyway. Because sitting there beside him, her face illuminated by the sun, she looked like beauty personified. It hurt his chest just to look at her.

She slowly turned her face to his. Her eyes were soft, her lips slightly parted, but it was her breathing he noticed most of all. It was shallow, as though it was caught in her throat. A slow flush worked its way up her neck.

Verboten, he reminded himself. It didn't stop his body from reacting to her.

"Beauty's only skin deep," she whispered.

But it wasn't, not with her. Maybe he'd thought that when they first met, but right now he could see so much more to Ally Sutton than just a pretty face. There was a fragility to her that made him want to protect her from everything, along with a strength that made him know she wouldn't accept that at all.

"It is," he whispered, the ocean breeze lifting his words. It lifted her hair, too, whipping it against her face. He leaned forward and gently pushed it away from her cheek, his fingers trailing across her skin.

She was still staring at him with those big blue eyes, as if he was some kind of God. It made him want to beat his chest, pick her up, and carry her back home. His muscles flexed with the memory of how she'd felt when he'd held her. Warm, soft, everything.

"Beautiful," he said again. "Kind. Funny. Clever." He traced his finger down from her cheekbone, along her jaw, and up to her mouth, trailing it across her bottom lip.

He could feel her stilted breath on his finger. One of them was trembling – he could feel it in his fingertips – but he wasn't sure if it was Ally or him. Maybe it was both of them, because this moment was so full of everything.

He dropped his forehead, his brow resting against hers, and cupped her jaw, his fingers brushing against the soft skin of her neck. Her eyes were wide as she stared into his, and for a moment he wanted to drown in them. Her close proximity pushed any good sense he had left out of his mind. Everything about this felt inevitable. It was only a matter of how long he could last out.

Right now he was barely hanging on by a thread.

"Ally," he whispered.

His lips were only a whisper from hers. When he said her name again he could feel her bottom lip quiver. He was full of her. Surrounded by her. Everything else around them faded into nothing as the spotlight of his desire fell firmly onto this woman. All those thoughts about how wrong it was. How he was her boss, how she was so young, they all seemed to dissolve into the air. His mind couldn't concentrate on anything but her.

"I want to kiss you," he said, his voice full of grit and need.

She blinked and looked up at him again, her face tilting a little until he could feel the warmth of her mouth only a brush away from his.

"Why don't you?"

Right now he couldn't think of a single damn reason. But still he hesitated, savoring that moment between thought and action. He was standing on the edge, teetering as gravity fought against sanity. Then he stroked her neck with his thumb, closing the gap between them to brush his warm lips against hers.

It wasn't quite a kiss, but it was definitely an intention. He felt her breath catch, watched her close her eyes as she melted against him. He did it again, this time parting his lips against hers, sliding his other arm around her waist so he could pull them closer together.

She hooked her arms around his neck, arching her back so her face was angled perfectly against his. He deepened the kiss, still cupping her face as he moved his mouth with hers.

Ally threaded her fingers through his hair and let out the smallest of moans, the sound vibrating against his lips like a tiny concerto. Desire punched him in the gut like it was ready for a fight. It rose up through his belly, filling his chest, before it pulsed its way down to his thighs. Still holding her tightly, he slowly traced a line of fire along her bottom lip with his tongue. She tasted like everything he never knew he wanted.

She arched her back even more, pressing herself against him, the soft swell of her breasts pushing into his muscled chest. His body ached to scoop her up again – the way he'd done when he first brought her home – and carry her some place away from prying eyes where he could show her exactly how she made him feel.

"Nate." His name was a sigh against his lips. He opened his eyes to see her staring into them, but then they suddenly darted away. "We have company," she said, pulling back from him.

He turned to see a little boy – no more than three-years-old – standing next to them. He was holding an ice cream cone, but it was melting and turning his hand sticky. A bead dropped onto his yellow t-shirt. He was entranced by Ally's crutches, reaching out a finger to touch the metal. He left a grubby brown fingerprint on them.

"I'm so sorry. He keeps running off." A woman ran over, grabbing the boy by his arm. "Honey, you have to keep licking it or it melts everywhere," she told him, lifting his hand up and running her tongue around the cone.

"*My* ice cream," the boy said, pulling his hand away sharply.

From the corner of his eye Nate could see Ally biting her lip, trying not to laugh. He took a deep breath in, trying to steady himself as he smiled at the woman who was apologizing once again.

"It's fine," he said. And it was. Even if his body felt cold in spite of the Californian heat. It missed the feel of her against him. "We were just heading out anyway." He looked at the little boy. "You should probably listen to your mom, though. She looks like she knows about ice cream."

"Mine."

Okay, then. The kid clearly didn't want to share. And who could blame him? He hadn't learned the ways of the world yet. Hadn't worked out that by not licking regularly, more of the ice cream was going to end up on him than in him.

Everybody in this world had to make their own mistakes – it was pretty hard to learn from somebody else's.

"You ready?" he asked Ally.

She nodded. He stood and grabbed her crutches, rubbing off the ice cream with his thumb. Passing them to her, he helped her up.

"Come on. Let's go home."

🎋 16 🎋

"Oh. My. God," Ember said, leaning into the camera. "I can't believe he kissed you. So what happened after that?"

"Nothing," Ally told her. "We got in the car and came home. Then Nate said he had to cook dinner, and Riley was in the kitchen with him so I told them I needed a quick nap and called you two."

The three of them were on a video call. Crazy, since they lived in the same town, but there was no way to get together tonight – and this was a crisis. Ally needed her friends like she needed air. If she didn't talk about what happened she thought she might explode.

"How long was the drive home?" Brooke asked. She was cooking dinner, her laptop angled so she could see them both from the stove. She stirred the sauce and turned the heat down, then added some pepper.

"Two hours maybe?" And they'd been the longest two hours of her life. So many thoughts had been rushing through her mind as she stared out of the window at the Pacific coast.

Was he going to say something? Would he try to kiss her again?

The answer to all those was a firm no. Instead, he turned on the music as loud as it would go and tapped his fingers on the wheel to the rhythm. And here she was, wondering if she was supposed to forget it ever happened.

How the heck could she do that when she couldn't stop thinking about that kiss?

"Maybe he'll talk to you tonight," Ember said, her face full of sympathy. "When Riley's in bed. He can't just pretend it didn't happen, can he? Not when it was as hot as you described."

"What did you do when Lucas first kissed you?" Ally asked her friend. "Did you talk about it?"

Ember shifted her eyes away, looking suddenly embarrassed. "I... um... went back to his cottage and then..." she trailed off. "Okay, I'm officially not answering that question."

"It was different for you guys," Brooke interjected. She was chopping vegetables, her knife slicing through stiff carrots. "First of all, you weren't working for him. Plus he doesn't have a daughter. There weren't as many complications as there are for Ally."

"My whole life is one big complication," Ally said, sighing. "I've no idea how I can go out and face him again without blushing like crazy. If I act like a loon then Riley will wonder what's going on, and that will only make things worse." She shook her head. "Ugh. Why can't this ground just swallow me up right now?"

"You'll be fine," Brooke told her, giving her a warm smile. "You're catastrophizing. If he kissed you then that means he likes you. There's nothing to be embarrassed about."

"But what if he doesn't like me the way I like him?" Ally asked. "Maybe he got carried away by the moment. We were having fun, sitting out looking at the ocean. Everything was beautiful. What if he regrets it?"

"Did he look like he regretted it?" Ember asked.

Ally thought back to that long car ride home. "I've no idea. He has this ability to make his expression totally blank. He'd make a killing at poker."

"It's probably the businessman in him."

"Well it's not very helpful." Ally sighed. "I wish I knew how he felt."

"How do *you* feel?" Ember asked, taking a sip of coffee. "Isn't that the important thing?"

How *did* she feel? It was almost impossible to tell. She felt high from the kiss and low from the aftermath and in between she felt completely confused.

"Would you kiss him again if he asked you to?" Brooke laid the knife down and stared at Ally through the square in her screen.

"Yes."

"And if he asked you on a date would you go?"

"Of course."

She could see Ember's eyebrows rise up in her part of the split screen. "Oh honey," she said, trying not to smirk. "You've got it bad."

"I have?"

"Oh yes," Brooke agreed. "One of the worst cases I've seen."

"You guys aren't helping," Ally protested. "It's not about me. It's about him. Who cares if I've got it bad when he's pretending that kiss never happened?"

"Then remind him."

"Maybe I should move out now," Ally said, ignoring the way Ember was wiggling her eyebrows. "Because there's no way I'm going to survive living here for another week. I'd rather hop up five flights of stairs every day."

"And down. You'd need to hop down them, too," Ember said helpfully.

They were both having way too much fun at her expense. "Guys, this is serious. What do I do now?"

"You do nothing," Brooke said, her expression thoughtful. "You just go out there and eat dinner and pretend that kiss didn't happen. He's not going to say anything in front of Riley, is he? So enjoy your dinner and wait to see what unfolds."

"And don't forget," Ember said, giving her a small smile. "He may not do anything while you're staying there with him. He strikes me as the kind of guy who wouldn't want to put you in an awkward position. Maybe he'll wait until you've moved back home."

Ugh. Ally hated waiting. She hated worrying, too, and right now her life was full of both of those things. The skin beneath her cast was itching like crazy, too, and she couldn't do a damn thing about that either.

Somebody tapped on her door. "Ally?" Riley called out. "Dinner's almost ready."

"I'm coming," she replied, then quickly turned to the laptop screen. "Guys, I gotta go," she said, talking quietly so Riley couldn't hear her. She was supposed to be napping after all.

"Me too," Brooke agreed. "I got a hungry boy sitting at the table waiting on me."

"And I've got a guy who's calling for take out," Ember said, grinning. "Message us later, okay? I want a full status report."

"There won't be anything to report," Ally told her.

"Well message even if there isn't. Now go, you got dinner to eat."

Ally leaned forward to switch the laptop off. Thank God for her friends. They might not have been much help with

Nate, but at least she knew they were always there for her. They were like sisters to her, and she loved them so much.

Twisting her legs on the bed, she put her feet on the ground and grabbed the crutches resting on the wall. Slowly she pulled herself to standing, taking a deep breath to try and steel herself for what was to come.

"Wish me luck," she murmured to the empty room. She had a feeling she was going to need it.

"How was your trip?" Riley asked as she sliced into the steak Nate had broiled for them. "Did you guys have fun?"

Ally looked down at her plate. The whole room was silent. She could hear the beat of her heart and nothing else. But there was no way she was answering first. Let Nate handle this one. Riley was his daughter, after all. And right now, Ally had no answer for her.

Nate cleared his throat. "It was good."

"Was it good for you?" She turned to Ally. "Or did he make you listen to his playlist? I swear it's a form of torture. I keep threatening to report him to the Geneva Convention."

Ally coughed loudly. Riley didn't really want the answer to that one. "Um. Yeah. It was fine," she said.

Riley frowned. "You two must be exhausted. I've never seen you so quiet."

"It was a long day," Nate told her, then quickly changed the subject. "How was school? Did you get the grades back on your English assignment?"

"Not yet, but the teacher promised us we'd have them tomorrow. And school was good." Riley put her fork down and looked up at him. "Actually, I have something to ask you. My friends are going to the movies on Saturday night and they've asked me to join them. We'll only be gone for a few hours." She looked up with hope in her eyes. "Can I go?"

"You're still grounded," Nate reminded her. "It's been less than two weeks since you tried to jump off a cliff. So the answer's no," he said firmly.

"But it's only a few hours. Laura's mom's going to take us and pick us up, so you don't have to worry about me being in a car with a teenage driver." She pulled her lips between her teeth, worrying at them. "Please, Dad. I really want to."

Ally looked up, curious.

"The answer's still no," Nate said again, his voice sharper. "Maybe another time."

"God!" Riley cried out. "That's so unfair. Do you know how hard it is to make friends when you're new in town? They'll probably never ask me again."

"Riley." His voice was a low warning.

"Don't *Riley* me. I don't believe this. You took me away from all my friends when we left Seattle. You don't want me to be happy, do you? You don't care if I don't have anybody to talk to. I bet you like it when I'm miserable." Her eyes flashed with an anger Ally hadn't seen before. It made her breath catch.

"I don't."

Riley glared at him, her eyes flashing. "Could have fooled me." She pushed her plate away, the silverware rattling loudly against the china. "And your steak tastes like rubber." Standing up, she folded her arms across her chest, her eyes narrowing as she stared at him. "I'm not hungry," she said, letting out a big huff. "I'm going to my room."

She stomped out of the kitchen, slamming the door, and Nate stared after her, his jaw tight and eyes narrow.

Ally blew out a mouthful of air. It had been weird watching them go at it. As though she was being transported back through the years, to her dad's old blue-and-yellow kitchen where they'd had their most electric arguments. She could feel Riley's sense of injustice, but strangely, she could feel Nate's frustrations, too.

"Are you okay?" she asked softly.

He raked his fingers through his hair. Like Riley, he'd abandoned his half-eaten steak. "Apart from being the worst father in the world? Yeah, I'm great."

"You're not the world's worst father," she told him. "You're coming from a place of love. Riley might not realize that now, but she will one day."

"Did you realize that with your dad?"

Touché. Ally looked down at her fingers, suddenly fascinated by the oval of her nail beds. The air felt loaded and heavy, as though it was full of conversations neither one of them wanted to have.

"I'm running out of ideas." His voice was low. "I can't seem to make her happy at all. I know she's still grieving and it takes time, but I can't stand seeing her so angry." Gone was his heated expression, replaced by a lost look that tugged at her. "What should I do?"

"You're asking *me*?" She shook her head. "I'm not that experienced with kids. I wish I could help you."

"I'm asking you as someone who was in Riley's place. What did you need from your dad? Should I be stern, should I let her get away with stuff? Tell me, because I have no idea."

She took a moment to consider his question. "When I was in Riley's place I felt isolated. As though nobody understood me at all. When I was with my friends I wanted them to treat me like anybody else would. I wanted to go out with them and be a teenager because as soon as I got home and my mom wasn't there, reality was going to hit me all over again. And it hurt like hell every time it did."

Ally wasn't looking at him. She couldn't. There were too many memories and emotions pushing at her chest. "But more than being isolated, I felt so damn afraid. I was a kid and yet I had to come to terms with the fact that my mom wasn't coming back. I had to leave the only home I felt comfort in and move in with my dad. And unlike you, he had a girlfriend at the time, and she made it clear she wasn't happy with having me there." She rolled her shoulders, trying to loosen her tight muscles. "I was so scared he was going to make me leave. That he was going to choose her over me. And I guess it could have gone two ways – I could have tried to be the best kid ever and make him want me. But," she lowered her voice, "what if he still didn't?"

Nate leaned forward, but remained silent.

"So instead I went the other way," she told him. "I kept pushing and pushing to see what the boundaries were. How bad did I have to be to make him throw me out? I needed to know. I was so used to the worst happening; it felt like it was only a matter of time before I lost my dad, too."

"But somehow I didn't lose him. Not then, anyway. His girlfriend moved out after a couple of months, and it was just the two of us for the next few years." She took another deep breath in, the air pushing through her tight chest. "And I'm guessing right now Riley's trying to see how far she can push you. She'd never admit it to anybody but she's scared. She wants you to love her unconditionally, but she's afraid that you don't. She's too old to ask for hugs, but she still wants you to offer them, even if she rejects them nine times out of ten. But more than anything, she wants to believe in you. She wants to believe you'll always be there for her. But she believed that of her mom, too, and life stole that certainty away from her."

She lifted her hand to wipe the tear that had begun its long roll down her cheek. Her other hand was flat on the table, resting near her water glass.

Nate's voice was soft. "I'm so sorry." And when she looked

at him, he really was. Empathy molded his features as though he understood every emotion rushing through her.

"It happened a long time ago." She took a deep breath. "And as it turned out, my dad left anyway."

"You want to talk about it?"

She shook her head. "No. We're talking about Riley."

"So what should I do?" he asked her. "How can I make things right?"

"You take each day at a time. You understand that however you feel, her emotions are about ten times as big and she has no experience in dealing with them. You show her love, but you also show her that love means sometimes saying no." She raised her eyebrows. "It also means saying yes, sometimes. And admitting when you're wrong."

"So you think I should tell her she can go to the movies?"

He was close enough for her to smell his cologne. She shut her eyes for a moment, trying not to get distracted. It was important, for Riley and for Nate.

Maybe, just maybe, her terrible experiences might help somebody else. And wouldn't that be amazing after everything she'd been through?

"I don't want to tell you what to do as a father, that's not my place. But if you're considering it, I could make a couple of phone calls and check that Laura's mom really will be driving them there and back. I know pretty much everybody in Angel Sands, or at least I know somebody who knows them."

"You'd do that?"

"After everything you've done for me? Of course I would."

"Thank you."

Every time she looked at him her heart ached a little more, remembering how perfect that kiss on the beach had been. The details were etched into her mind. The soft whisper of his breath against her lips. The silkiness of his thick, wavy hair as she threaded her fingers through it. But more than anything, she could remember the way he made her feel. The way desire and need tugged at her every time his lips touched hers.

She needed to get over this and fast. He was obviously not going to talk about it, and she wasn't ready to open herself up and spill her guts to him. That kiss they'd shared earlier might have been the best one she'd ever had, but for him it was a mistake.

Taking a deep breath, she pushed herself up to standing, grabbing the crutches she'd rested on the table. "I'll go and make some calls," she said, needing to put some space between herself and Nate. Because right now all she could think about was that he was the best kiss she'd ever had.

Nate shut the door to his office and slumped in the black leather chair. Right now it felt like the only room where he could truly be alone. The only room that didn't hold a high note of Ally's fragrance, and the only one that Riley didn't enter unless she knocked first – even at her very worst when she was rebelling against everything.

He reached down to pull out the bottom drawer, before he curled his fingers around the neck of the bottle he had stashed down there. It was still three-quarters full. He twisted the lid open to pour himself out a splash. No ice, no water, just pure bronze liquid. Lifting the glass to his mouth, he closed his eyes, tipping the whiskey in. It slipped down way too easily, warming his stomach, and he let the burn soothe him.

He could hear the occasional squeal from Riley as she spoke into her cellphone, no doubt telling her friends that her dad had relented and she was allowed to go with them to the movies. Ally had been right; banning his daughter from going out with her friends had been foolish. He didn't want to make her life any harder than it already was.

And then there was Ally.

He shook his head and poured himself out another mouthful of whiskey, swallowing it as quickly as the first. Then he tightened the lid and put the bottle back into the drawer.

What the hell had he been thinking, kissing her? He dropped his head into his hands. It was bad enough that she was an employee, she was also more than a decade younger than him, and living with him, too. He knew how stupid it was to have feelings for her – the kind of feelings that would engulf him if he let them.

Hadn't he learned from his mistakes with Stephanie? She had been younger too – not as young as Ally, but the difference was enough – and from the start it was clear she wanted different things than he did.

She wanted to have fun. To go out and be seen by people that mattered to her. She wanted to be a twenty-something woman, not somebody burdened by a step-daughter and all the crises and tears that were brought with it.

He and Stephanie had been at totally different stages in life. They'd both thought it didn't matter, but it did, more than either of them had ever anticipated. Ally was even younger, and she'd want different things, too.

It could never work.

He lifted his head and leaned back on the smooth leather chair, letting a sigh escape his lips. What a damn mess he'd made of things. He'd behaved like a teenager at the beach with Ally, not thinking through the consequences. Just living in the moment, tasting the pleasure of her lips, letting desire mold his every move when common sense should have prevailed.

Yeah, well he wasn't a teenager – far from it. He was a grown man with the ability to control himself. He'd made a mistake, given in to primal needs, but that didn't mean he had to do it again.

How long was it until Ally's elevator would be repaired? Just another week or so? He could hold out until then, couldn't he? Once they weren't stuck under the same roof things would be so much easier. He'd be able to breathe without inhaling her fragrance, to relax in his living room without his eyes being drawn to her. And maybe, just maybe, he'd be able to sleep without waking up every hour, his body damp with sweat, his heart pounding against his chest.

Two weeks maximum. He could do this.

❧ 17 ❧

"I need your help," Riley said, walking into the living room and collapsing on the sofa next to Ally.

Ally pressed pause on her game and put the controller down on the arm of the sofa. "What's up?"

"I have nothing to wear. *Nothing.*" She gave a dramatic sigh. "What do you wear to the movies in California anyway?"

"Pretty much the same as you wore in Washington, but with less layers I'm guessing." Ally smiled. Since Nate had spoken with Riley and agreed she could go out with her friends, she'd been like a different child. Her happiness had been infectious. It had almost taken Ally's mind off that kiss, and the fact that neither she nor Nate had mentioned it in the two days since.

Almost being the operative word.

It wasn't as though they'd had a chance to be alone. In her new happy state Riley had been much more sociable, spending time with them in the kitchen while dinner was being cooked, and slumping in the living room with them until it got late. A few times Ally would look over at Nate and see him staring at her with a question in his eyes, but he'd look away again and she'd be the one left with all the questions.

"Jeans then. I should wear jeans, right?" Riley asked.

"Jeans sound good. It can get cool in the movie theater with the air conditioning on."

"But what should I wear on top? And should I have my hair up or down?" She lowered her voice. "Apparently, some of the guys from my math class are going to the same movie. I don't want to look out of place."

Ally raised an eyebrow. "Is there one particular guy you're worried about?"

"Maybe." Riley bit down a smile. "But you can't tell Dad because I'd just die."

"I won't."

"So?" Riley said. "What top should I wear?"

"Let's go and look in your closet," Ally suggested, grabbing the remote control to switch the television off. "And if you don't have anything that works we can look in mine. We're probably the same size."

"Apart from your legs. Those are about ten million inches longer than mine."

"Ah, but your legs are better. They actually work without crutches," Ally pointed out.

An hour later, Riley was almost ready for her trip out. Nate was working in the coffee shop. So when Riley had asked if Ally could do her make-up she'd agreed.

"There you go," she said, running a mascara wand through the younger girl's lashes. "All done. You look gorgeous." Gently, she turned Riley's head until she was facing the mirror. She really did look good. Her almond-shaped eyes were to die for, especially when they were highlighted with neutral shadows that had sparkle to them.

"Oh my God! Thank you," Riley said, hugging her. "You're amazing."

"Any time. It was fun. And it's not as though I get to go out much anymore, is it?"

Riley immediately looked guilty. "No," Ally said, "I'm not talking about my leg. I just go out less than I used to because I'm not a teenager any more. A lot of my friends have families and partners. It gets harder to find time when we're all free."

"But you still go out on dates, right?" Riley asked. "I mean you're not ancient or anything. Not like Dad."

Ally laughed. "Now there's a backhanded compliment if I ever heard one. And yeah, I've been out on a few dates. But not so many recently."

"Why not?"

"I was busy with work. Plus there's the problem of supply and demand."

Riley looked confused. "Supply and demand?" she repeated. "What the hell does that mean?"

"I've been single for a long time and Angel Sands is a small town. The number of available guys I haven't dated before decreases every day." Ally shrugged. "Maybe I'll end up an old maid."

"But you're beautiful," Riley said. "You could have any guy you want."

"Well, thank you." She gave Riley a small smile. "But it doesn't always work that way. And anyway, we were supposed to be talking about you and this guy. What's his name and how old is he? I want to know all about him."

She may have been terrible at dating, but she was great at changing the subject. And as Riley began to tell her about Leo Frischmann, the blonde-haired football God from her Math class, Ally was almost certain the sixteen-year-old girl in front of her was having better success with the opposite sex than she was.

"Hey, where are you?" Ember asked, her soft voice drowned out by loud music echoing through the phone line.

"At home. Well at Nate and Riley's home," Ally corrected herself. "Where did you expect me to be?"

"At the beach, the same place we always go on the first weekend in October."

"It's October?" Ally looked around the living room, searching for a calendar or clock that could tell her the date. She'd completely lost track of time since she'd been laid up with a broken ankle. "Seriously? I swear it's only just September."

"That's the first sign of getting old. Losing track of dates." Ember's voice was full of amusement. "Anyway, get your butt down here. The cookout's started, there's a band playing, and it's only an hour or two before the fireworks start."

For as long as Ally could remember, the town of Angel Sands had thrown a beach party on the first weekend of October, declaring it the end of the summer season for all the businesses that lined the beach. It was when many of the smaller shops closed up until the following spring, and their owners took a chance to recover from the busy summer rush.

It wasn't as crazy as the Angel Day Fair that opened the summer season every May, but Ally, Ember, and Brooke loved it anyway. It was a chance to catch up with old friends, to say goodbye to workers who only stayed in Angel Sands for the summer, and to enjoy the fireworks that the local Business Guild put on for their appreciation.

Ally looked at her watch. Riley had left for the movies an hour earlier, and Nate was still at the coffee shop. The house was completely empty. "I can't come," she said, "Nobody's here to bring me, and I'm still not able to drive."

"No problem, I'll send Lucas over. Come on, it's a tradition. We always watch the fireworks together." There was a shout followed by a cheer. "It wouldn't be the same without you."

"Okay," Ally agreed, glancing down at the old t-shirt and shorts she was wearing. "Give me twenty minutes to get ready?"

"Of course. I'll tell Lucas to come over for you in a minute. And while we're waiting for you, I'll get the drinks ready."

"What's going on out there?" Nate asked Brad as he emerged from the kitchen in the coffee shop. The sound of music was carried up on the breeze from further down the beach, near Paxton's Pier, if Nate had to guess. "It sounds like somebody's having a party."

"It's the beach party," Brad said, frowning. "I told you this morning, remember? That's why we have extra staff on today, to cope with the influx of customers."

"You said it was the end of the season," Nate agreed. "But I didn't know there was music."

"And fireworks," Brad said. "They start right after sundown. You should go and see them. This town knows how to throw a party."

Jeff came through the double doors, mopping his red brow with a cloth. "You should be here for Angel Day," he said, sighing as he leaned on the counter. "Now that's something to see."

"Angel Day?" Nate repeated. His mind immediately went to what Lorne Michaels had told him when they'd first met. Something about an Angel leading a captain home.

"Yeah," Brad said, nodding in agreement. "It's when we commemorate the town's creation every May. It's a lot of fun."

"Can I close the kitchen up?" Jeff asked him, his face still as red as beetroot. "I promised to meet my wife and kids down there."

"Sure," Nate agreed. "You can head out, too," he told Brad. "I'll close up here."

"You coming down after?" Jeff asked. Nate blinked – it was the first time Jeff had ever asked about anything other than whether he could go home.

"Um, yeah. Maybe." Nate glanced at his watch. He could call Ally and see if she wanted to go down and watch the fireworks. Then he grimaced. No, that was a really bad idea. The memory of what happened the last time they were together on a beach rushed into his mind. He swallowed hard as he tried to push it out again. "What time did you say the fireworks were?"

"Just after eight, when the sun goes down."

A few minutes down at the pier wouldn't hurt. In fact, they could only be a good thing. Riley was out tonight, and being alone with Ally in the house really wasn't a good idea.

Because there was willpower and there was *willpower*. Nate might have had the first, but the second seemed elusive, especially whenever he was close to Ally Sutton.

"You made it!" Ember ran forward to embrace Ally, who was balancing on her crutches on the boardwalk. "And you look gorgeous. You're the only woman I know who can rock a dress like that when you've got a foot in plaster."

Ally looked down. She was wearing a white strappy sundress, the bodice cut close to her body, the skirt flowing from her waist to halfway down her thighs. Her long hair was down and wavy – thanks to the braid she'd worn it in ever since she'd washed her hair that morning – and she'd put a little make up on for once. It was a party, after all.

"Thanks. Though I'm not sure about the shoes." She grimaced as she looked down. On her good foot she was wearing a white tennis shoe. She didn't trust herself in anything else – walking with one good leg was hard enough, trying to do it in sandals was asking to fall over.

"They go with the dress perfectly," Ember said, grinning.

"I got you both a drink." Lucas came up to join them, carrying two bright pink cocktails, balancing them in his hands as he gingerly walked from the bar further along the boardwalk. "I saw Brooke over there, too. She's getting a hotdog for Nicholas, but said she'd be over to join you in a minute."

"How are the fireworks looking? Is it safe?" Ally asked Lucas, smiling at him as he passed her the drink. As a firefighter he always saw the danger in everything. The fireworks were probably going to kill him.

"I took a look at the set up. It's as good as it gets," Lucas said, his voice serious. "They're setting them off from boats out in the ocean, so hopefully that will lessen the risk."

Ember glanced at Ally, widening her eyes. Ally stifled down a grin. Lucas was a great guy – funny, kind, and strong as hell, which came in handy when you were a woman living on your own. He was always doing favors for Ember's friends – helping them out with home improvements, lifting things that were just too heavy for them. When he wasn't at work, that was.

His seriousness about safety was kind of endearing, even if she and Ember did giggle about it occasionally.

"And how are you doing?" he asked her, glancing down at her cast. "Any news on when it's coming off?"

"It's a couple more weeks until my next appointment. Then they'll x-ray it and decide what to do."

"How about the elevator? You got news on that?"

"It'll be another five days before the right part is in the country," Ally told him. "After that, it's a matter of how long it takes the engineer to fix it."

"So you'll be staying with the hot coffee guy for at least another week," Ember said, not bothering to hide her grin. "Sucks for you."

"Hey," Brooke called out to them, running up from the shoreline. "You made it." She threw her arms around Ally, giving her the tightest of squeezes. "I'm so glad you're here." Brooke looked back over her shoulder to the ocean. "I can only stay a minute. My mom's keeping an eye on Nick and you know what that means." She wrinkled her nose.

Brooke's mom was more at home in high society than at the beach. With her beautiful clothes and perfectly coiffed hair she rarely went near the ocean, claiming the salty air was so bad for her complexion.

Ally hugged her back, so happy to see her friends again. Though they caught up most nights either on Facetime or by messaging, she'd missed being able to spend time with them.

"Ally." A thick, weathered voice came from her left. Lorne was standing there with his wife, Marcie. "I didn't think you were coming."

She smiled at the old man, her heart warming even more at the sight of him. She wasn't kidding when she said she thought of him as a second father. Leaning forward she hugged him just as tight as she'd hugged Brooke, then gave his wife a kiss on the cheek. "I decided to get out of the house. It's getting claustrophobic there."

And lonely, she thought to herself.

"How are you feeling? That ankle giving you any problems?"

Ally took a sip of her cocktail, letting the fruity liquid

wash over her tongue. "Nothing that a couple of drinks won't fix."

Lorne laughed. "That's my girl." He lowered his voice. "Have you heard from your dad recently?"

Ally blinked. Her dad? No, she hadn't heard from him. She hadn't even thought of him for days. Not since that afternoon with Nate and the kiss they'd shared on the beach. Her mind had been too full of her current problems to think about her old ones.

"Oh." She covered her mouth with her free hand. "He's still blocked in my phone." Her eyes widened with shock. In all the craziness she'd forgotten to unblock him. Yes, she was still angry at him, but she was also an adult. She'd never intended to ignore him for too long.

"That explains why he keeps calling me to ask how you are. I couldn't understand why you hadn't told him about your ankle."

"He knows about my accident?"

"I didn't realize it was a secret. He's worried about you, Ally. I know you're angry with him, but you should at least listen to what he has to say."

Lorne was right. As angry as she was at her dad, she could hear him out. He'd given up a lot for her over the years, she owed him that. "I'll unblock him when I get home."

"You've always been a good girl."

"It doesn't mean I've forgiven him," she told him, her voice thick. "It'll take more than a few phone calls for that."

Lorne nodded slowly. "I know, sweetheart."

The music started up again, a local band taking the stage as the loud bass vibrated through the PA. Lorne gave her another squeeze and put his arm around his wife's waist, saying hello to Ember, Brooke, and Lucas before the two of them walked away.

Ally took another mouthful of cocktail, and tried to push

down the anxiety talking about her dad had brought up. On the positive side it gave her something to worry about other than Nathan Crawford. That had to be a good thing, didn't it?

Nate glanced at his phone as he walked through the throngs of people lining the boardwalk beside Paxton's Pier, the sound of music and excited conversation filling his ears. A message from Riley flashed across the screen.

Just finished up dinner. Going into the movie now. Laura's mom promises to have me home by 11:30. Love you, xxx

He quickly tapped out a reply. *Have fun. Love you too xx.* He was still on high alert, worried about something going wrong, but he'd spoken to Laura's mom who seemed like she had everything under control. He rolled his shoulders, his muscles stiff beneath his white cotton shirt, and tried to let his jaw loosen up.

"Nate, you came. I wasn't sure if you would."

He looked up to see Lorne Michaels standing there, along with Frank Megassey, and two women who were almost certainly their wives. He gave them a smile that all four of them returned.

There. Being friendly wasn't so hard after all.

"I heard there were fireworks. I thought I'd check them out before I headed home."

"Riley not here?" Lorne asked. He'd met Nate's daughter a few times, when Nate had sent her to the shop next door with a drink for the old man. He was becoming very fond of his lattes.

"She's at the movies with friends."

"And of course Ally's already here. She's looking well. You're obviously taking care of her." Frank gave him a slow nod, his eyes full of approval. "You did a good thing taking her in."

"Especially when her dad left her all on her own," the woman standing next to Frank – his wife? – added

"He didn't leave her," Lorne pointed out, looking irritated at the woman's suggestion. "He went away for a while. That's all. And she's a grown woman. She doesn't need her daddy around her constantly."

"Daughters can be tough," Frank agreed. Then he looked at Nate. "I expect you know all about that."

Nate let out a little laugh. "Yeah, I do."

"Oh look, there's Ally." Nate followed the direction of Frank's arm, frowning as he tried to pick her out. There were so many people here.

But then he saw her standing next to her friends about fifteen feet away. She was holding a glass with pink liquid in it, her beautiful blonde hair tumbling over her bare shoulders.

His stomach tightened. So much for avoiding her. And there was a part of him that didn't want to because, damn, she did things to him. Made him feel things he hadn't in a long time. She breached boundaries he didn't know he had, and it scared him.

"Such a nice girl," Lorne's wife was saying. "She's always taken care of you, hasn't she, Lorne? And she always has a smile for me whenever I see her. Such a shame what happened to her when she was younger."

With his eyes still on Ally, Nate inclined his head to listen to the conversation going on around him. He held his breath so he could hear a little better.

"Losing her mom?" Frank's wife asked. "Yes, that was so sad."

"She had such a bright future ahead of her," Frank agreed. Somebody had moved in front of Ally, blocking his view.

Nate frowned, willing them to move. He wanted to look at her again, to drink her in.

"Did you know she used to compete for the state?" Frank asked. "Man, she could make running look easy." It took Nate a minute to realize Frank was talking to him. Reluctantly, he pulled his gaze away from Ally's direction.

"She did?"

"Yup. There was talk of her eventually meeting Olympic standards. She was that good."

"So what happened?"

Nate took in a deep breath. His heart was hammering in his chest. He blamed the lack of oxygen after not inhaling for so long.

"Her mom died. After that her heart wasn't in it anymore. She refused to do all the travelling it required. Said she didn't want to leave her dad." Frank lowered his voice. "Such a shame for her."

"She was still good, though," Lorne pointed out. "She got offered a full athletic scholarship at Cal State."

Nate glanced to his right. The man had moved out of the way. There she was again, the last of the sunlight illuminating her hair, making her skin glow like she'd just stepped off a catwalk. He lowered his gaze, taking in her legs and that cast, swallowing hard when he thought about all she'd lost.

Not just her mom, but her future too. The desire that he'd been feeling for her ever since the first day they'd met mingled with something else, something softer that he couldn't quite define.

Even from this distance he could feel the pull toward her. The only question was how long he could fight it.

Nate pulled his car into the driveway, pushing the button to close the gate behind him. The fireworks had finished half an hour ago. He'd looked around for Ally, intending to offer her a lift home, but there was no sign of her among the crowd of people spilling out from the boardwalk. So he'd headed back to the café and picked up his Lexus, and driven home through the dark California streets. He must have beaten most of the traffic because he'd made it home within ten minutes. Thank God, because he was exhausted.

There were a few lights on in the house – one in the hallway and another in the living room – but apart from that it looked deadly quiet. Climbing out of the Lexus, he walked up the steps, the metal keys in his hand rattling against each other.

He let himself into the house and pulled the front door quietly closed behind him. It was quiet. Maybe Ally hadn't made it home yet. He wasn't sure whether to be relieved or disappointed, because his mind was full of questions he wasn't ready to ask her.

"Ally?" he called out. There was no reply. Frowning, he put his bag down on the polished wooden floor and kicked his shoes off, then headed for the living room.

As soon as he pushed the door open he saw her. She was slumped on the sofa, her eyes closed, her lips slightly parted as she breathed rhythmically in her sleep. She must have left before the fireworks had started, or at the moment they'd ended.

He stood and watched her for a moment, trying not to feel like too much of a creep as his eyes took her in. She was so damn beautiful it made his heart pound. His lips tingled with the memory of her taste. He squeezed his eyes shut, trying to center himself.

He was her boss, her friend. He couldn't be anything else.

"Nate?"

He waited for her to say more, expecting her eyelids to

open any minute. But they didn't. Instead she muttered something unintelligible and turned her head, letting out a huff of breath like she was blowing out a candle.

He willed for her to say his name again, but her steady breathing returned and the room was filled with silence. For a second he wondered what the hell he should do.

Wake her up and help her get to bed? No, he wasn't quite ready to take her to that room again. It had been hard enough painting her nails in there the other day, and that was before they'd kissed.

He wasn't going to stay around while she was sleeping, either. Because yeah, he might not have been a creep yet, but give it a minute or two. No, he'd go and grab something to eat and do a couple more hours reading on the reports his team had sent in. Maybe by then Riley would be home to help Ally to bed.

He almost made it to the door before she spoke again.

"Nate... please."

Damn. There was no way he could walk away. Not when she was saying his name. He was too damn curious to hear what else she had to say.

When he turned to look at her, she'd shifted positions again. This time she was laying on her left, her body angled toward him. She gave a little huff again, her lips pursing together.

"Ally?" he said, giving her one final chance to wake up.

"Wha—?" She lifted her head, her eyelids heavy, and her brow pulled down. "What time is it?" she asked, staring up at him.

"Just after nine. I'm sorry to wake you." He reached up to scratch the back of his neck. "I saw you at the boardwalk. Did you leave after the fireworks?"

She ran her tongue along her bottom lip. "Just before. I

got tired and my leg started to ache," she said, her voice still thick with sleep. "Lucas brought me home."

"You missed some good ones." He kept his voice soft. His whole body felt tense, as though he was contracting every muscle. "Are you feeling okay now?"

He watched as she straightened herself up. Then her face wrinkled up. "Damn."

"Are you okay?"

She nodded quickly. "My leg's so itchy. Right above my ankle where I have no way of getting to it." She shuddered. "It comes and goes, but right now it's killing me. I don't suppose you'd have a knife strong enough to cut this cast off?"

"I'm not sure your doctor would approve." He was glad of the distraction. "Are you sure you can't get it with your fingers?"

"I've tried, but the gap isn't big enough." She jammed her fingers into the rim of her cast to demonstrate. "Maybe you could just chop my leg off."

"Have you tried a knitting needle?"

"What?"

"That's what my mom did when I was a kid and had my arm in a cast. She'd push it down and it felt like heaven."

"Well, I don't have a knitting needle." She looked at him hopefully. "Do you?"

"Nope. But I have an idea. Stay there." He ran to the kitchen and pulled a chopstick from the drawer, coming back to the living room a few seconds later. "It's not as strong as a knitting needle," he said. "But if we're careful it could work."

"I'll try anything once." She took the chopstick from him, and jammed it down between her leg and her cast. Her brows knitted together as she moved it from left to right. "Damn, I can't quite get to it."

"Do you want me to try?"

She nodded, handing him back the chopstick.

Gently he took her leg, his warm fingers circling her calf. He held it steady as he pushed the long stick inside, moving it to the left as she directed.

"Right there. Scratch me," she said quickly.

He did as he was told, moving the chopstick up and down.

"A little harder."

He raised an eyebrow but said nothing, increasing the pressure of the wood against her skin.

"Harder, please."

Okay, then. He wasn't getting turned on by this. Not by the feeling of her skin, the aroma of her body, nor by the way she breathed out the words. Nor was he imagining her breathing those words out while she was lying beneath him in his bed.

Nope. Not at all.

"Oh God, that's good."

Her innuendos were killing him in the most delicious way. He could feel the need for her pulse right through him.

"Don't stop, not yet," she gasped. "I might need you to do this all night."

This time he couldn't help but chuckle. It was either that or groan. He slowly lifted his gaze to hers.

She smiled back at him. "Sorry. I couldn't help it. You're just too good at this."

"Ally?"

"Yeah?"

"If I kiss you will you shut up?"

Ally's mouth dropped open and she stared at him with those big blues. "Probably not. But you should do it anyway."

He tried to remind himself of all the reasons this was a bad idea, but his brain had an answer for every one of them.

I'm her boss.

Not right now. You're not even at the shop.

She's too young.

She's an adult. And look at the way she's staring at you.

She's staying at my house.

Convenient, hey?

Dammit. He didn't have any room for a relationship. Look what happened with Stephanie.

Stephanie who?

His pulse started drumming through his ears, silencing everything except that constant need. He pushed himself up from where he was kneeling, moving closer to her. His hand was still on her calf, and he slowly feathered his fingers up higher, past her knee and to her lower thigh. Her skin was so tender, so delightfully inviting. Before he knew it, he was stooping down to press his mouth to the soft flesh there.

"I thought you were going to kiss my lips," she whispered.

"I am. But I like to do a thorough job," he murmured against her skin. "Give me a chance." He kissed her leg again, then lifted his face until it was level with hers. Reaching out, he brushed her blonde hair out of her face, then cupped her cheek with his palm. "Are you sure you're okay with this?"

"I've been waiting for the past few days."

"So have I. And I've also been thinking about what a bad idea this is. And yet I'm going to do it anyway."

"That's basically my life's mantra."

"Looks like it's turning into mine, too."

"Welcome to the dark side," she said, before he finally pressed his mouth to hers. "I think you're going to like it here."

🦋 18 🦋

Damn, the man knew how to kiss.

His lips were warm and soft as they moved against hers, making her breath catch in her throat as he ran the tip of the tongue along them, before sliding it against hers. Not too hard, not too gentle, just enough to send pleasure shooting through her, as he cradled her face with the palm of his hand.

Time passed like a foxtrot; quick quick slow, until she had no idea how long they'd been kissing. It could have been ten minutes or half an hour. Her lips felt tender and swollen, her skin tingling from the brush of his beard growth against her. All she knew was she didn't want it to stop. Not when it felt this good.

Nate dragged his lips from hers, sliding them to her throat. His hand moved down, tracing the line of her collar-bone where it emerged from her dress. "Can I?" he whispered, his fingers hovering at the top button of her dress. Below it were five more, leading to the waist band. He looked up at her with those deep eyes, and for a moment she was lost again.

"Yes." She nodded. "Yes, please."

He unfastened the buttons, pressing a kiss to her skin between each one. As he released the last, and pushed her dress open, she felt a shiver slide down her spine.

"Are you cold?"

"Not at all."

Their eyes connected, and she felt electricity jolt through her veins. He gave her a half smile, then looked down at her exposed chest. His pupils dilated as he took her in. Thank God she'd worn a pretty bra today – a scrap of white lace with demi cups that pushed her up in all the right places. Nate must have liked it too, because he reached out to touch the swell of her breasts.

"So beautiful."

He cupped them, taking their weight into his palms. He was taking his time, in no hurry at all to do anything but savor her. It was tantalizing and excruciating, making her want to beg for more.

Dropping his head, he pressed his lips against her stomach, his mouth warm and firm as he dragged it up the center of her ribs. He stopped at the fabric bow attached to her bra, then moved his lips to her breast.

"Oh!" Pleasure shot down to the tip of her toes.

"Is that good?" he asked, glancing up.

"So good."

He smiled again, then did the same to her other breast, until they were peaked and tender. She could feel his hardness pressing against her, right at her center where she needed it the most.

"You taste like orange juice," he muttered against her skin. "Sweet and bitter and everything in between." She loved the way his voice was so thick with need.

His hand moved down, past the hem of her dress, his fingers feathering against the sensitive skin of her inner thigh.

His touch was delicate, and yet she could feel it vibrate through her body. Making every muscle clench.

"Is this okay?"

She was slick with anticipation. Her breath was ragged with need. And yet he still took his time, circling around her, avoiding the part of her that needed him the most. His mouth moved against hers, capturing her gasps with his lips, his tongue, swallowing them down as if he couldn't get enough. Even with her leg in a cast she was able to move her hips to his maddeningly soft rhythm, closing her eyes to will him to move his fingertips higher... higher... just a half an inch more.

Oh!

"Nate," she cried out, desire making her breathless. The way he was touching her was so maddeningly delicious. He was bringing her to the edge with his fingers and mouth, dangling her there until she couldn't hold on any more. One more step and she'd be falling...

"It's okay," he whispered, his lips moving against her mouth. "I've got you."

She opened her eyes to see him staring at her, his lids heavy with desire. His intensity took her breath away. Her head tipped back as she teetered at the edge, puffs of breath escaping her lips, arching her back and curling her toes as she finally reached the crest.

He held her as she fell, his breath short as she cried out his name, sensation overwhelming her until she had to squeeze her eyes tightly shut.

It must have been thirty seconds or more before she was able to open them again. Her entire body was still pulsating with pleasure. Nate was beside her on his oversize couch, his eyes dark as he stared at her. "Wow," she breathed, when she finally regained her ability to talk.

He smiled, pressing his lips to the tip of her nose.

She bit her lip and moved her hand to press against his stomach. "It's your turn," she said, her voice thick with the pleasure he'd given her.

He slid his palm on top of her hand, pressing it to him. "It's okay," he said, still looking into her eyes. "I'm good."

"You are?" she frowned. When was the last time a guy refused reciprocation from her? She wasn't sure one ever had. "But you're..."

"I'll deal with that later. Right now I just want to look at you."

If her face wasn't already red with pleasure, it would be flushing. And yet there was no edge to his voice. No sign that he was anything but happy to have given her pleasure without receiving it back. She wasn't sure what to say in response.

He pressed his lips to hers with the briefest of kisses. "Stop overthinking."

"How do you know I am?"

He raised his eyebrows. "Your legs are tense as hell. I bet you want to run right now." He pulled her bra cups up so they were covering her breasts, deftly refastening the buttons on her dress. "You're wondering why I don't want you to touch me, right?"

She nodded.

"Because I don't want you to think I made you come for any other reason than I wanted to. It turned me on like crazy to watch your pleasure and hear you call out my name. But it's getting late, and Riley's going to be home soon, which means we don't have a whole lot of time. And when you touch me, I'll want you to do it all night. A quick hand job isn't what I need from you right now."

"When I touch you..." she repeated.

"If, then."

She smiled into his eyes. "It's definitely when," she whispered. "There's no if about it."

He swallowed, making his Adam's apple bob in his throat. "Okay, then. But right now I need to calm myself down. How about I make us both some coffee, and we play Echoes of War?"

"Sounds good to me," she replied. And what just happened between them? Well she'd think about it later, because right now she needed a distraction.

"I'm back," Riley called from the front door. "No arrests, no underage drinking. We didn't even have an orgy. You'll be proud of me."

Nate pressed pause on the game they were playing and gave Ally a wry smile. She bit her lip, reminding herself to act natural – whatever *that* was. She didn't really have long enough to think about it because less than five seconds later Riley was bounding into the living room, the biggest smile on her face.

"Oh my God," she said, looking from Nate to Ally. "Have you guys been playing that game all night?"

"Pretty much," Nate said, sounding so much more nonchalant than Ally felt. "We went to watch the fireworks then came home to play. How was the movie?"

"Not as lame as your evening. We had fun even though the movie was awful." Riley dropped into the chair beside the sofa.

"Where did you eat?" Ally asked her. Her voice sounded strange. She cleared her throat, trying to get rid of whatever was making it all croaky, and tried to ignore Nate as he grinned at her.

"At the mall. Laura's mom treated us all." Riley looked down at her hands, her brows pulling together as if she was thinking something through. Then she looked up. "Something interesting happened," Riley said, biting her lips as she glanced at her dad. "Do you remember Charlie Prince?"

"I've never heard of him," Nate said.

"It's a her. And she comes in the coffee shop almost every day after school. Anyway, she was supposed to be going on the school trip to Los Angeles next week, but she's come down with mono and she's not allowed at school per doctor's orders. So there's going to be a place free, and I was wondering if I could go instead."

From the corner of her eye Ally saw Nate frown. "Why haven't I heard about this trip before?"

"Because it was full before we even moved to Angel Sands." Riley shrugged. "But now it isn't."

"Then give me the details. When is it, how many teachers are going, what will you see? And more importantly, how much is it going to cost me."

"That I can tell you. Charlie's mom's happy to offer it for half price, which means a hundred and fifty dollars. You'll get rid of me for four days, three nights, so I figure that's a great value all round. And if you really want to make me work for it, I'll come to the shop every weekend to pay you off." She smiled expectantly at him. "So can I go?"

"I'll think about it."

Her smile dissolved. "Well you need to think fast, because if I don't snap it up somebody else will."

"I said I'd think about it." Nate's voice was firm. "You won't be able to do anything about it until Monday anyway."

"But if I'm going I need to get some new clothes. The trip starts on Tuesday. There's not much time." She tipped her head to the side. Was she batting her eyelashes? Ally couldn't quite tell from where she was sitting.

Nate took a deep breath in, then muttered something to himself.

"What?" Riley asked, leaning forward.

"I said you're supposed to be grounded."

"Apart from school," Riley said, still full of cheer. "And this is *definitely* school. I can promise not to have any fun at all if it helps?"

Ally sniggered. She couldn't help it. Sometimes Riley reminded her so much of herself as a teenager.

"You're no help," Nate told her.

"Sorry." But Ally couldn't get rid of the grin.

"That's what happens when you spend your night killing soldiers," Riley said. "Father daughter arguments become entertainment."

"We're not arguing," Nate protested.

"Not yet. But only because you haven't said no. I'm keeping the big guns waiting until then." Yep, Riley really was batting her lashes. Ally wasn't sure how much longer Nate would be able to hold out.

He closed his eyes and shook his head, letting out a sigh. "Okay, you can go."

Wow, that was quicker than she thought.

"Seriously?" Riley sounded genuinely shocked.

"What? Did I make it too easy for you? You can go because it's educational, and because you proved yourself trustworthy tonight. But I've still got a close eye on you."

Riley launched herself at Nate, throwing her arms around him as she thanked him profusely. "I need to call Charlie," she said, pulling herself away. "And then I need to start packing. What do people wear in LA, anyway?" She looked at Ally. "Oh God, there's so much to do." She turned on her heel and ran for the hallway, raising her hand in goodbye. "Laters, people."

Ally slowly turned to look at Nate. "You've made somebody very happy."

"That's what I live for." He raised an eyebrow. "On the

plus side, we only have to listen to that level of crazy for the next couple of days."

After that, Riley would be gone. *For three nights.* The realization struck Ally like a ten ton truck.

She was going to be alone in the house with Nate, and the mere thought of it made her heart pound.

❧ 19 ❧

Leo just asked me to sit next to him on the bus. That's a good sign, right?

Ally bit down a smile as she read Riley's text, then immediately hit the reply button.

It's a great sign. Now relax and try to enjoy yourself. L.A. is an amazing city.

Maybe she needed to take that advice herself, because she felt herself shiver as Nate's tires crunched on the driveway, quickly followed by the slam of his car door as he climbed out.

A few seconds later he was opening the front door and walking up the hallway. His face split into a smile as he looked into the living room and saw Ally there. She grinned back as a thousand butterflies decided to beat their wings in her stomach. "How was your day?" she asked as he slumped on the sofa next to her.

"Busy." He ran his hand through his thick brown hair. "I have some investors and my management team coming down to check out the Beach Café, and I'm planning to pitch the Coastal Coffee idea to them. So, I spent most of the day running numbers and creating slides for the presentation, which left them one short behind the counter."

"I could probably come back to work, you know," Ally suggested, glancing down at her leg. "I'm much more mobile than I was, and not in any pain. If I did some short days I could make a difference."

"Our insurance won't cover you like that. Even if it was a good idea, which it isn't."

Ally sighed.

"What's with the rush to get back? Are you getting bored of saving the world?" Nate asked, his voice teasing.

"Something like that. I miss people and talking, and conversations. I even made Brooke take me grocery shopping with her today so I could get out."

"There must be a lot of things you could do with your time," Nate said, his brows knitting together. "All those things we put off because we're too busy working."

"Like what?"

He ran his finger along his jaw, deep in thought. "I've always wanted to hike the Appalachian Trail."

"Well that would be a great idea if my leg wasn't in a cast." She smiled ruefully. "Can you think of anything else?"

Nate was silent for a moment. "No," he said. "I can't think of anything I'd want to do that wouldn't involve full use of both my legs." His expression softened with sympathy.

"You know what I miss the most?"

"Apart from the coffee shop?"

She laughed. "Yeah. And apart from running."

"In that case, you've got me stumped."

"I want to walk on the beach as the sun goes down. Feel the warm sand against my toes, let the waves lap over my legs as I make my way along the shoreline. I don't even want to run. Just an hour without this damn cast and those crutches and I swear

I'd be happy." She sighed, remembering how beautiful the beach had looked on Saturday night. She'd stayed safely on the boardwalk, but her whole body had itched for the sand. "Ignore me. I'm just feeling sorry for myself. You're the one who's had the busy day, you should be relaxing, not listening to my tales of woe."

"Maybe I find your tales of woe relaxing." He glanced out of the glass doors that led from the living room to the deck. "The sun looks beautiful tonight," he murmured.

She followed his gaze. The orange ball of fire had almost hit the horizon, and it was licking long flickering flames into the darkening ocean. Everything looked still out there, as though the rest of nature had stepped back into the wings while dusk took center stage.

When she glanced back, he was looking straight at her. There was that darkness in his eyes again. They made her shiver.

"Let's go," he said.

"Where?"

"To the beach."

"I can't use my crutches on the beach," she told him. "They'll sink."

"We'll do it the old fashioned way. Just you and me."

He held his hand out and she took it. The next moment he was sliding his arm around her waist, pulling her to standing. Then they were walking – well he was, she was hopping, really – over to the glass doors which he pulled open, letting in the evening air.

It smelled of salt and ozone. She closed her eyes and breathed it in. He helped her onto the deck, and down the steps. His hold gentle and yet so reassuring.

It didn't take long for them to walk through his yard, past the lilacs and the sagebrush to the iron gate that separated the house from the beach. Nate released it with his free hand, pushing it open with his hip as he held her waist in his palms to help her down the steps to the sand.

"We should take our shoes off," he said, helping her sit on the wooden step that bordered the sand. "Or in your case, shoe. It'll be easier that way." He tugged at the laces of his oxfords, pulling them off one at a time. He then pulled his socks off and stuffed them inside. Ally followed suit, sliding her sandal off, and putting it next to his shoes on the steps.

"Let's hope nobody throws them in the trash," she teased.

"I still owe you a pair of running shoes for that." The hint of a blush stained his cheeks. She'd never thought of men as beautiful before, but the word was so perfect for him. Looking at him felt like staring at a perfectly sculpted statue. He made her heart hurt in such a good way.

"I think I'm the one who owes you," she said, her voice soft.

He stood and reached for her again, pulling her up until she was balanced. She could feel his shoulder muscles flex beneath his shirt where she held him.

"Ohhh..." she sighed as her foot sunk into the sand. It still held the warmth of the day, but didn't burn like it sometimes did. "God, I've missed this."

"You want to head down to the water?" he asked.

"We can't. Not with my cast. The doctor said I couldn't get it wet."

"You won't get it wet," he said, pulling his arm tightly around her waist, encouraging her to lean on him. "I promise."

He was staring at her intently. "Okay, then," she breathed, her whole body reacting to his closeness.

They took their time walking down the sand. Not just because it was harder to balance on the uneven ground – though that was reason enough – but because they were in no hurry. The spectacle ahead of them was only getting better as the burnished sun sank into the ocean.

"We should stop here," Ally murmured. The waves were kissing the sand two feet ahead of them. Any further and they'd be lapping over her cast. "This was always my favorite part of the day when I was a kid," she told him, her eyes trained on the horizon. "Dad used to let me play by the ocean while he closed up the café for the evening. When he was done he'd bring down a drink and a bag full of whatever he hadn't sold that day and we'd eat it overlooking the sunset." She smiled, remembering the way the sandwiches had tasted – a little stale, a little crunchy from the grains of sand that inevitably got into them, and yet good enough that she'd always eat it all up. "It would be the one time of the day when it was only him and me. No customers, no fellow business owners popping in to chat with him."

"Do you miss him?"

"I guess I do. But it's weird because I'm angry at him, too. I'm not sure if I want to hug him or scream at him." She breathed in a fresh lungful of salty air. "Although right now I'm not doing either because we're not talking."

Nate inclined his head, looking at her through the corners of his eyes. "Why not?" he asked. "Because he sold the café?"

"Partly," she admitted. "But also because he left without thinking about what it would do to me. I worked like crazy trying to keep that place running, and he sold it anyway."

"But he made sure you still had a job," Nate pointed out. "It was part of the contract."

She'd unblocked her dad the day after the fireworks, but hadn't had the energy to message him. There was plenty of time for that. The sea breeze lifted the ends of her hair, making them dance against her skin. She wrinkled her nose as they tickled her lips. "And there was me thinking you employed me because you thought I was a fabulous manager."

CARRIE ELKS

"You are." The corner of his lip pulled up into a half-smile. "Normally when I buy a place I bring in a new team. But I'm glad your dad asked for you to stay. Otherwise we wouldn't have met."

Her eyes caught his, and she felt the connection between them like a fist to her chest. She filed away her thoughts about her dad in the little compartment in her head she saved for things she wasn't ready to process right then. She'd worry about him another day, because right now all she could think about was Nate.

She could hear the beat of her pulse as the blood rushed through her ears, mixing with the lapping of the waves as they pushed against the shore. Her chest felt too full to breathe, yet her lungs were desperate for oxygen. And all the while they were staring at each other, their eyes locked together as his arm pulled her against him, tipping her head up so their lips were only a breath apart.

"Damn!"

A crashing wave came in from along the shore, spraying foam toward them on the sand. Before she had time to react, Nate was scooping her up into his arms, lifting her out of the way of the water as it soaked his tailored pants.

Still holding her, he ran up the beach. Ally wrapped her arms around his neck, biting down on her lip in an attempt not to laugh at the expression on his face. But the impulse got the better of her as she collapsed into a series of giggles.

They made it up to the steps where they'd left their shoes. The bottom of his pants clung to his legs, flecks of sand covering the dark blue fabric where he'd kicked it up as he ran.

"Are they ruined?" she asked, as he scooted down and helped her sit on the bottom stair.

"I've no idea," he said. "It doesn't matter anyway. I've got more pairs."

She reached out to touch his cheek. "My knight in shining armor," she murmured. "Always ready to save a damsel in distress." She traced the line of his jaw, feeling the sharpness of stubble against his smooth chin. "Thank you for saving me." She glanced down. "And I'm sorry about your pants."

"At least one of us got to paddle today." He moved his hand over hers, pressing her palm to his face. Slowly, he turned so his lips were pressed against the center, kissing her hand before he looked at her with heavy eyes.

"Do you want to go inside?" he asked.

She could tell from the tone of his voice that he wasn't just asking if she wanted to walk back to the house. Her heart raced as she considered the real meaning. Did she want to go inside and shut the world out so it was only the two of them? Was she ready to carry on where they'd left off a few days earlier?

When, not if.

"Yes, please," she said, more certain than she'd ever been before. "There's nothing I'd rather do than go inside with you."

❧ 20 ❧

They didn't even make it inside before the urge to kiss her overwhelmed every cell in his body. They stopped at the door, where he spun her around, pressing her back against the glass as he inclined his head to brush his lips against hers, tasting the warmth of her gasp as she arched herself into him. She was clinging to his neck, her body sandwiched between the door and his firm chest, making certain there was no possibility of her losing her balance.

He slid his arm around her waist, pressing his palm into the dip of her back. Curling the other around her jaw, he angled her face so he could kiss her harder.

Her lips tasted of salt and strawberries, an intoxicating combination. She filled every sense he possessed. He welcomed it, wanting to be so full of her he couldn't think properly. The need to possess her pushed everything else away.

Their first kiss had been delicate and sensual, as they'd sat on that bench overlooking the beach. Their second had been full of desire – to connect with her in a way that showed her exactly how he felt.

This third time? It felt like a communion. Their lips moved together as though choreographed, their bodies melting into each other until he wasn't sure where she ended and he began. And from the way her breath hitched as he threaded his fingers through her silky hair, she felt the same urgent need he did – to come together and never part.

She was still in his arms when he unlatched the door and slid it open. He helped her inside, hooking his arm around her, keeping her steady as she lifted her cast high enough to clear the doorway.

"You okay?"

She nodded, her eyes sparkling. Her lips were already pink and swollen from his kisses. He loved that he'd done that to her. "I'm more than okay," she said.

"Do you want to stay out here? Or should we go to my room?" He eyed her carefully. He was desperate to touch her, to taste her, but only if she said yes.

Her smile widened. "Your room?" she said, raising an eyebrow. "I've never been in there before."

Yeah, well he wanted her in there now. He could picture her on his bed, her blonde hair fanned out against the dark blue sheets, her wide eyes staring up at him as he took every inch of her in. His mind was full of the memory of her from the other night; the way her thighs were warm against his arm as he touched her, the way her breasts tasted as he worshipped them with his mouth. He wanted to feel that again, to feel her tighten against him as she reached her peak, her body melting as she rode a wave of pleasure.

He let out a mouthful of air. If he kept thinking that way tonight was going to be over before it had even begun.

"Come on. It'll be faster if I carry you."

She didn't protest as he scooped her up into his arms, her legs dangling, and arms wrapped around him. Her eyes were as heavy as his, reflecting back the desire that had taken over his body. As far as he was concerned he couldn't get to the bedroom fast enough.

When he laid her down on his bed – freshly made this morning, thank God – she looked just as delicious on there as he'd imagined. But she had way too many clothes on. He licked his dry lips, wondering where to start. His hands ached to feel her thighs, her chest, her waist.

"Nate?" she questioned when he hesitated a moment too long.

Time to stop over thinking this. He'd passed the point of no return days ago. Climbing onto the bed, he slid his body over hers, and the first thing he touched was her face. It was right, because that was where *she* was, the very essence of the woman he couldn't get out of his mind.

He kissed her, savoring her with his lips and tongue. His hands slid down to her waist, pushing her tank up so he could feel the warmth of her skin against his palms. She moaned into his mouth, just the slightest of noises, and yet it vibrated right through him. One of her legs was hooked around his waist, pulling him closer, the other – her bad one – was splayed out. And her hands, oh God, her hands, they were pressing against his ass, dragging him in, until the sensation of her against him was driving him crazy.

As if she could sense it, she tugged at his top, helping him pull it off. In the end, he had to kneel up and lift it over his head, throwing it on the floor.

Her pupils dilated as she took him in, her gaze scanning up and down his chest, and he loved seeing her reaction to him. She reached out and traced her finger from his collarbone and over his chest, then to the ridges of his abdomen where a tiny line of hair led into his shorts.

Ally had a look of absorption on her face as she pushed her finger into his waistband. It was enough to make him hard as hell. He held his breath as he waited to see where she went next.

She was still staring at his waist as she bit her bottom lip, her teeth sinking deliciously into the plump flesh. Then she was unfastening his waistband, loosening it enough to push his pants wide open, revealing cotton shorts that barely restrained his desperate excitement.

"Can I touch you?" Her gaze flickered up at him.

Swallowing hard, he nodded.

Releasing her lip, she slid her hand into his shorts and curled her fingers around his length, and the pleasure of her touch made him gasp.

She moved her palm up and down, her touch gentle and yet crazy-inducing. He closed his eyes for a moment to savor the sensation. It was getting hard to breathe, to think, to do anything but try to resist the pleasure she was building inside of him. There was no way he was going to let things end before they'd even begun.

"Come here," she whispered. "I want to taste you."

He opened his eyes to see her crooking a finger at him. She didn't need to ask twice. With one hand still circling him, she reached out to touch the tip of him with the thick of her tongue, and the warm wetness made him shudder.

"Closer," she whispered, lifting her head. Her lips made a circle around him, and she was taking him in. Every bit of him enveloped in her velvet mouth, and he had to grab at the bedcovers to ground himself.

"Stop," he whispered when he could feel the quickening inside him. "I don't want to..."

Her eyelids flickered open as she slowly released him, and he felt himself relax.

It was his turn to tease her. He pulled off her tank and kissed his way down to her chest, his mouth closing around her. He nipped and sucked until she was gasping for more. Biting down a satisfied smile, he pulled her shorts down, followed by the scrap of pink she called panties, taking care to hook them over her cast.

Her bare breasts were pressed against his chest, her thighs warm against his hips, and he could feel the slickness of her against his own excitement. It was as much as he could do to reach across to his bedside table, and pull out a packet he hadn't used in way too long.

She nodded, even though he hadn't asked her the question, and he opened the foil and rolled it on himself, before letting him relax against her. "If I hurt your leg, you need to tell me," he said, gritting his teeth to keep his control as he centered himself against her.

"I will," she said softly. Her lips were tender when he kissed her again, and the feel of them was enough to make his chest tighten. He slid inside her, gently at first, then harder, until she took every inch of him in. He groaned against her shoulder, stilling himself for a moment as pleasure overwhelmed him once again. He was going to have to take this easy, concentrate on her. It was the only way to control himself.

He pulled his hips back and pushed in again, and this time it was Ally who moaned. She slid her hands down his back, to his behind, pulling him closer, harder, deeper, until she cried out again. Their kisses were frantic, their breaths shallow and short, their bodies moving in a rhythmic dance that made every muscle inside both of them tense.

It was Ally who fell first. She released his lips to gasp for air, her head falling back as she called out his name. Within seconds he followed her, sinking deeper into her than he ever thought possible.

He never wanted the feeling to stop.

The first thing Ally saw when she woke up were her crutches propped up against the bedside table. Nate must have put them there some time in the night – or was it morning? She blinked and pushed herself up on her elbows, looking around his room. The mattress beside her was empty, the palest of light bathing it through the floor length windows. She knew from the color that the sun hadn't quite risen up behind the mountains, which meant it couldn't be any later than five-thirty in the morning.

She sat up and swung herself around, then slid her arms over the crutches, lifting herself up to standing.

"Are you okay?" Nate asked her, walking back into the room. He was drinking from a huge mug. His hair was mussed up, his t-shirt crumpled, and the dark cotton shorts he was wearing made her want him all over again.

"I was just wondering where you were."

"I couldn't sleep, so I made some coffee. You want some?"

She shook her head, smiling as she sat back on the bed. "No. I want you to come back to bed."

He slid onto the mattress beside her, placing his half-full cup on the table. "I was thinking what a great idea it was for Riley to go on this field trip," he said, turning on his side to face her. "And wondering whether there are any others she can go on."

Ally laughed. "You've changed your tune."

"Yeah, well maybe I've been a bit too much of a helicopter parent. She's proved she's trustworthy. I should give her more of a break."

"You won't hear any argument from me." Ally slid her hand around his waist.

Nate winced at the sudden coldness from her palms. "You're freezing." He pressed his hand over hers.

"It's cold in here without you."

He kissed the tip of her nose. "It's sixty-five degrees already."

"That might be warm to a Seattle guy, but this California girl feels the cold." She shivered to make her point.

"You want me to warm you up?" He didn't wait for her answer before he pulled her against him.

She tugged at his t-shirt. "This should go," she told him. "I need direct body heat or else I might freeze to death."

There was a smirk on his face as he pulled it over his head, messing his thick hair up even more. Then he put his arms around her, laying back on the mattress until she was nestled against him, and pulled the covers up over them.

She pressed her lips to his chest, breathing him in. Nate swallowed. "Did you sleep okay?" he asked.

"I was out like a light for the night." She smiled against his skin. "Well, all three hours that were left of it." She looked up at him. "How about you?"

"Like a dog. You wore me out."

"That's what happens when you get old."

Nate barked out a laugh. "Enough of the old. I'm not that ancient. I still have all my own teeth."

"I know." She closed her eyes, remembering how they felt as they scraped softly against her breasts. God, she really could do it all over again. "How old are you, anyway?"

"Didn't your dad teach you it's rude to ask?"

"I just want to know our age difference. For science." She shrugged.

"Since you asked so nicely, I'm thirty-nine."

She lifted her head up. "You got the big one next year?"

"This year."

"Wow." She nodded. "Are you going to ask me how old I am?"

"I already know. You're twenty-seven. I've seen your resume, remember?"

"So that makes it twelve years between us. Soon to be thirteen. I guess it's not so bad, is it?"

"It depends, I guess," he said, his brows furrowing as he thought it through.

"On what?"

"On what we both want out of life."

She reached out to trace her finger across his chest, moving it in circles. "What do *you* want out of life?" This conversation was getting deep, especially since it wasn't even six in the morning. It made her chest feel tight, as though she was only a few sentences away from panicking. She held her breath and waited for his answer.

He shrugged. "Pretty much what I have. A healthy business, a happy daughter, nobody telling me what I should or shouldn't be doing. I like my life." He turned his head, looking at Ally. "How about you?"

She was still tracing her fingers along his skin, her circles getting smaller as she reached the thin line of hair leading down from his navel. Running her finger over it, she smiled as he gasped. He captured her hand to stop her teasing.

"I want to be happy," she told him. And it was true. Okay, there was so much more that she wanted, but she wasn't sure she could talk about it without looking crazy. She wanted somebody to love her and be loved. Wanted a house on the beach just like this one. She wanted her father to explain why he'd sold the café.

"Happiness I can do," Nate said, as if he sensed her sudden tenseness. Did he know that all she wanted to do right then was to run for ten miles, and then maybe ten more? "I know one way to make you very happy indeed."

She smiled as he pushed her until her back was against the

mattress, then pressed his lips to her throat, making her shiver.

Yes, he could do happiness, and she'd take whatever he had to offer. Because if there was one thing life had taught her, it was to grab onto the happy whenever it made a fleeting appearance.

❧ 21 ❧

"Honey, it's your dad. I'm calling to see how you are. Lorne told me your ankle's broken and I've been worried sick about you. Do you want me to come home? I'll get on the next flight if you need me, you just have to say the word."

Ally closed her eyes as the voicemail continued, feeling her chest get tight. He must have called when she was with Nate this morning, before she'd turned on her phone.

"I'm so sorry I didn't tell you about the café. There's no excuse for it, except that I'm a foolish old man who didn't want to upset you. Yet I ended up doing it anyway."

He sounded lost. It reminded her of the way he'd been right after he and her mom had divorced and he'd pick her up from school then sit in the car as if he had no idea what to do next.

"There's so much I want to say and I know you probably don't want to hear it. Please call me back whenever you're ready to talk, or even if you're willing to listen."

He cleared his throat. "I love you, sweetheart. More than

anything else in this world. So call me, please. I just want to know you're okay."

Ally lifted her hand to wipe the dampness from her cheeks. For a woman who rarely cried she was so emotional lately.

She and Nate had two more nights together before Riley got back and she was determined that nothing was going to spoil it. She'd call her father back after that, when she had more time and space to think about things.

It had been too long since they'd spoken, and she knew it was mostly her fault. Firstly for blocking him – ugh what a stupid thing that was – and then for waiting for him to make the first move.

When Riley was back, she'd talk with him like the grown-ups they both were. She owed him that, at least.

"I have your clothes and I'm willing to exchange them for information." Brooke was standing at the front door, a bag in her hand from where she'd been back to Ally's place to pick up a few more things. Her blonde hair was pulled back into a messy bun, and she was wearing a pair of jeans and an old t-shirt; her standard uniform for when she volunteered at the animal shelter. It was one of her favorite places in the world.

"What kind of information?" Ally asked, leaning against the doorjamb. It was late in the afternoon, and she was all alone in the house.

"How many times, was it good, and did you remember to practice safe sex?"

Ally glanced over Brooke's shoulder, though there was clearly nobody else there. It was a gated house – nobody got in or out without either a code or a press of the button from inside the house. "I guess you'd better come in."

Brooke grinned. "I thought you'd never ask."

Ally turned on her crutches and made her way up the hallway to her bedroom, where Brooke placed the bag on top of her bed. "Oooh," Brooke said, turning to her with a grin. "This bed is cold. When was the last time you slept in it?"

"Was everything okay at my apartment?" Ally asked, deliberately ignoring her question.

"Yep. You had some mail; I put it in your bag. Oh, and I saw your super in the lobby. The part came in earlier than expected. The elevator will be fixed the day after tomorrow."

"It will?" Ally felt her brows knit together at the thought. "Oh, that's great. Do you have long enough to sit for some coffee?" she asked.

"Sure. Though I have an assignment due at the end of the week, so it'll have to be a quick one."

They walked into the kitchen, and Ally grabbed them a couple of mugs from the cupboard in the island. "How's school going?" she asked.

"It's tough. But I keep telling myself it's only a few more months." Brooke leaned across the kitchen counter. "After that the real fun begins." She was studying for her degree in Veterinarian Technology. All her life she'd dreamed of working with animals. Before she became pregnant with Nick, she'd been offered a coveted place in Vet school, but having a baby had put an end to all those plans. Ally was so proud of her friend for going back to study, with a plan to become a Veterinarian Technologist – not quite a Vet, but the job was still made for Brooke. Ever since they were kids she'd been obsessed by animals.

Ally turned on the coffee machine and listened as the water tank began to heat up, steam making it rattle. She was caught up thinking about the fact that the elevator would be repaired soon and she'd be able to move back home in two days time. The thought didn't excite her as it would have done a couple of days ago.

"There were a few voicemail messages on your home phone for you," Brooke said as Ally passed her a mug of coffee. "I wasn't sure if you'd want me to listen to them or not. But then I was worried they might be important." She gave Ally a soft smile. "They were all from your dad."

Ally bit down on her lip and winced. The skin there was still tender from this morning. "I finally remembered to unblock him," she said. "He left a voicemail on my phone. I'll call him back over the weekend."

"Good idea," Brooke said, raising her eyebrows. "You don't want to ruin your alone time with Nate."

Great minds thought alike.

"So, are you going to answer my questions or what?" Brooke asked. "I need all the details about you and Nate. I'm living my life vicariously through you. I can't remember the last time I was even asked out, let alone did anything exciting with a guy."

"Your mom tries to set you up all the time," Ally pointed out. "Wasn't she pestering you to go out with some lawyer the other week?"

"I'm really not interested in her friends' sons." Brooke wrinkled her nose. "I can see it now. Breakfast appointments at the salon, lunch with the Women's League at the Beach club. Evenings entertaining whatever clients my husband is desperate to land." She shuddered. "There's no way I'm turning into my mom."

"I'm glad to hear it." Ally grinned. "And since you're clearly going through some kind of crisis, I'll answer one question and one question only."

"That's a lie. You're dying to tell me all about him."

Ally held her finger up. "One."

Brooke laughed. "Okay, okay," she said, narrowing her

eyes. "Give me a minute to think about it." After a moment she lifted her head up and smiled. "Okay, I got it."

Ally sighed. "Why do I not like the sound of this?" All those times she'd been the interrogator and it had been Brooke or Ember with wide eyes beneath the bright light of her scrutiny – she'd never thought the situation would be reversed.

"It's not that bad. But I'm really curious now," she said, biting her lip to stifle her smile. "What's the best position to have sex with your leg covered in a plaster cast?"

Ally sighed, deciding to brave it out. "Every position you can imagine," she told her friend. "I'd hate to choose between them."

❧ 22 ❧

Nate flicked at the button on his dashboard to accept the incoming Bluetooth call. "Hello?" he answered, pulling the Lexus into the parking lot opposite the coffee shop. There were only a few cars scattered here and there this early in the morning. Mostly business owners and surfers – everybody else was still tucked up in bed.

"Hello, stranger. Long time no talk." Kirsten's warm tones came down the line. "I was beginning to think I didn't have a brother."

"Sorry." He winced, even though she couldn't see him. "Things got kind of hectic around here." He glanced at the clock on the dash. It was right before seven. Enough time to open up and get himself ready for his video meeting later today with his investors. "What time is it there?" he asked as he pulled into a space.

"Almost ten. I just finished my first lecture. I figured I have enough time to grab coffee and ream you out for not calling me."

"What coffee did you get?"

She laughed. "That's such a *you* question. I got an Americano with room because I'm not loving the way they make cappuccinos at this place. When are you going to open up a Déjà Brew in Boston?" She paused, and Nate could hear her take a sip of her drink. "It's the home of coffee. We need you here."

"Seattle's the home of coffee, and we've already got shops there."

"Six hundred thousand Bostonites would beg to differ."

He flicked the ignition off and rolled his neck. Christ he was tired. And too old to be getting by on only a couple of hours sleep two nights in a row.

But damn was it worth it.

He smiled, thinking of the way Ally had looked as he left her this morning. All sated and warm and everything he'd dreamed of. It had taken an act of will to leave her and actually drive to work.

"So, I texted Riley last night and she told me she's in L.A.," Kirsten said, bringing Nate out of his thoughts. "I feel like I'm out of the loop. The last time we talked she was grounded. So what's she doing there and how come you let her go?"

"One, she's on a field trip. Two, because I'm the world's best father."

Kirsten sighed. "I need details, Nate. Tell you what, I'll send you an email full of questions the way I do when I'm doing a practice deposition. How does that sound?"

"Horrific?"

She chuckled. "How are you doing, big brother?"

He glanced up at the mirror to look at himself. His hair was still wet from the shower he took after he finally dragged himself away from Ally. His face was freshly shaven, and in spite of the shadows beneath his eyes they somehow looked brighter than they normally did. "Good," he told his sister. "I'm good."

"You sound it," she said, a smile in her voice. "I knew a change of scene would be perfect for you both."

He glanced out of the windshield. Yeah, Angel Sands was pretty – and being close to the ocean was definitely good for the soul. But the way he was feeling had nothing to do with the beautiful beach, and everything to do with the woman who'd somehow limped her way into his life, smashing everything up and making it new again.

"Listen, I need to go and open the shop," he told Kirsten. "I've got some meetings I need to prepare for. How about Riley and I Skype with you this weekend? I'll have a bible in my hand ready to swear to tell the whole truth."

"Skype sounds good," Kirsten said. "I'll have my questions ready, too. Did you want me to submit them beforehand?"

"Always." His sister never failed to make him smile. For the briefest second he considered telling her about Ally. But then he shook his head and pushed that crazy notion away.

What would he tell her anyway? That he'd been sleeping with one of his employees? Or maybe he could tell his sister – his *baby* sister – that Ally wasn't that much older than her. What was it, a year or two? If he thought she was being curious now, imagine what she'd be like with that kind of information.

Nope. Best to keep quiet about it and get on with things.

"Bye, sis."

"Goodbye, big brother. Talk to you this weekend."

If he'd have thought about it too much her words would have sounded like a threat. Instead, he ended the call and decided not to think about it at all.

"Hello, darling, how was your day?" Ally asked as he walked into the hallway. She was standing there waiting for him, a huge grin on her face as she held out a glass of red wine.

"What's this for?" he asked, taking the glass. His eyes crinkled as he smiled back at her because, really, she was a sight for sore eyes after his long day. Her wavy blonde hair was down, the tips skimming the dark blue tank she was wearing. He let his eyes scan down her body, taking in the way her blue-and-white striped skirt stopped mid thigh, revealing her toned, tanned legs. Was it wrong that he wanted them wrapped around him, cast and all?

She leaned to the side, adjusting her weight on her crutch. "You've been working so hard, the least I can do is pour you a drink when you get home."

"Am I in the middle of some fifties housewife fantasy?"

"Do you want to be?" Ally lifted an eyebrow. "Because I can grab you a pipe and slippers."

"Ah, no." He bit down a laugh and reached for her, running his fingers down her soft curls. "When it comes to relationships I prefer mine to be equal. Sometimes me on top, sometimes you."

"Right now it's mostly you," she said, glancing down at her leg. "But as soon as this cast is off, then all bets are off."

Nate blinked, trying to get the image of Ally riding him out of his brain. But it refused to disappear, sending shoots of excitement down between his legs. Jesus, he'd just got home. Couldn't his body give him a break for a minute?

"I've got something to show you," Ally said, inclining her head toward the living room. "This one took a little longer to set up, but hopefully it's worth it."

He followed her down the hall and through the doorway to the living room. Looking around, he tried to see what was different, but for the life of him nothing stood out.

"Not in here. Out there."

He looked out of the glass doors to the terrace and blinked. There was a bed on the deck, covered with a roof of sheets, tiny little lights surrounding it, blinking on and off. In the distance, the sun was going down, painting the sky a deep purple.

"Where did that come from?" He looked back at her, bemused.

"It's your bed. A couple of friends carried it outside for me." She rolled her lip between her teeth.

"And you made a fort?" he asked, walking across the living room to the open doors. The warm evening breeze embraced him, a hint of salt lingering in the air. "I haven't seen one of those for years." He loved that she'd made it for them. There was something so sweet about it that curled around his heart.

"I thought we could sleep outside tonight," she said from behind him. "When I was a kid my dad used to let me do it sometimes, though it was in the hills and not by the ocean." Her voice was soft, full of memories. "There's something amazing about the sun waking you up so you can see the first light of dawn." She paused for a moment, as she took a deep breath. When he turned his head to look, her expression was hesitant, as though she was expecting him to laugh at her. "Riley will be home tomorrow, and my elevator will be repaired the day after that. So it's kind of our last night together. I wanted to make it special."

Something in her voice made him stop short. A wistfulness that wrapped around him in a silken thread, pulling tighter until he was finding it hard to breathe. "Ally, I..." He wanted to tell her that it wasn't their last night. It was only the beginning. But would he be making promises he couldn't keep?

He hadn't thought about what would happen when Riley

came back. Hadn't imagined where this thing between them would go. He felt his chest contract as he remembered Stephanie and her demands. One thing he'd learned – girl-friends and bereaved teenage daughters rarely mixed.

But after the last few nights they'd had together he couldn't bear to let her go. Every time he looked at her his heart skipped a beat.

"Maybe we should try it out," Ally said, as though she could sense his conflict. She followed him outside, and Nate kicked his shoes off, climbing onto the mattress and scooting across. A moment later she joined him, propping her crutches against the bedframe and lifting her legs onto the bed.

They both lay back and looked up. Close up he could see the roof wasn't a cotton sheet at all; it was a semi-transparent curtain that made the sky above them shimmer. "This is just for some privacy," she told him, nodding up at the fabric. "When we go to sleep we can pull it off so we can see the stars in our dreams."

"Did you do this often when you were a kid?" he asked. The need to know more about her was like an itch right at the center of him. Impossible to scratch, but he was going to try anyway. He reached out to trace his finger down her bare arm, smiling as she shivered in spite of the warm evening.

"Not that often. But when we did I used to get so excit-ed." The corners of her lips curled up. "I can remember Dad dragging my bed out onto the grass, letting me set it up with so many cushions you couldn't see the covers. We'd sit outside and he'd tell me all about the different stars. My favorite story was always that of Orion. The way he boasted about killing every wild beast on Earth." Her smile widened. "I guess I learned from an early age that pride came before a fall." She turned her head to look at him. "Did you ever sleep out beneath the stars with Riley's mom?"

"Natalie? No, never. She wasn't the outdoorsy type." He leaned over and pressed his lips to Ally's bare shoulder. "We weren't together for that long anyway. Just a couple of years."

"Can I ask you what happened?" Ally was hesitant and Nate could tell. He brushed his lips to the base of her throat.

"Of course you can ask," he said, his voice thick. "But it won't put me in the best light."

"Did you cheat on her?"

"No." He frowned. "Nothing like that. I just wasn't there for her or Riley when they needed me. Too busy building up the business. At that point I was at the shop from seven to seven every day, and Natalie was at home with a tiny baby going crazy. I kidded myself that I was doing it for all of us, but looking back I was a selfish son of a bitch. Too young to understand what Natalie needed of me. Too stupid to realize I'd made this tiny beautiful human who wanted me around. And when she gave me an ultimatum, I was cocky enough to think she would back down. So I chose the business over my family."

He closed his eyes for a moment, his lips still pressed to Ally's throat. He could smell her shampoo – floral and light – and a deeper note of the perfume she sometimes wore. She filled him up in a way he'd never been filled before. Made him feel needy yet peaceful too.

"It turned out I made a much better ex-husband," he said. "And I learned to be a better father. When Riley was a little girl I'd pick her up every Friday and keep her until Sunday. Those were my favorite days of the week."

"You took her to work with you?"

"Sometimes. But we'd done a lot of other things, too. Go to the zoo, the movies, make crazy meals together like choco-late nachos." He smiled. "And you already know about our beauty salon nights."

"I do." She grinned. "And while we're on that subject, my nails could do with some fresh polish."

He laughed, pulling her closer against him, feeling the warmth of her skin press against his shirt. "You've still got your tie on," she murmured, reaching out to unknot it with her hands. She slid it out of his collar then unfastened his top buttons. "There, that's better."

Curling into him, Ally slid her hand under his shirt and pressed the flat of her palm against his chest, her head nestled into the crook of his arm. He could hear her soft breaths, matching the rhythm of the waves as they hit the shore. He closed his eyes, wishing he could keep this moment forever.

"Are you hungry?" she asked, her voice muffled by his chest. "I can make us something to eat if you are."

"Not for food, no."

Her breath caught. "For something else?"

Yeah. Something else entirely. The only thing that left him empty and aching when he couldn't have it. He inclined his head until his lips were almost brushing hers. Just a heart-beat away from tasting everything he wanted.

"For everything else," he said, closing the distance between their mouths. His body began to pulse with that familiar rhythm only she knew how to play. He cupped her face with his hand, angling her so he could deepen the kiss, his tongue sliding against hers until she let out a tiny moan. "I want to taste every inch of you," he whispered, dragging his lips across her jaw. "Then I want to do it all over again." He lifted her tank top, pulling it over her out stretched arms and throwing it onto the deck beside them. He scooted down and pressed his lips against her belly, slowly making his way up to her perfectly rounded breasts.

God she was delicious. Falling for her would be as easy as breathing if he let himself.

It was the last night they'd be able to be this free and easy in his beachside house and Nate was determined to savor every moment of it. And from the sound of her sigh as he lifted her breast out of her bra and ran his thumb over her nipple, Ally was thinking exactly the same thing.

❧ 23 ❧

Ally pushed herself onto her elbows, frowning as she looked around her. Something had awoken her, but she couldn't work out what it was. They were surrounded by darkness, and the air had cooled considerably. She pulled at the sheet that they'd kicked to the bottom of the mattress, tucking it around Nate who was sleeping soundly.

She had no idea what time it was. Her watch was in the living room. She didn't have her phone either – it was somewhere in the house, forgotten thanks to an evening spent in Nate's warm arms. Under him, next to him, even over him once or twice, with the help of his strong hands. Every muscle in her body ached deliciously, a reminder of how frantic they'd been.

The stars were bright. She looked up, pleased that they'd removed the gauze curtain when they finally finished their love-making, and saw Ursa Minor twinkling back at her. Then heard the crash of a wave as it rushed its way to shore.

She was never going to forget this night. Bringing the bed out here had been the best idea ever. And thanks to Lucas and his friend Griff popping over earlier in the evening, it had been pretty simple, too. Ember had raised her eyebrows at the request, but said nothing, though her knowing look as she left the house led Ally to believe she'd be facing an inquisition in the morning.

Not that she cared. It was so worth it.

She turned on her side, propping her chin on her hand as she watched Nate's bare chest rising and falling with his slow breaths. His lips were slightly parted, his dark hair messed up by a combination of her fingers and the pillow as he slept. Her chest felt tight when she saw how beautiful he was. Beneath the moonlight his skin looked like it was sculpted from stone, the ridges of his muscles enhanced by the shadows cast by the sky above.

It didn't get any better than this.

A loud bang reverberated from the driveway, bringing her out of her sweet reverie. Her heart went from zero to sixty in seconds, and she sat straight up, clutching the sheet to her chest. The motion-activated lights came on, shining down on her and Nate, though he was still in deep sleep.

She reached out to wake him up when she heard a voice.

"Ally?"

Her racing heart stopped dead. Ally slowly turned her head, holding her breath without realizing it, and saw Riley standing only a few feet away.

For a moment she was paralyzed, not a single muscle moving. And then, as though somebody had flicked a switch, her heart started hammering all over again. Was this what it was like to have a heart attack? Her fingers tightened around the sheet she was clutching against her chest – the same sheet that was pooled around Nate's waist.

Around *Riley's dad's* waist.

"Riley," she said, her voice ragged. "We weren't expecting you home until tomorrow."

Nate stirred against her but didn't waken. Ally wanted to

shake him until he did, but then Riley would see Ally touching her dad and... *oh God, this was terrible.*

"Riley, honey? Are you okay?" Ally asked. Riley began to shake her head, her face crumpling as tears welled in her eyes. Riley continued to shake her head but said nothing, her lips parting to gasp in oxygen. She lifted her hands up, her palms cupping each side of her face. The way she was staring at them with wide, horrified eyes reminded Ally of Munch's *The Scream.*

"It's okay..."

"Huh?" Nate muttered, finally opening his eyes. He slowly pushed himself up, taking a sharp mouthful of breath as he saw his daughter standing there.

"What are you *doing*?" Riley said, her voice soft at first. Then louder. "Oh my God, what's happening here?" Her eyes widened further as she took in the pile of clothes pooled at the side of the bed. "Dad... Ally," she whispered, her mouth falling open. "I've gotta go." She turned on her heel and ran back the way she came – through the gate that led out to the driveway.

Nate tugged at the sheet, pulling it from Ally's grasp, then let it go as soon as he realized what he'd done. "Shit." He clambered over the mattress, grabbing his pants and pulling them over his naked body, and slid his feet into his shoes.

"I need to..."

"Go," Ally whispered. Her stomach was churning. It was only thanks to the fact she hadn't eaten anything for hours that she wasn't bending over and vomiting. Nate ran across the wooden platform, calling Riley's name, the nighttime swallowing his voice. Ally grabbed her own clothes, taking longer than Nate to get dressed, thanks to her cast and the fact she couldn't run around topless.

She heard the sound of an engine, followed by the screech of wheels. By the time she'd made it across to the gate on her crutches, Nate was turning back. "She's gone," he said, his voice short. "I'll follow her in my car."

"Gone? How? Where?"

"I don't know, Ally," Nate said, his voice short. "I'm not a fucking mind reader."

She blinked at the anger in his voice. Her chest felt so tight it was impossible to breathe in the lungful of air she so desperately needed. "Whose car was she in?" she asked, trying not to wince at the darkness in his eyes.

"I've no idea." He shook his head again. "Christ, I can't believe she saw that."

Neither could Ally. Her whole body shivered at the thought. How would she have reacted if she'd seen Marnie and her dad like that as a teenager?

Pretty badly.

He reached in his pocket and pulled his phone out, frowning as he looked at the screen. "I left it on silent after my meeting," he told her, turning it so she could see the screen.

Ten missed calls from Riley's teacher.

"Oh God," she whispered, covering her mouth with her hand. What the hell had happened? Her brain was too messed up to think straight.

Nate turned his back to her, his eyes as dark as the night. "I'll call the school from the car. Stay here in case she comes back." He pulled his shirt on, deftly fastening the buttons. "Call me if she does."

"Okay." There was so much more she wanted to say, but none of it sounded right to her ears. How sorry she was. How she couldn't believe this had happened.

Somewhere deep inside was that tiny part of her that wanted to ask him why he was so angry at her, but she knew she could never ask him that.

Her hands were shaking as he walked back into the house.

A few moments later she heard the slam of the door. She was still holding her breath as the car engine came to life with a roar, then the familiar sound of him reversing out of his parking spot drifted through the air. When she heard the creak of the main gates, she made her way back to the big glass doors, glancing at the messed up bed that had seemed like such a good idea only a few hours before.

Right now it felt like the worst idea in the world. She pressed her lips together, trying to stop herself from crying. What on earth had Riley thought, seeing the two of them naked beneath the sheets? The same thing she would have thought if she'd caught somebody she'd considered a friend sleeping with her own father.

Betrayed, disgusted, but most of all completely devastated.

And now Riley had run off to God only knew where – and it was all Ally's fault.

"Riley? It's me. Again. Call me back as soon as you can. We're so worried about you." Ally took a breath to try and calm down her pulse that hadn't stopped racing since Riley had caught them on the terrace. "I'm sorry," she whispered into the mouthpiece of her phone. "Please come home."

She'd been calling Riley for the past half hour, but every time it clicked straight to voicemail. It was the middle of the night, it was dark, and Riley was all alone somewhere.

Please let Nate find her. Or let her come home. Ally squeezed her eyes closed for a second, sending up a silent prayer. Surely somebody had to be listening up there.

When she glanced at her phone again, she saw the notifications flashing at the top. She slid her finger to drag them up, and saw a voice message that had been received hours earlier.

From Riley.

It felt as though Ally's heart had risen up from her chest and into her throat. Her fingers shook as she keyed in her pin. Why hadn't she had her phone outside with her last night?

Because you were too busy, the little voice in her head told her. *Too concerned about being in Nate's arms to care about his daughter.*

She closed her eyes as her voicemail connected.

"Ally?" Riley's voice was tremulous. "Can you call me?" A tiny sob echoed down the line. "Please..." A loud click was followed by nothingness. How long ago had Riley tried to call? Ally quickly brought up her call log to see the message was left at nine the previous night. It was almost three-thirty in the morning now. If Riley arrived home at two–thirty, then she must have left Los Angeles almost as soon as she'd failed to speak to Ally.

She jumped when her phone rang out – loudly this time, thanks to the full volume she'd been sure to switch on.

"Any sign of her?" Nate asked as soon as she picked up the call.

Ally swallowed. "No. But she left a voicemail last night."

"What did she say?"

She tried to ignore the impatience in his voice. He was just worried. "Nothing. Just asked me to call her." She took a ragged breath in. "But Nate, she was crying. So upset." She pulled her bottom lip between her teeth, biting into it. "What's happened to her?"

"The school realized she was missing around midnight," Nate said. "After they couldn't get ahold of me they got the police involved."

She covered her eyes with the palm of her hand. "Do they know how she got here?"

There was a pause. "She stole her teacher's car."

"Oh shit." Ally felt his words like a punch in the gut.

"It's not the first time she's been in trouble. I've just spent the last ten minutes persuading them not to press charges. The only problem is she's still got the damn car somewhere. She could be anywhere by now."

Ally was trying not to hyperventilate. The thought of Riley driving in the state she'd been in made her hands shake like crazy. She'd passed her driver's test back in Seattle – that much she knew from Nate – but she was still a new driver. Anything could happen. Anything at all.

"So what do we do?"

"I don't know," Nate admitted, his voice tight. "I'm just driving around looking for a car that matches her teacher's. Any friends she has here are still in LA. She's not at the coffee shop or by the beach. I just drove up to the cliff where..." his voice faded. "Yeah, she's not there either."

"She's not going to do anything stupid, is she?"

"She already has," Nate said. "So many damn times I've lost count." His words were so sharp she could almost feel them cut. "I don't know where my daughter is and it's fucking killing me."

"Come back here," she said, trying to keep calm. "I'll call the police here in Angel Sands. They have way more manpower than we do, and they can spread word into neighboring towns, too."

She could hear the soft rumble of the engine over his Bluetooth connection, and the sound of his indicator, as he must have taken a turn from the road. Finally he sighed, and she imagined his shoulders slumping as his fingers tightened on the wheel. "Yes," he said. "Please do that."

"She'll be okay," she whispered, as much to herself as to him.

"I just want to find her," he said, his voice cracking. "Make her safe."

Of course he did. He was her dad, after all. And wasn't that what any good father would want to do?

❧ 24 ❧

The doorbell rang sometime after four that morning. Nate had come back from searching for Riley, his expression dark, and he'd hardly said two words to her before he made his way to the office. That's where he'd been since – making phone call after phone call, emerging once to pour himself a cup of black coffee before disappearing back in there again. He looked like hell. They both did.

Ally made her way up the hallway on her crutches, opening the door to see two uniformed officers standing there. "Thank you for coming," she said, standing back to let them in. "The living room is the first door to your left."

Nate must have heard the doorbell from the office, because by the time they reached the room he was there, shaking their hands. She looked at him as soon as she walked through the doorway, but he seemed to be studiously avoiding her eyes.

"Can I get you a drink?" Ally asked the two officers as they sat on the easy chairs facing the sofa. "Coffee or orange juice, maybe?"

"No thank you, ma'am."

"Nate?" she asked, looking at him. He shook his head but still wouldn't look at her.

Okay, then. She gave them a nod and went to turn away.

"Miss Sutton?" the male officer said. He looked to be around her father's age. "Could you stay, too? We may have some questions for you."

Ally pressed her lips together and nodded, sitting on the sofa next to Nate, though there was at least a foot of distance between them. He was still looking at the older officer, his back as straight as a poker, his jaw tight. He looked so uncomfortable and nervous it made her stomach churn.

"I'm afraid we still have no news on your daughter's whereabouts," the older officer told them. "All our cars have her details, and a photograph thanks to the one you sent over. And I can confirm that none of the local hospitals have had admissions that match Riley's description."

Ally let out a mouthful of air.

"We have a few questions that might help us find her." The female officer leaned forward, flashing a brief smile as she pulled out a pencil and notepad from her pocket. "Obviously you're her father, Mr. Crawford. And Miss Sutton is Riley's stepmother, is that right?"

"No." Ally shook her head. The officer's cool eyes gave nothing away. "I'm just a... friend."

"But you're living here right now?"

The corner of Nate's jaw was dancing rhythmically as he ground his teeth together. Ally felt herself begin to flush.

"I hurt my leg," she said, looking down at the cast as though they hadn't noticed it as soon as they walked in. "I've been staying in the spare room while I recuperate."

"Okay." The officer wrote something on her pad. "You said that Riley came home at little after two this morning, then left right away. Did something happen to make her leave?"

It was as though a snake had wrapped itself around her chest, making it impossible to breathe. "She, um…"

"She found me in bed with Miss Sutton," Nate said, his voice low. He kept his gaze firmly on the officer. Ally winced, wanting to crawl into a hole and die there.

"But you're not in a relationship?"

This was excruciating. Ally shifted on the sofa, moving her leg in an attempt to get comfortable, but it did no good. Nate was showing no emotion at all.

"It's not unusual for teenagers to run off for a while," the male officer said. "Especially in a situation like this one." His gaze flickered to Ally then back to Nate. "We'd usually expect her to return within twenty-four-hours, once the novelty of running away wears off."

"She was very upset," Ally said. "She'd tried to call me the previous night and left a tearful voicemail."

"Can you let my partner hear it?" the officer asked, standing up. "And in the meantime, can you give me a few more photographs, Mr. Crawford? I assume you keep some around here."

"I have a good one in my office."

"Great. Let's go take a look. And if you can also give me the contact details for any other members of your family, just so we can alert them that she may be headed their way."

Ally watched as the two men left the room, leaving her alone with the female officer. Taking her phone out of her pocket, she dialed her voicemail again, putting Riley's message on speakerphone for the policewoman to hear.

"She really did sound upset," the officer said as the message ended. "Do you know if something happened in Los Angeles?"

"I've no idea. She has a friend, Laura, she may know. And there's a boy she likes, too. His name is Leo."

The officer gave a rueful smile. "In ninety-nine percent of

cases like this there's always a boy or girl." She took note of their names on her pad. "Please try not to get too worried. There's every chance we'll track her down before the day is up. It's almost textbook, really. Emotional teenager discovers her father has a girlfriend?" She shrugged. "When they suddenly realize their parents have a sex life it shakes them up and makes them mad."

A shiver went down Ally's spine. She'd been that teenager once. Hated Marnie as much as she'd hated her right back. She'd demanded his time, his money, his constant attention. Which meant that when Ally needed him he wasn't there.

Just like Nate hadn't been there when Riley needed him. Because he'd been naked beneath the sheets. With Ally.

The embarrassment felt like being covered in shards of glass.

Nate walked back into the room, swiftly followed by the other policeman.

"We've had a lead. Mr. Crawford's credit card was used two hours ago to buy a single plane ticket to Boston."

"Where my sister lives," Nate said.

"We're pretty sure she's headed there."

"Has the plane taken off yet?" the female officer asked. Ally looked at Nate. His face was as tight as ever, his breath as shallow as hers.

"Half an hour ago. We're requesting the flight manifest now."

"I'm going to pack a bag and head to the airport," Nate said, his eyes landing on Ally's. "I've called Kirsten to let her know."

"Kirsten's your sister?" the officer asked. She made another note.

"That's right."

"We're calling the Boston Police Department, too. Riley

should have a big welcoming committee waiting for her at the other end."

Ally waited for relief to wash over her, but it didn't arrive. All she felt was that same churning feeling in her stomach that had been going on all morning. At the thought of Riley – so upset by seeing Ally and her dad that she had to jump on a plane to escape.

"We'll head out to the car and make a couple of calls while you pack," the male officer said. He inclined his head before he made for the hallway, his partner following right behind.

It was just the two of them again. Nate raked a hand through his thick hair, curling his fingers around the back of his neck. There were shadows beneath his eyes and his skin looked pale in spite of the California sun outside. "I should go grab a bag," he said, still hovering by the door.

"Yes." Ally nodded.

"Can you stay here again?" he asked, his tone business-like. "Just until I know she's safe. If she isn't on that flight, or if something goes wrong I need somebody here."

"Of course I can." Her voice was soft. "Whatever you need, I can do it."

"I'll let you know when I get to Boston." He still wasn't looking at her.

"I'd appreciate that. I want to know she's safe." She moistened her lips with her tongue. "Nate?"

"Yeah?"

"Can you tell her I'm sorry?"

He frowned. "What are you sorry for?"

A humorless laugh escaped from her lips. "I don't know," she said, her brows knitting together. "For not answering her call. For not being here when she needed me." *Because I took your attention away when she needed you the most?*

"I'll tell her." He gave a short nod. "I should go. They're waiting for me."

A moment later he was headed to his bedroom – the one that was still minus a bed. A loud creak told her he was opening his closet, no doubt throwing clothes into his overnight bag.

And then there was one. Just Ally, this huge house and all the dark thoughts that threatened to rain down on her.

Her chest ached with a sense of loss she couldn't quite understand. Because she hadn't lost anything had she? Or at least she hadn't yet.

"Okay, everything's back where it belongs." Lucas walked into the living room where Ally was sitting with Ember and Brooke. Griff, Lucas' best friend, was hovering behind him, having come over to help carry the bed back from the patio. "We'll head out and leave you ladies to it." He winked at Ember who smiled back at him. "See you later, babe."

"Thanks for all your help," Ally said. Her voice was fragile as glass. "I appreciate it."

"Any time." He gave her the softest of smiles. He really was a good guy. No doubt Ember had filled him in on all the gory details while they were on their way over. "If you need anything else, call me, okay?"

"I will."

The two of them left, heading out to Griffin's truck, where their surfboards were stashed in the flatbed. It was strange, knowing that normal life was still going on while Ally felt as though she was at the center of a storm. Surfers still surfed, teachers still taught, even the coffee shop was still open. For most of Angel Sands it was just another Friday.

Not for Nate and Riley, though. Or for Ally.

"What time is Nate's plane due into Boston?" Brooke asked, checking her watch.

"Any minute now. He got on the first flight out once the police confirmed Riley was on the earlier plane."

"And his sister was going to meet her?"

"Along with some police officers. They were going to escort his sister to the arrival gate so she doesn't have to wait in the hall." She gave a wan smile. "I guess she's there already."

"At least you know she's safe." Ember reached out for her hand. "What a mess this all is. You must be exhausted after everything that's happened. Maybe you should go lie down."

Ally shook her head. "I couldn't sleep even if I wanted to." Not with all these thoughts racing through her head. Every time she thought about Riley seeing them out on the deck it made her feel sick. Not because of her embarrassment, but because she hated to think what Riley must have thought of her.

She came home because she was upset and wanted Ally's support. Then she found her in bed with her father. She must have felt so alone, so betrayed. Exactly the same way Ally would have if she'd been in her place.

Her phone buzzed and Ally grabbed it.

Made it to Boston. Riley's safe with Kirsten. I'm heading there now.

That was it. Nothing else. Ally stared at his words, trying to take them in.

"Is that from Nate?" Brooke asked. "Is everything okay?"

"Um, yeah I think so. He's made it to Boston and Riley's with his sister."

Ember squeezed her hand. "That's great news, isn't it?"

Ally nodded. She had to press her lips together to stop herself from letting out a sob. Of course it was great news. It was such a damn relief. But there was still that self-loathing deep inside that seemed to be slowly eating its way out.

"She's safe and that's the main thing," Brooke said, smiling at her. "Though I bet Nate will be reaming her out when he sees her. Man, it's tough being a parent sometimes. One day we'll all be talking like this about Nick and wondering where I went wrong."

"It's tough being a kid, too," Ally said. "Poor Riley. First her mom dies, then she moves here and has to make a whole bunch of new friends. And now..." She couldn't say it again. She could think it, though. Riley had been let down by the two people she thought she could trust.

"And now she's safe." Brooke finished the sentence for her in an entirely new way. "They'll be back later and this will all be forgotten in a week."

"I'll be back in my apartment by then." Ally smiled wanly. "That'll be a good thing for everybody."

"But you'll still be seeing Nate, won't you?" Ember asked. "This doesn't change things between the two of you, does it? It's embarrassing, yes, but it's not the end of the world."

"I don't know." Ally shook her head. "I guess we'll have to wait and see what happens next."

Maybe tomorrow she wouldn't see that expression on Riley's face every time she closed her eyes. The confusion that morphed into hurt and disgust before she turned on her heel and ran away.

Yeah, maybe tomorrow would be a better day. Because God knew that today was pretty much rock bottom.

❧ 25 ❧

Nate pressed the buzzer to his sister's apartment, and glanced at the policeman standing next to him. He'd picked Nate up from the airport, driving him along the freeway to Kirsten's apartment in Bay Village. The weather in Boston was a contrast to the warmth of Angel Sands, and he found himself shivering. And worrying about Riley once again. He could guarantee she hadn't worn appropriate clothing.

"Hello?" Kirsten's voice echoed through the speaker.

"It's Nate."

"Come on up."

"Would you like to come, too?" Nate asked the policeman.

"No, sir. I'll let you go see your daughter. I'll call in to your local PD to let them know she's safe."

Nate reached for the man's hand, shaking it vigorously. "Thank you," he said.

"Any time."

It only took a couple of minutes for him to catch the elevator up to the eighth floor, where Kirsten's two bedroom apartment could be found. He knocked softly on the door and she opened it immediately, her lips curling up into a smile when she saw her brother standing on the other side.

"She's in the spare bedroom sleeping it off," she said quietly, standing back to let Nate into her apartment. "I don't think she slept at all for the past day or so, and it's caught up with her."

"That makes two of us." Every muscle in his body ached from a combination of the flight and the worry. But it was his head that hurt the most. The pounding headache that had begun with Riley's surprise arrival back in Angel Sands hadn't dissipated at all.

"You want to see her?" Kirsten asked.

"You read my mind." The urge to check on her, make sure she was okay, was overwhelming. He'd spent the last five hours feeling completely helpless, buckled up in an airplane while his daughter was here in Boston.

"You go and I'll go make us some coffee." Kirsten walked into her small kitchen, leaving Nate in the hallway. He pushed the door of the guest bedroom open, just enough to look inside. Sure enough, there was Riley curled up on the bed, her face resting on her hands, her eyes closed as she rhythmically breathed in and out.

His arms twitched with the need to touch her. To hold her. To make sure she really was okay. But Kirsten was right, she needed this sleep. His own needs would come second.

"There you go." Kirsten slid the mug into his hands as he joined her in the kitchen. "It's not Déjà Brew standards, but at least it has caffeine in it."

"Just what I need." He took a sip and closed his eyes as the bitter liquid coated his tongue. "This is damn fine coffee."

"I bet you haven't had anything to eat or drink all day." She rolled her eyes at him. "Oh, and I made you a sandwich."

'Have I told you lately that I love you?"

She cocked an eyebrow. "Nope."

"Well I do." As soon as he glanced at the sandwich his stomach gurgled. Kirsten was right; he hadn't been able to manage anything on the plane. "Thank you for all you've done," he said, putting his mug down to give his sister a hug. "I know Riley will be thankful, too."

"She's not in a good way right now." Kirsten nodded at the door to her living room. "Maybe we should talk in there." She picked up his sandwich and her own coffee, and he followed her in, sitting down on a cozy chair.

"Take a bite," she said, pointing at the sandwich. "That way I can talk without you interrupting me all the time."

"I don't interrupt."

She gave him a pointed look. "You just did."

If she'd been fifteen years younger she'd have stuck her tongue out at him the way she used to. Strange to think how grown up she was now. The age difference between them didn't seem so important any more. At one point he'd felt more like her father than her brother, thanks to their parents' messy divorce when Kirsten was seventeen, but now she was a friend more than anything. Somebody he could rely on when life got tough.

"Okay, I won't interrupt again, I promise." If she wanted to talk, he'd let her talk.

As soon as he took a bite Kirsten leaned forward. "There's this guy she's fallen for at school. His name's Leo. And apparently she spent the whole trip to LA thinking he was going to ask her out on a date."

Nate opened his mouth, but she lifted her finger up to quieten him. "Okay, so her friend offers to go and talk to him. Laura I think her name is. So yesterday, after they've had their dinner and they're given some free time, this Laura heads for Leo's room and leaves Riley on her own in her hotel room. *For two hours*." Kirsten raised an eyebrow. "So of course Riley goes looking for her. And when she finds them, this

Laura and Leo are kissing like crazy in the recreation room. And Riley's standing there devastated because pretty much the only friend she has in her new school has betrayed her with the boy she likes."

Nate sighed. "Not a great friend."

"Nope. So Riley's really upset and doesn't know what to do and tries to call – what's her name, Ally?"

"Yeah."

"But Ally doesn't answer. And there's no way Riley's going to sleep in the room she's sharing with Laura because she's way too upset to even look at her. She goes to her teacher to ask for help, but the teacher tells her she can't swap rooms and to be an adult about things." Kirsten winced. "Great teacher."

"I guess I'll be talking to the school, too."

"Yeah, well this teacher also happened to have her car stolen by your daughter, so I wouldn't be too angry about it."

Nate swallowed. "The car's been returned to her. Unharmed. And the teacher will be recompensed for the inconvenience. I even had the gas topped off."

Kirsten caught his eye. She was biting her lip. Any minute now she looked as though she was going to burst into laughter. "Riley really messed up this time, didn't she?"

"She's going to be grounded for the rest of her life. And possibly after that."

"The poor kid. Life really sucks for her at the moment."

"She can join the club." Nate let his head fall back onto the stuffed armchair, closing his eyes to try and calm himself down. Like Kirsten, he felt the strange need to laugh. Possibly because what he really wanted to do was cry.

"I haven't got to the best part yet," Kirsten said. Nate lifted his head to look at her. "You know, the piece where she gets home and finds her *dad* in bed with some smoking hot blonde who's been staying with them." This time she really did laugh. "Oh Nate, you've been a bad, bad boy."

He closed his eyes, trying to block out the regret that was churning in his stomach. "Shut up."

"Is it serious between the two of you?"

He opened his eyes, taking in Kirsten's gentle concern. He had no plans to get into this conversation right now. Especially with his sister. "I don't know. We were having some fun while Riley was away."

"Not so much fun now though, I bet?"

He shook his head. "No."

"I thought you were done with relationships after Stephanie. I never thought you'd be back to sowing your wild oats so soon."

A sudden tiredness washed over him, making every muscle in his body ache. "You know what? I think I might take a nap, too. I've been awake since two-thirty this morning." He stood and stretched his arms, as if to underscore the fact he wasn't just attempting to evade her questions. Though if he was honest, that was a pretty big reason to close his eyes. "Can I hit your bed for an hour?"

Kirsten's smirk was replaced by a look of concern. "Oh God, I'm sorry, you must be exhausted. Of course you can, the bed's all made up. And if you want to shower first there are fresh towels in my bathroom."

He felt as though he'd just dodged a bullet. One heading straight for his heart. As much as he loved his sister, right now she was the last person he wanted to talk to about Ally. Okay, the second-to-last person. The last person was sleeping in the guest room.

"Sleep tight, big brother." Kirsten smiled at him.

"I'll give it my best shot."

"Nate?"

He opened his eyes, looking around the darkened room. Whoever just spoke was standing in the doorway, silhouetted against the light spilling in from the hall. "Kirsten?" he said, his voice croaky. "That you?"

"Yeah. I'm heading out to dinner with a couple of friends. I thought it would give you a chance to speak to Riley without me here cramping your style. I'll only be gone a couple of hours."

"What time is it?" He sat up and looked at his crumpled clothes. He was wearing the same t-shirt he'd grabbed that morning before the police arrived, along with a pair of old jeans.

"Almost six. Riley's stirring but she hasn't woken up yet. Or at least she hasn't shown her face outside the guest bedroom. If you need me to be out any longer just message me. Otherwise I'll bring you both something back to eat on my way home."

"Are you okay with us staying here tonight?" He felt more awake now. Sitting up, he swung his legs around to touch the floor, and something about the movement reminded him of Ally.

He pushed that thought right out of his mind.

"Sure. I can take the couch."

"I'll take the couch," Nate told her. "I'm not throwing you out of your room as well as imposing on you. I'll book us a flight home for tomorrow."

"Home?" she asked, smiling. "Which one?"

"Angel Sands."

She gave a little chuckle. "I thought you might say that. And I'm glad. I know things have gone spectacularly wrong these past couple of days, but it really seemed like Riley had turned a corner before then." Kirsten pulled a jacket on. "Anyway, I'll speak with you later. Call me if things threaten to explode. And whatever you do, don't let Riley leave. God only knows when you'd find her again."

"Wasn't planning on it."

Kirsten left with a wave, pulling the front door closed behind her. Nate sat on the edge of the bed for a moment, blinking his way back to full wakefulness.

He might have slept the afternoon away, but it hadn't done anything to improve his mood. He needed to get himself into a better one and fast. There was only room for one teenager in this apartment, and it certainly wasn't him.

Maybe coffee would help. He walked across Kirsten's bedroom, glancing at himself in the darkened mirror. His hair was a mess, his face was worse, and he looked like he'd slept for hours in these clothes.

He really did need coffee and fast.

"Kirsten?" Riley's voice was sleepy as she pushed the guest room door open. Nate stopped in the hallway and held his breath for a moment. Then she walked out, her hair as messy as his, her face red and creased where she'd been sleeping on it. "Dad?" Her eyes widened. "When did you get here?"

"A couple of hours ago."

"Why didn't you wake me?"

"Kirsten said you were beat. I was pretty tired myself. I thought we could both use the rest." He kept his voice even. There was time for shouting and time for calm. This was definitely one of the latter occasions.

Riley opened her mouth and closed it again, reaching up to smooth her hair back from her face. Watching her gesture was like looking in the mirror. How often did he do that when he was feeling uncomfortable?

"You okay?" he asked her.

She nodded. Then her face crumpled. "I'm sorry." Her bottom lip wobbled. "I was so stupid. I don't know what came over me."

Nate cleared the distance between them in a second, put his arms around in two. Then he pulled her close, shutting his eyes and breathing her in. And for a moment – just a moment – he finally felt some peace.

She was safe. *Thank you, God.*

"You need to stop making decisions on impulse," he said, his words muffled by her hair. "Because every time you do, it makes things worse. What part of stealing your teacher's car seemed like a good idea last night? Or flying to Boston without stopping to talk to me first?"

"I don't know." She buried her face against his t-shirt. "It all seems like a blur. I can't remember making those decisions. By the time my thoughts started working it was like I'd already made them and I was in the middle of a horror story where things keep getting worse."

"That's exactly what this is like," he said. "One of those movies where the heroine goes into the haunted house even though everybody tells her not to."

"I'm the heroine, aren't I?" she asked, sighing. "The one that's too stupid to live."

"Well you're still alive. So that's something." He hugged her a little tighter. "But you're also in big trouble, kid."

"I know. And I'm never leaving the house again anyway, so you can ground me all you like."

"You'll be leaving it to apologize to your teacher. And to go for a meeting with your principal."

She tipped her head up to look at him, her eyes wide. "Have they kicked me out?"

"I don't know," he told her. "Do you think they should?"

"I would if I was them. I'm nothing but trouble." She looked so young as she stared up at him, the light catching her face. He wished he could freeze time, or even better turn it back. To those years when he could always keep her safe. "I bet mom's turning in her grave right now."

"Your mom would be worried about you. The way I am." Nate sighed. "And Ally's pretty distraught as well." Just saying her name made his stomach contract.

Riley winced. "Oh God, she must hate me."

"She doesn't hate you, she's concerned. And embarrassed that you saw..." he cleared his throat. "What you saw. She asked me to give you a message, to tell you she's sorry for not answering your call."

"It's not her who should be sorry." Riley shook her head. "I'm so ashamed. You must all hate me. I'm sorry, Dad. Sorry for everything. And I know I've said it before and messed up again, but this time I mean it." She circled her arms around him again, hugging him tight. "I'm sorry I messed up your night with Ally."

"You didn't mess anything up. I did. I'm sorry you had to see us there. It won't happen again."

She looked up, her eyes shiny with tears. "I knew there was something going on between you. All those long looks and silences whenever I walked into the room. I'm not a kid, Dad. I know sexual tension when I see it."

He stifled a groan. Just what he needed. Another member of his family he really didn't want to have this conversation with. "There was nothing going on, not really."

Riley grimaced. "Whatever it was, I never want to see that again. Keep it behind closed doors, thank you very much."

Nate's stomach gave a loud rumble. Riley stepped back and looked at him with mock-horror. "When was the last time you ate?" she asked him.

"Kirsten made me a sandwich. How about you?"

"No idea. I wasn't hungry when I got here." She frowned. "I am now though."

"Kirsten said she'd bring something back later," Nate said. "But maybe we should head out and get some dinner now."

Riley nodded. "I'd like that," she said, giving him another hug.

For the first time all day Nate felt his headache begin to ease off. Yes, Riley was in big trouble, and yes, she was going to be punished, but right now he wanted to hold his little girl and protect her from the world.

And the mess they'd all caused in the past twenty-four hours? He had no idea how to handle it. He'd let his daughter down so badly, again, and he hated himself for it.

When was he going to get this parenting thing right?

✵ 26 ✵

It was almost midnight when her phone rang. Ally had been sitting alone in the big beach house for hours, her body sinking into the soft leather sofa, her leg propped up on the matching footstool.

Ember had offered to come over after work, and Brooke had suggested staying with her to keep her company, but Ally had batted off their suggestions, telling them she was tired and wanted to sleep for a while.

It wasn't really a lie. She *was* tired. Exhausted, even. But there was no way she was getting any sleep tonight.

"Nate?" she said breathlessly as she lifted the phone to her face. "Is Riley okay?" She missed the smell of him, the feel of his arms around hers. Missed everything feeling perfect... until it wasn't. And didn't that make her heart ache just a little bit more?

"She's fine." He sounded as drained as she felt. "She was sound asleep when I got to Kirsten's place."

She waited for him to say something about not calling earlier, but he was silent. "I've been worried," she said, breaking the silence that hung between them. "When you didn't call I started to think the worst."

"I'm sorry. I can't always call when you need me to." There was an edge to his voice that made her breath catch in her throat. "I had to speak to the police and then to Kirsten and Riley. She's my first priority."

Ally licked her lips, trying to ignore the way his words made her feel. As though she was of no importance. Of course she wasn't, not compared to his daughter.

Didn't stop it from stinging though.

"But she's okay?"

"I said she's fine."

Ally bit her lip. "Did you talk to her about..." she trailed off, the excruciating memory of Riley seeing them washing over her once again. "About us?"

"What about us?"

"About what she saw," Ally said, keeping her voice as even as she could. "When she came home. Did you explain it to her?"

"What's there to explain? She saw us naked. She freaked and ran away." He cleared his throat. "So no, I didn't try to make excuses or explain things away. There are no excuses."

With every word he was building a wall between them. It was already so high she could barely see over it. The closeness of the past few days felt like something she'd only imagined.

But she hadn't, had she? It was real, so real for the few days they were alone together. Before that, even. From the moment they'd met outside the coffee shop the connection had been there.

"Is there anything I can do to help?" she asked him, still trying to work out why he sounded so mean. "I could talk to Riley, maybe?"

"You really think that's a good idea? She saw you... us... together. It would only make the situation worse."

Ally squeezed her eyes shut. For a moment she was a teenager again, listening to Marnie complaining that she'd used up all the hot water, that she'd eaten the last cookie, or anything else that made Ally look bad in front of her dad. Would she have wanted to talk to Marnie in the same position? Not at all. She couldn't wait to see the back of her.

Maybe Nate was right. She'd only make it worse if she got involved with the situation. But she felt so damn impotent here, knowing Riley's world was falling apart and it was her fault.

Or at least partially.

"I don't know..." she said, covering her face with her hand. "I just want to make things better. Maybe if I found the right words she'd understand. I know this is my fault."

"Can you quit making this all about you?" Nate sighed. "It's been a long goddamned day and it's a stupid time in the morning here. I just wanted to let you know she's okay."

"I'm sorry, I—" She tried to think of the right words but they scurried away, hiding in the depths of her mind. Of course he was tired and angry, she would be too in his position. Yes, he was being an asshole, but it was understandable.

He was exhausted, afraid and he had Riley to think about. He was like a tiger growling because he didn't know what else to do.

"Christ." He let out a long sigh. She imagined him pulling at his hair the way he sometimes did when he was out of patience.

"When are you coming back?" she asked him. Maybe if they talked about something different he would calm down. She hated to think of him so irate.

"I don't know. Tomorrow maybe. Or the next day. I need a bit of time alone with Riley first."

"I thought you were at your sister's place."

"We are."

She took a deep breath in. The whole conversation was laying heavy on her. Nate's refusal to talk about the situation was making her feel so uncomfortable, yet she didn't know quite how to word it.

"Maybe once Riley's back we can talk about this. All of us. It's not healthy to sweep it under the rug."

As soon as she said the words she knew they were the wrong ones. The silence that followed was so loaded she could almost hear it screaming. She squeezed her eyes shut, wanting to hit herself with the damn phone she was talking into.

Stupid Ally. She never could say the right thing.

"I..." Nate trailed off, as though he was looking for the right words. Maybe she should have done the same. "Ally, I can't do this right now," he finally said, his voice low and thick like it was full of molasses.

"Do what?"

"Talk to you about this. I'm so tired and my head's messed up and I need to be alone right now."

Her breath stuttered. "What does that mean?" she asked him. "I don't understand. Surely we need to talk about Riley and what to tell her about us?"

"I'm sorry, Ally, but there is no *us*. I can't think about us right now. I took my eye off the ball. I spent too much time chasing you that I didn't even see my daughter was spinning off the rails again. I need to just concentrate on her for a while."

She gasped at the impact of his words. If he'd slapped her it couldn't have hurt any worse. Tears stung at her eyes, heating her skin as they began to roll down her cheeks.

"Okay," she whispered through the tears. Her chest began to ache, as though there was a huge weight pushing down on it, making it hard to breathe. "Okay," she repeated, more to herself than to him.

"Ah, Ally." He let out another sigh. She waited for him to say something else, but it didn't come. Just his soft breaths, so more measured than her own. Her hands shook as she held the phone against her wet cheek.

"I need to go," she said, trying to hide the wobble in her voice. "It's late here, too." And neither of them had slept for almost twenty-four hours. It was a shock either of them could speak at all.

She wasn't going to beg. Not while she had some semblance of self respect left. It hurt like hell to have him speak to her like this, but she wasn't going to let him know that.

"Ally," he said again. And once again she waited, her teeth gritting together when she realized he wasn't going to follow it up. That's when the anger began to rise inside her, replacing the sadness and the indignation. This man had slept with her, he'd listened to her worst fears, confided some of his own. And yet right now he was treating her like a stranger. No, worse than that. He wouldn't talk to a stranger the way he was talking to her, not without risking getting his face punched.

She looked around the large living room, taking in the beautiful walnut polished floor, the expensive furnishings, the original paintings that had been expertly chosen to complete the look. This wasn't home. It was far from it — so far she couldn't quite remember what she was doing here.

She took a deep breath and reached up with her free hand to wipe away the tears that were spilling down her face. "The superintendent of my apartment called earlier. The elevator's finally fixed." She didn't wait for a response. "I'll move out tomorrow morning," she said, trying to keep her voice as mild as possible. "That way when you and Riley get home I won't be here."

"There's no rush."

Yes there was. If her whole body hurt now, it was going to hurt so much more when she saw them in the flesh. She didn't trust herself not to break down in front of them, and there was no way she wanted to make this situation worse than it already was.

Nate had made it clear that Riley came first, and that was how it should be. And if the way he did it was cruel and unfeeling? Well, she was a big girl now. She could handle it.

"It's fine. I'll be gone by the time you're back."

"I can help you. Or call somebody..."

"No. I have friends. I'll ask them for help."

He was silent again. As though her last words had sunk in.

"I'm going to bed," she told him, more than ready for this conversation to end. "Thanks for letting me stay. And good luck with Riley. She's a good kid, try not to be too hard on her." She licked her lips, tasting the salt of her tears. "Good-bye, Nate."

She didn't wait for him to reply. There was nothing he could say that would make her feel any better. Pulling the phone from her face she ended the call and leaned back on the sofa, closing her eyes.

She was alone again. Completely and utterly. But that was okay. She'd been alone before and survived it. This time she was going into it as a pro.

Shit.

Nate's hands curled into fists. He wanted to hit something. *Anything.* But it was in the middle of the goddamned night here in Boston and any sudden movement was sure to wake Riley or Kirsten up.

He wasn't quite sure what the hell had just happened. There'd been something in Ally's tone that had reminded him of Stephanie. Something about the way she'd said 'us' that had put him on edge. As if she was trying to make him choose again. Between the woman he'd desired and the daughter he'd promised to always take care of.

It was a no-brainer. And Ally should know that.

He shook his head, still not able to understand how the conversation had gotten so messed up so quickly. But his brain couldn't focus on it no matter how hard he tried. No big surprise, really – it was after three in the morning here in Boston. California seemed like more than half a world away. Those nights with Ally seemed like a hazy dream.

And his actions like a nightmare.

He dropped his head into his hands and leaned back on the couch. Kirsten had made it up, tucking a crisp white sheet over the cushions, putting two plump pillows on the armrest. On top there was a thick red comforter, enough to block out the chill of the Boston night.

All he could think about was the previous night. How connected they'd been, how he'd held her and felt so much warmth, not just from her skin but from being with *her*. The memory of the break in her voice as he told her there was no 'us' made him feel sick. His heart ached at the thought of her all alone in his house, thinking he didn't care.

The problem was he cared too much. He was in danger of losing his daughter because of it. He couldn't let it happen. While they'd been talking on the phone it had felt like that conversation with Stephanie all over again. She wanted to talk about their relationship while all he could think about was losing his daughter.

Yeah, but she isn't Stephanie, is she? She's never once asked you to choose between her and Riley. They love each other, any fool could see that.

There was a truth to that voice in his head that made him want to punch something. His chest felt as though it was being torn in two. He'd messed up and he kept making it worse. And he had no idea what to do next.

What the hell had he done?

Should he call her back? He looked at his phone, at the time reflecting on the screen. It was so late it wasn't funny. More importantly, he was beyond tired. Beyond exhausted. It was as though his body was running on fumes, each part of him slowly breaking down until he was going to stop all together. The entire apartment was silent, save for the creaking of the old pipes and the loud insistent beat of his heart. He cleared his throat just to hear some noise.

If he called her back he'd probably make it worse. His brain wasn't working properly, that much was clear. No matter how he looked at things he had no idea how to make both his daughter and the woman he cared for happy. He needed to get Riley home and safe, and then he could work things out. Find a way forward from this mess he'd found himself in.

A mess of his own damn creation.

Ally was different, that little voice he hated so much whispered from deep inside his mind. *She was kind and funny and for some reason she liked you. You're a dipshit, Nate Crawford.*

The truth of those words made him hate himself a little bit more.

He'd dug himself a hole so deep he wasn't sure how to climb out of it. And in doing so, he might have lost the best thing that had ever happened to him.

❧ 27 ❧

When Ally walked into her apartment building it felt completely wrong. Though it had only been a few weeks since Ally was last there, everything felt so much smaller. As she made her way into the elevator, Ember and Lucas following close behind, Ally had to swallow down the feelings of panic that threatened to envelope her.

Was it possible to develop claustrophobia over the course of a few days? Because right now it was all she could do to keep herself breathing.

"Are you okay?" Ember asked, tipping her head to the side. "You look ill."

"I'm fine." Ally nodded as though that would convince her friend. "Or I will be as soon as the elevator takes us to my floor. I don't trust this new part they installed yet."

Lucas smiled. "I checked the maintenance log. It's all good."

Ember rubbed his arm. "My hero." She glanced at Ally. "I knew having a firefighter around would come in handy."

"Is that the only reason you keep me around?" He lifted

an eyebrow. Ally watched as the two of them stared at each other, their eyes filled with love. It made her heart ache.

"That and the fact you're great at carrying bags," Ember told him, glancing down at Ally's suitcases. There were only three of them. It didn't seem a lot to show for the past few weeks, but then Ally was carrying most of the baggage inside of herself.

She wasn't quite ready to unpack those dark thoughts yet, however heavy they felt.

The elevator pinged when they reached the fifth floor. After a pause that made her hold her breath, the doors slowly slid open, revealing the hallway that led to her apartment. It was darker than she remembered – the interior lit by dim spotlights. Such a contrast to the light-filled beach house she'd just left.

There was a musty smell inside her apartment that would disappear with the opening of a few windows. Unopened letters were scattered across the wooden floor – no doubt pushed under the door by some of her neighbors; their mail was always getting mixed up. But apart from that everything looked the same way it had a few weeks ago. Before she'd been butt-dialed by Riley and ran out of the door. Maybe if she sat down in her living room and closed her eyes for a moment, she could pretend that it had never happened.

That she hadn't gone running in the rain to stop Riley from jumping.

That Nate hadn't brought her to his home and taken care of her.

That Ally hadn't fallen for him so badly every part of her ached. Especially the bones that were knitting themselves back together beneath her cast.

It was probably a good thing she couldn't run at the moment, even though every muscle in her ached to move. Because if she put her running shoes on and made her way down to the beach she wasn't sure she'd ever be able to bring herself to stop.

Lucas walked into the living room. "I put your bags on your bed. You need some help unpacking?"

She gave him the biggest smile she could muster. "No, thank you. I'll empty them later. It'll give me something to do."

"You don't look well. Should we call your doctor?" Ember asked. "Maybe you shouldn't have moved out so soon. I could call Nate and tell him you're going back there?"

Ally shook her head. "No, I probably just need to lie down."

Lucas walked into the kitchen and poured her a glass of water, bringing it back and putting it in Ally's hand. "When did you last take some painkillers?"

"Um, I'm not sure. Yesterday I think." Or was it the day before? Anyway, the hurt she was feeling right now couldn't be touched by a pill. And yet when Lucas grabbed her purse and brought it back to her, she dug through it until she found the bottle of pills the doctor had described her. Two pills, four times a day, as needed.

She took the bottle from him with a wan smile. "I'll take some later if I need to. It doesn't hurt so much any more." She glanced down at the printed instructions. There was no mention of whether they could mend a broken heart.

"When is Nate coming back?"

"Today some time I guess." The thought made Ally's chest tighten, enough to push all the breath from her.

"Is he going to call you when he's home?" Ember asked. "Otherwise maybe you should come and stay with us. I don't want to leave you on your own."

"He's not going to call." Her voice broke on the last word.

"What?" Ember looked over at Lucas, and he shrugged. She brought her gaze back to Ally. "Why not?"

"Because it's over between us."

Ember's brows dipped as she took Ally's words in. "But why?" she asked. "You're just moving out of his house, not finishing your relationship with him."

She sat silently as Ally filled her in. Lucas was still hovering in the space between her tiny kitchen and living room, looking awkward as Ally spilled her guts. Ember, on the other hand, reached for her hand, folding it between her own.

"He made it clear that things were over between us," Ally finished, biting her lip in an attempt not to cry. "He was so angry and short with me. I can't see any way forward for us."

Ember squeezed Ally's hand. "Are you sure he meant that he wanted to end it? Maybe he was just trying to cool things between you. A lot has happened in the past few days. He must have been going crazy when Riley disappeared."

"I know." Ally felt her tears sting against her cheek. "And I tried to be there for him, I really did. But the way he talked to me on the phone..." She lifted her free hand to wipe her tears. "I should have known it was never going to work. When does it ever work out for me? Everybody leaves eventually. My mom, my dad, Nate..."

"I'm still here," Ember reminded her.

Ally squeezed her hand back. "I know. And thank God you are."

"And so are Lucas and Brooke, and all the people in town who stop me constantly to ask how you're doing."

"Frank Megassey gave me the third degree when I went to buy some paint the other day," Lucas said.

"And maybe Nate didn't mean what he said. You know what phone calls are like. It's so easy to misunderstand somebody. Just give things time and see what happens." Ember looked over at Lucas. "Sometimes they're worth it."

"Sure," Ally agreed, though she held out no hope. He was

doing what any good dad would do – putting his daughter first.

And if the way he did it was cruel and hurtful? Well, she could handle that. "I'm beat," she told them. "I might take a nap before I start to unpack."

Ember nodded. "Rest will probably do you some good. You want me to stay?"

"No. I should be on my own for a while. Get used to being back in this place." Somehow she found the right muscles to form a smile. "You guys go and enjoy the rest of your day off. You don't get enough of them. I'll be fine once I get some sleep. You don't need to worry about me."

"But I do. Worry, I mean."

"Well you don't need to. I've been through worse than this and survived. I can take a little heartbreak."

Ember hugged her tightly. "I know," she whispered. "But I wish you didn't have to."

Yeah, Ally wished that, too. If hopeless wishes were dollars she'd be a millionaire by now. It was time to stop wishing for things that were never going to happen, and concentrate on getting herself better.

She had a broken ankle to mend, as well as a broken heart. One of them seemed easy – some rest, some time, and a plaster cast to keep things all together.

The other one? Not so simple. And in the meantime she'd learn to live with the pain.

Ally's eyes flew open, her heart banging against her chest as she looked around the unfamiliar room, trying to work out what was happening. She'd been having a dream, one where she couldn't stop running even though her body ached and her lungs were screaming with pain. Every time she thought about slowing down her legs kept moving on.

She blinked, her eyes slowly becoming accustomed to the dark of the room. Pursing her lips, she blew out a lungful of air, but it did nothing to slow the racing of her heart. The memory of the dream lingered. It mixed in with the ache that had been in her chest ever since that phone call with Nate. Both of them reminded her that she was alone. Just Ally. She should have learned from experience she couldn't rely on anybody else.

Nate. The thought of him was physically painful. She took another breath, holding it for a few seconds before releasing it. Her heart rate was slowing, but her body was still on high alert. She tried to turn in her bed, wincing as the cast knocked her good foot. In the end she had to lift her thigh with her hands to move it, but still she wasn't comfortable.

Maybe this was her life now. Discomfort everywhere.

The kitchen clock was ticking, a constant click that only made her feel more alone. It couldn't be any earlier than five in the morning. There was nobody she could talk to, nobody to call. Right now it was only her.

And she hated it.

Grabbing her phone she scrolled through the notifications. A few friends had posted on Insta since she'd fallen asleep last night, but just looking at the photographs made her feel even worse. She looked at her last message with Ember and Brooke and for a moment she considered calling them just to hear a friendly voice.

No. That wasn't fair to them. They both had their own lives, and they both needed to get up early in the morning. As much as they loved her, neither of them needed to hear her tales of woe right now.

Her eyes scanned down the list of chats. She could see

Riley's message from when she'd been in LA. Ally squeezed her eyes shut at the memory of that night.

And then she saw *his* name. She didn't need to click on the chat to see what was said. She could remember every conversation they'd had by heart. Even the written ones. Anyway, the last thing he'd sent her was the message saying he'd arrived in Boston. The kind of message that happened every day between couples – they probably never thought twice about it.

But for a moment in time she'd felt like one of *them*. Taken care of, maybe even loved.

And now it was gone.

It hurt. So much. Even breathing in made her wince with the pain. She'd heard of heartache but never thought it was a real, physical thing. But unless she was dying, that's exactly what she was feeling.

Shaking her head, she pressed the trashcan icon and deleted those messages. Then she blocked him, the way Ember had shown her. There was no way her heart could stand any contact from him right now.

Her eyes fell to one final contact, lingering there as she tried to block out the pain. Then, without letting herself think about it too hard, she pressed her finger down on it to make a call.

It went straight to voicemail, like she knew it would. And maybe it was better that way for now. There was so much emotion involved. She needed to talk without feeling afraid of being hurt again.

As soon as the message ended she took a deep breath, letting the oxygen surge through her. It was time to talk. Beyond time. And if he'd broken her trust before it didn't negate the love she knew he felt for her.

"Daddy? It's Ally. Can you call me back when you get this message?"

❧ 28 ❧

Her dad had called her back while she was asleep, leaving a message that he'd call again that afternoon. It was strange, but she felt so much calmer now. And unwilling to hide away from the world forever.

She was stronger than that. Amazing what sleep could do for the soul.

The elevator was still working – thank God – and it came up to floor five as soon as she called it. Within moments she was in the lobby, then walking outside to what was another beautiful California day. She stopped and closed her eyes, letting the sun's rays warm her face.

It was only a five-minute walk from her apartment to the boardwalk, but with crutches it was more like fifteen. She was so used to being able to cover small distances with speed, it was frustrating to be so slow. By the time she made it to the oceanfront she was feeling overheated. Leaning her elbows on her crutches, she lifted her thick hair from her neck and quickly braided it, closing her eyes as a cool breeze danced up from the ocean and kissed her skin.

Déjà Brew was the first shop she came to. It was at the

end of the boardwalk, after all, taking up the prized corner position that made it so accessible both from the road and the beach. Sneaking a glance through the window, she swallowed hard, her breath coming a little easier when she saw that Nate wasn't there.

She wasn't ready to see him yet. Not ready to smile and pretend he was just a boss. But at least she wasn't hiding away either. There was a sense of pride in that.

"Ally!" A gruff voice called out from the shop next door. Lorne was sliding diving masks onto a rack, and he smiled as soon as she caught sight of him. She couldn't help but smile, too. He was wearing a pair of pink board shorts and a white t-shirt that proclaimed he hoped he died before he got old.

God, she loved him.

She made her way over, her crutches slapping against the concrete. As soon as she reached him, Lorne gave her a huge bear hug, as though he knew inside that she needed it before returning to his work.

"So, Lorne cleared his throat as he slid the last mask onto the rack. "You hear from your dad?" he asked, trying – and failing – to keep his tone light.

Ally bit down a smile. "I called him last night and left a message."

Lorne visibly relaxed. "Oh thank God. He's been calling me every day to see how you are. The wife thinks I'm having an affair."

The thought of Lorne being unfaithful to his wife made her want to laugh again.

"Well, you'll be able to stop being in the middle now," she told him, reaching out to touch his arm. "Thank you for being there. For both of us."

"You're like a daughter to me," he said, his voice thick. "I'll always be there for you. And as for your dad, he might be an old reprobate but he's my best friend." Lorne shrugged. "I just want you both to be happy."

Ally's throat tightened. Happiness felt far too out of reach right now. She'd settle for getting out of the bed in the morning and putting one foot in front of the other – even if it meant leaning on crutches for a while.

She might not be happy but at least she had some strength. She knew her own worth. And it was more than being shouted at through a phone line by a man she'd allowed herself to be vulnerable to.

"Thank you," she whispered, leaning forward to give him another hug. He was warm and kind and for a moment she allowed him to chase all the other emotions out of her head.

There was plenty of time to think about them later.

———

"It was good to see you," Kirsten said, squeezing Nate tight. "Even if it was just a flying visit."

"We'll try to make it longer next time." An announcement came over the loud speakers that he couldn't quite hear, but it reminded him that they needed to join the long line through security. "And maybe we'll give you some more notice, too."

She smiled, the corners of her eyes crinkling up. "Hey, what are sisters for? If you ever need anything I'll be here. And of course for Riley, too."

"When did you grow up?" he asked her. "Weren't you fifteen the last time I saw you?"

Her grin widened. "I'm pretty sure in your imagination I'll always be fifteen. Just like Riley will. But you know what? I grew up and she will too." She raised her eyebrows. "And then who are you gonna swoop in and save?"

Strange how his thoughts turned to Ally. He deliberately steered them right back. "Myself?"

"It's been a long time coming." The grin was gone, replaced by a serious expression. "Eventually you'll have to actually figure out what you want, instead of building your life around us."

"That's exactly what I want." He released her and stepped back, taking another glance at the ever-growing security line. "You and Riley." He shrugged. "My family. That's all that matters."

"And how about this blonde woman?"

"Ally?" Saying her name made the shame wash over him again. He remembered the messages he'd sent that morning, and the fact there was no read receipt for any of them. And the calls he made that were diverted right to voicemail. "I think I've burned my bridges there."

Kirsten tipped her head to the side, scrutinizing him. "What do you mean?"

Nate glanced over at the news shop where Riley had run to buy some gum to take on the plane. Like him, his daughter was tired, and clearly edgy about going back to Angel Sands and facing the music. But she'd be okay. He'd make sure of it.

As for him, he had no idea.

"It doesn't matter." He didn't want to think about it. He'd gotten hardly any sleep last night after the way he'd spoken to her. Okay, so he'd been completely wrung out from Riley's disappearance, but that didn't give him any right to take it out on Ally. He sighed, hating himself more than ever. Another thing he'd messed up in his life.

"I got a pack of gum for you, too," Riley said, her breath heavy from running back from the news store. "In case you decide to drink coffee on the plane." She wrinkled her nose. "Is there anything worse than coffee breath?"

"Nope." Kirsten shook her head. "Come here, you." She reached for her niece, enveloping her in the biggest hug. Nate stood back and watched them, his chest feeling tighter than ever as Kirsten dipped her head to whisper something in Riley's ear.

"Okay," Riley said softly. "I will."

"You ready?" he asked his daughter.

"If I say no can we stay here forever?"

"Nope." He liked the way she said 'we' though. It made the band around his chest loosen a little.

Giving his sister a wave, Nate put his arms around his daughter, and the two of them walked over to join the back of the security line.

It was only a little over twenty-four hours since he'd flown out here, and yet Angel Sands – and Ally – felt like a lifetime ago. There was part of him – that childlike part he'd left behind so long ago – that was as afraid to return as Riley was. Afraid of how he'd feel when he saw Ally again. Afraid he'd make a fool out of himself in front of her.

But he'd left his childlike self behind so many years ago. He was a man now, not a scared little boy. And if Riley could go back and face the music then he could, too.

Even if the thought of it made him feel sick.

───────

Her apartment hadn't gotten any less lonely since she'd left it this morning. Maybe that's why Ally spent so long avoiding coming back. She'd whiled away half the day with Lorne, helping him out in the shop and talking to the customers. Later she'd joined Ember and Brooke in the diner – the three of them stuffing their faces with burgers and fries as her best friends did their best to cheer her up.

But none of that was enough to stave off the screaming silence of her home as soon as she'd returned to it. Glancing at her watch, she saw it was almost nine o'clock. Maybe she should call it a day and settle down to sleep.

Things would be better tomorrow. They couldn't get any worse, could they?

She was about to turn out the living room light and head for her bedroom when she heard the rap at her door. It had to be a neighbor – she hadn't buzzed anyone in. Taking a quick glance at herself in the mirror fixed on the entranceway wall she smoothed down her hair and grimaced at her wrinkled clothes. The jeans and t-shirt she was wearing had been freshly pressed that morning, but a day of working with Lorne and eating with the girls had taken its toll.

Sliding the chain into place – a woman living on her own could never be too careful – she peeped through the little round glass to see who was on the other side. She had to squeeze her other eye shut to focus, but when she did she almost jumped.

What was *he* doing here?

Her fingers shook as she unlatched the lock and slowly pulled at the handle. The man on the other side waited patiently, his eyes fixed on hers as she tugged the door ajar.

"Oh." She stared at him for a moment. The dark hair splashed with grey, the tired look on his crumpled face, and the brightness in his eyes that never failed to make her heart feel warm, even though the rest of her was wary. "I didn't know you were coming back."

"I got the first flight out after I got your message." Her dad shifted from one foot to the other. "You sounded upset."

She nodded and pulled the door open wider. He lifted his arms to hug her, but thought better of it, pulling them back to his sides. She wasn't sure if she was relieved or not. A bit of human contact would be good about now.

"Would you like a drink?" she asked him.

"Coffee would be good. It's been a long trip."

About eight hours or so, from what Ally knew. No wonder he looked exhausted.

She made them both a cup of coffee, adding a splash of cream the way her father always liked it and her dad carried them into the living room. When she was settled in the chair he handed her a mug then sat on the sofa opposite.

Her father closed his eyes as he swallowed a mouthful of coffee. "Damn that tastes good." He put his mug down and looked up at her. "How are you doing?"

The weight of his question laid heavily on her. He'd always been her person, the one she could confide in. He'd known from the start how badly her mom's death had affected her. He'd held her when she cried, cheered for her when she ran. He'd been her biggest fan and her strongest protector.

But not for the past few months.

"I'm not doing so good," she admitted.

He took a deep breath, his warm eyes still on hers. "I'm so sorry to hear that." He leaned forward to put his half-drunk mug on the table between them. "And I'm really sorry that I'm the one who caused it."

She opened her mouth to tell him he wasn't, but shut it. Because truthfully it was partly his fault. Not because he'd sold the café to Nate – although that was why the man had entered her life – but because he'd hurt her first, and that made her current pain even worse.

He slid his fingers together, wringing at them. "I've been a bad father. I know it." He looked up at her through his lashes. "Lorne knows it, too, and hasn't wasted any time telling me."

"That's the best thing about friends," Ally said, thinking of Brooke and Ember. "They always tell you the truth."

Her dad gave a little chuckle. "That's no word of a lie."

She sat up straighter. What was it she'd told herself that morning? She was strong in spite of her pain. Or maybe because of it – she'd been through worse and gotten through it. And she owed it to herself to tell the truth.

"You did hurt me," she told him. "Not because you went

away, but because every time I asked you for help you made things worse. Then you sold the place without even asking me how I felt. After all those years working there, keeping the café going. You made me feel like I was nothing to you."

He shook his head. "Baby, I'm sorry. So damn sorry. I hate that I hurt you. There's no excuse for my actions."

"So why did you do it?"

"Sell?" he asked. She nodded. "Because I had no choice. It was either that or the bank was going to foreclose."

Her breath caught in her throat. "I didn't know that. I knew things were bad, but..."

"I should have flown home to tell you face to face. Like I'm telling you now. But I was a damn coward, I never could stand to see you cry. Knowing I was the one causing it..." he trailed off, shaking his head. "It killed me."

"You could have come home then," she told him. "After the call."

"I wanted to, but I was still chicken shit." He had the good grace to look embarrassed. "I kept trying to call you but you never answered. Then when I talked to Lorne he told me to give you some time. I was ready to take the first plane home when I heard about your broken ankle, but Lorne said to stay where I was. That you were being taken care of."

Her thoughts immediately turned to Nate. To the way he'd helped her for those few weeks. To his warm skin and soft words.

The pain was visceral.

"When I heard your message this morning I could tell from the sound of your voice that something was wrong." He half-smiled. "It was time for me to stop being so damn weak and face what I'd done. And I know it may be too late. That you might not ever forgive me. But I'm asking you to anyway, because I love you, sweetheart."

The way he said it made her heart swell up. She'd never

seen her father so vulnerable before. It was as though they'd swapped roles and suddenly she was the strong one.

For some reason that felt good.

"I'm so sorry you got hurt," he told her, looking down at the cast on her leg. "And I'm even more sorry I wasn't here to help you." He pressed his lips together in sympathy. "You've had a hard few weeks."

For the first time Ally laughed. It wasn't loud, but it was something. "You could say that."

He shook his head. "I've failed you too many times. I keep letting you down and it kills me."

"When have you failed me?" she asked. "Before now I mean?"

"When your mom and I split up. I'll never forget your face when we told you." His voice wobbled. "You were so tiny and so sad, and it was all my fault."

"It wasn't your fault. I just didn't understand that yet."

"Then your mom died. You kept looking at me as though I could make everything better. And when I couldn't you used to get so upset. It killed me to see you that way. If I could have given you a better dad I would have."

"I didn't want a better dad," she said, her voice rough. "I never did. I only ever wanted you."

A tear rolled down his cheek. "You deserve so much better."

"I thought you didn't love me. That you didn't care what happened."

"I've always loved you. And I've always cared. But I worry about you, too. Remember when you got your place at college and then refused to go?"

She nodded. "I remember." How could she forget? They'd paid her first term's tuition, packed up his car. She'd even bought the bedding for her dorm room. And yet she'd found herself refusing to go, stomping back up to her room, not listening to him as he tried to reason with her through her closed door.

"I felt like such a failure then, too. And looking back it was all my fault you didn't go. I hadn't taught you how to be okay by yourself. Hadn't showed you how to work through things. I'd kept you close and thought I could protect you forever." He rubbed the palm of his hands over his face, wiping away his tear. "But I couldn't. Not that way."

"So you just cut me loose instead?"

"Not on purpose, but I guess that's what happened. And I don't blame you for hating me for it. But you'll never hate me as much as I hate myself, I can promise you that." His eyes softened. "I should have told you how damn proud I am of you. How amazed I am by your strength. Life keeps knocking you down and you keep climbing back up. I've never met anybody as strong as you are."

This time it was Ally's eyes that filled with tears. His words were like oil on the troubled water of her soul. She'd missed him so much, and she was angry at him. But more than anything she wanted to believe.

In him. In his words. And mostly in herself. She wanted to be the person he was describing.

"Can you forgive me?" he asked her.

"I think so," she told him, glancing down at the coffee she hadn't taken a sip of. "But it might take some time."

He swallowed. "There's something else I need to tell you."

"What?"

"I had another reason to sell the café. I had my annual health check a few months ago, and things aren't working as well as they once did." He shook his head. "Now don't you go worrying over this, but my heart isn't as good as it used to be. The doctor wants me to slow down. Getting away from all the stress seemed like the right thing to do." He pressed his lips together. "But now I see how selfish it was, too."

"What's wrong with your heart?" Ally asked, her mouth dry. She hadn't expected him to say that at all.

"Nothing to worry about. It's just slowed down a bit. Needs some medicine to keep it going the way it should. According to the doctor, I've got years left in me as long as I follow his advice. And I'm so sorry, honey, because I was scared to tell you about that, too. I didn't want to see your reaction, so I ran away."

Tears stung at her eyes. She took his hand in hers. When had it gotten so wrinkled? She'd spent her whole life idolizing this man, thinking he was invincible. It felt like a kick in the gut to know he wasn't.

"Okay," she said, nodding. "Okay. Do you need to relax now? You've had a long flight. You shouldn't have risked your health just to see me."

"As long as I keep taking the pills I'm going to be fine."

Thank God. He was her dad, warts and all. He'd been there for her after the divorce, and he'd held her tight when her mom had died. And when he had to choose between her – his unruly teenager daughter – and the woman he was dating. Well, it was Ally he chose to keep.

The way Nate had chosen Riley. And rightfully so.

Some cuts healed. Others became scars you wore with pride. But sometimes they festered. If he hadn't chosen her, then Ally's would have festered, too. Until they hurt every time she touched them.

She was a grown woman. Twenty-seven years old. Way past the age that she needed a constant parent. Her dad was fallible, but so was she. And he was right, they kept pulling themselves up anyway, and moved forward no matter how much it hurt.

"How long are you back for?" she asked him.

"For good. I'm not planning on travelling anymore."

Ally licked her dry lips. "Do you have somewhere to stay

tonight?" she asked him. He'd rented his house out when he'd left town.

"I'll check myself into a motel. I just wanted to check on you first."

She shook her head. "No need. You can stay here. That's if you're okay with sleeping on the couch."

"Are you sure?" His brows knitted together. "I don't want to cause you any trouble."

She stood, grabbing her crutches to steady herself. "Yeah, I'm sure. I'll grab you some linens and a towel. I bet you could use a shower right about now." She made her way to her bedroom, and began to pull some sheets and blankets out from her dresser, making a pile of them on her bed ready to take back out to him.

It had been a hell of a day. Two days, really. Was it really that short of a time since Riley found them laying out on the deck? She shook her head, trying not to dwell on what had happened.

She'd lost one man and gained another. And though her dad wasn't a replacement for Nate, she was glad he'd come home.

Because she didn't feel quite as alone anymore.

❧ 29 ❧

ossip moved faster than the speed of light in Angel Sands. It was no surprise to Ally when Ember called to tell her Nate was back. Or at least that's what Frank Megassey had told Deenie Russell, who'd told her son Lucas, who'd passed the message on to his fiancée in case she needed to warn her best friend.

Having social media was pointless around here. By the time you opened your phone up to look all the news was old.

"Has he not called you to tell you he's home?" Ember asked, her voice full of concern.

"I don't know," Ally admitted. "I haven't checked my voicemail."

It was over, she knew that much. It was time to take control of her life again, because it was the only way to get through the pain. Maybe she was finally growing up.

"You look pretty," her dad said as she walked out into her living room. He was piling up the sheets and pillows she'd loaned him, putting them on the arm of the sofa. "Going somewhere?"

"Only if you can give me a ride." She passed her car key to

him. Might as well put him to work. She didn't want to get herself all messed up before she made it to the boardwalk this time.

"Your wish is my command."

She was still getting used to having him around. After their heart to heart yesterday, the awkwardness between them had almost disappeared.

"Where are we going?" he asked after he'd helped her into the car. Her small Fiat was so much more difficult to get into than Nate's Lexus. One more reason to look forward to getting this damn cast off.

"To the coffee shop. I just need to drop this off." She held up a white envelope with Nate's name scrawled across it. "After that I want to catch up with everybody. Being unable to drive I feel like I've been gone for an eternity."

The beach was packed by the time they made it to the parking lot. Her dad had to drive around twice before he found a space, managing to squeeze her car in between a beaten up truck and a sports utility vehicle.

Once out of the car, he looked up at the café and blinked, as though some sand had blown into his eyes.

"It looks different," he said.

"Yeah."

He took a deep breath in, holding it for a moment before blowing it all out again. "But good. It looks good."

Ally followed his stare to the freshly painted façade, and the blue and white sign that proclaimed it was a Déjà Brew outlet. It did look good – inviting and professional and everything the Beach Café hadn't been. It was busier than they'd been in years. The line for coffee was spilled out onto the boardwalk, and from the look of it there wasn't a spare seat in the house. If anybody had any doubts if a chain could work in a place like Angel Sands, their answer was right here.

A strange feeling of pride washed over her. Because some of that success was down to her.

"How long until you go back to work there?" her dad asked, as they walked across the parking lot.

Ally bit her lip. "I'm not."

"What?"

The note she'd written out earlier was clutched tightly in her hand. She rubbed her thumb over the thick paper. "I'm not going back. It's time I took a new direction. I've been working there for years after all."

Yeah, her heart hurt a bit at the thought. But there was no way she could work there after everything that had happened.

She'd been afraid for too long. Of leaving the café, of leaving town, of losing the things she loved the most. But she'd lost so many things already and here she was still standing. It was time to let go of the past and start facing the future.

Whatever it might be.

"Are you coming in?" she asked her dad as they reached the end of the line.

"No, not now." He shook his head. "I'm not sure I'm ready."

She understood him completely. The café had been part of his life for much longer than it had been for hers. It must have been hard for him seeing the results of the sale he'd made. Of knowing that this little piece of earth and sand now belonged to somebody else.

"I'm gonna go and say hi to Lorne," he said. "Come find me when you're done."

Her dad made his way down the boardwalk, his gait slow as he took everything in. Then he turned and weaved in between the surfboards that led to Lorne's shop, giving her a wave when he realized she was still looking at him.

When he was gone, she turned back to the line. "I'm not buying anything," she told the girl nearest the door. "I just need to talk to someone. Can you let me past?"

"Sure." The girl stood back and held the door open, letting Ally make her way through on her crutches.

She wasn't sure he was going to be here. He might still be at home with Riley. But when she looked at the counter she could see him behind it, helping the baristas as they struggled to keep up with the long line of customers. He was at the espresso machine, filling two glass cups with dark liquid, his eyes narrowing as he took in the layers to make sure the coffees were good.

"Two lattes for Marc," he called out when he'd made them, passing the paper cups to the tall man waiting at the end of the counter. "What's next?" he asked Brad who was at the second register.

"A cappuccino and a iced tea for Sarah," Brad called back.

Ally shifted on her crutches, trying to get the guts to say what she needed to.

Maybe she'd give herself another minute as she watched him work.

But then he went to grab another glass cup from the stack on the machine, and his eyes lifted and looked around the room. Within a moment they'd locked in on Ally, and she felt her whole body heat up.

His hand was still hovering in front of the cups. Ally swallowed and attempted a smile. "Hi."

Nate blinked. "Hi. Are you okay?" He licked his lips. "I tried to call you... a few times. I sent some messages, too."

"I'm fine." Her voice was as strong as she could make it. "I can see you're busy but I just wanted to talk to you for a moment." She looked around at all the people crowding into the room. "This won't take long."

Nate glanced at the rest of the baristas, but none of them

were paying any attention. They were way too busy for that. "Yeah, we can talk." There was a warmth to his voice that made her heart skip.

"Is it ready yet?" a woman asked from the end of the counter. "I ordered a latte and an iced tea."

Sarah, Ally guessed.

"It'll be with you in a moment." Then he looked at Ally. "Don't go anywhere, I just need to make these drinks."

"I can wait."

It was a couple of minutes before he lifted the countertop and came out to see her. He looked as awkward as she felt. Ally took a deep breath, feeling the air expand her lungs, and tried to straighten her spine. She needed to get through this. She'd been through worse, after all.

"I need to give you this," she said, holding out the white envelope.

Nate's brows pulled together as he looked at it. "What is it?" he asked.

She took a deep breath. "It's my letter of resignation."

"*What*?"

A torrent of emotion washed over her. Exultation at finally taking control, sadness that this was how things ended up. But more than anything she felt strong and brave – and that thought bolstered her when she needed it the most.

She had to push the envelope toward him again before he got the message and took it from her. Still frowning, he slid his thumb beneath the seal and tore it open, pulling out the letter and skimming her words.

"You're serious?" he asked her.

She nodded.

"But what about us?" As soon as he said it his face dropped, as though he was remembering their last conversation. "Ally, we need to talk."

"No." She had to stay strong, she knew that much. She

couldn't let him talk about them or anything else. It would hurt too much. "I just need you to accept my resignation and them I'm going."

"What are you going to do for money?" he asked, shock still moulding his expression. "Have you got another job? You can't leave just because of what happened. You're a part of this place."

"That's my business."

He looked taken aback at the shortness of her words.

"I'm sorry," she said, hating every second of this. "I'm going to be working with Lorne for a while. He's getting old and needs a break. And while I'm working there I'll think about what I want to do next. I might see if they're recruiting at the new resort. I heard they were working on getting it back up and running."

"You could do that while you're working here."

She shook her head. "I really couldn't." Her voice was soft. "I hope I haven't left you too high and dry. I'd work my notice but I know you wouldn't have me with this thing." She glanced down at her cast.

"So that's it? We're done?"

Was he talking about her job or about them? She wasn't sure. But either way the answer was the same. "Yeah, I think we are."

Nate said nothing. His jaw so tightly clenched she could see the joint flexing in and out.

"Nate, the steamer's blocked," Brad called from behind the counter. "Can you take a look at it?"

"I'll be there in a minute."

"You should go," Ally said. "Before you upset the customers." She shifted her weight again, leaning back on her crutches. "I'll see you around."

"Ally, wait..."

"Nate, we're out of skim milk."

His eyes darted from Ally to the counter and back again. "I'll call you later. To talk about this some more…"

She shook her head. "I'd prefer it if you didn't." There were only so many times she could put herself through this pain. She needed it to end. "Goodbye, Nate."

Those words could have meant anything. A cheerful taking of leave. An easy way to close a conversation. But as they formed on her tongue and her lips before they made their way into the universe she realized that they were so much more. The end of something that had meant so much to her and losing it was supremely painful. She'd take a dozen broken ankles over this.

Without waiting to hear his response, she moved her crutches forward and walked toward the exit, making up in speed what she lacked in grace. And somehow she managed to stop the tears from forming until she made it outside into the warm summer air, lifting her hand up to wipe them impatiently away.

She'd done what she came here to do, no more and no less. So why was it that her heart was hurting more than ever?

Lorne looked up from the counter as soon as Nate stepped inside the store. He kept his watery eyes on him as Nate passed the racks of surf clothes and sandals, then wound his way through the aisles stacked with sunscreen and board wax. By the time he reached the counter Lorne had closed whatever magazine he was reading and had his hands clasped together, curving his mouth into a half smile.

"I was wondering when you'd be in," he told the younger man.

It was just before six that evening, the first chance Nate

had to leave the shop. Business had been steady all day –
something he'd usually be happy about.

But not today.

"I hear you've been poaching my staff," Nate said. There
was no malice in his voice. How could there be? This was
Lorne. He'd never shown Nate anything but kindness.

"Just one of 'em."

"The best one."

Lorne grinned, revealing a row of perfectly white teeth.
Nate found himself wondering if they were real. "I only take
on the best," he told Nate. "And anyway, I didn't poach her.
She came to me."

The door opened again, and Nate heard footsteps behind
him. Lorne lifted his hand in a greeting to whoever it was.
Nate turned to see a guy looking at a pair of flowered shorts,
lifting them up to his waist to see if they were a good fit.

"Why'd you take her on?" Nate asked him. "I thought you
were fully staffed."

"Because she's good at what she does. Plus she needed a
job." Lorne shrugged. "Friends help friends."

"She has a job. Well she had one." Nate shook his head.
"And maybe I need her there, too."

"Not what I heard." Lorne shrugged. "The way it was told
to me you didn't want her at all."

Nate dropped his face into his hands and leaned his
elbows on the counter. "I messed up," he admitted. "I said
some things I shouldn't have, and now I've no idea what to do
to make it right." He glanced up at the older man. "What
should I do?"

Lorne shrugged. "Don't ask me, ask him."

"Who?" Nate looked up, his brows pulled down in confusion. Then he saw the man who'd been looking at the rack of
shorts. He had to be in his early fifties, though it was hard to

tell. His hair was dark with a smattering of grey running through it, his skin smooth and tanned.

"Grant Sutton," the man said, holding his hand out. "I believe you know my daughter."

Nate immediately grabbed his hand and shook it. "Nate Crawford. I didn't realize you were back."

Lorne gave a huff.

"Why would you know? It was a snap decision."

Because it's something Ally would have told him only a few days before. Nate pulled his hand back from Grant's and he remembered all the things Ally had said about her father. Part of him wanted to berate the man, tell him how much he'd hurt her.

But then Nate had done exactly the same thing.

"I'm going to start pulling in the racks," Lorne said, grabbing his magazine and rolling it into a tube. "Can I trust you two not to resort to violence?"

Grant laughed. "You're as subtle as a ten ton truck, old man."

"Less of the old talk, thank you." He ambled out of the shop, pulling the door closed behind him, leaving the two of them standing next to each other at the counter.

Grant inclined his head at the two upholstered chairs in the shoe section of the shop. "You wanna sit down for a minute?" Grant asked. "I need to take the weight off these bones."

"Sure." Intrigued, Nate followed him over, settling down into the overstuffed armchair. Grant crossed one leg over the other, keeping his eye on Nate.

"I like what you've done with the café," Grant said to him. "Is business going well?"

"It's good." Nate looked at the man in front of him. From Ally's description of him he'd expected him to be old and haggard – worn down by the years of keeping the café open and dealing with a teenage daughter. Instead, he looked relaxed and sun-kissed.

"Does Ally know you're here?" Nate asked. He hadn't been able to keep the words from spilling out, no matter how hard he'd tried.

"Of course. I've been staying with her."

It hurt more than Nate had expected to not know what was happening in Ally's life. He wanted to ask so many more questions – how was she really doing? Was she going to be okay? Did she miss him as much as he missed her? He sat back in his chair, tapping his fingers on the edge of his seat. "It's nice that you've reconnected."

"I hear you have a daughter, too," Grant said.

"That's right. Her name's Riley."

The older man's expression softened. "It's tough bringing up a teenager on your own. Especially when you've got a business to run. I remember those days very well."

"It is tough," Nate agreed, "but it's what I signed up for when I became a father. And she has it a lot worse than me. Riley's the one who lost a mother."

Grant slowly nodded. "Yeah," he said, his voice gentle. "You spend all your time being mom and dad to them, and very little on anything else. I remember how draining it is. How are you holding up?"

Nate's spine stiffened at his unexpected question. "I'm fine. Just doing what I need to do."

"You shouldn't neglect yourself though."

"I'm not. And I'm sorry if it sounds insensitive, but the last thing I need is any advice from a guy who ran away and left his daughter to fend for herself. Did you know how hard things have been for Ally since you went away? How hard she tried to keep this place afloat." Nate shook his head. "It's nice to meet you, Mr. Sutton, but I have a lot to do." He stood up. "Have a nice day."

Grant didn't look surprised at Nate's outburst. "I deserved that. But it doesn't mean I'm not speaking the truth." He gave him a half smile. "I never wanted to hurt Ally. And I've made a lot of mistakes. Maybe you could learn a thing or two from them." He cleared his throat, covering his mouth with his palm. "I hear you and she had something going on."

Nate was still hovering by the chair. "Did Ally tell you that?"

"She didn't need to."

"Then there's really nothing to talk about." Nate went to walk away again, but his fingers were curled around the back of his chair and for some reason it was impossible to release them. As if his body wanted to stay right where it was.

"Did you know that when Ally's mom died I was dating a woman called Marnie?" Grant continued, ignoring Nate's gritted replies. "She used to work in Frank Megassey's store. That's how we met. She was a few years younger than me."

"Fifteen, or so I hear."

Grant laughed. "For a man who's not interested you seem to know an awful lot about me."

Nate shrugged but said nothing.

"Marnie wasn't interested in having kids. She didn't like to put roots down for long enough to have them. She'd been in Angel Sands for three years and as far as she was concerned, that was long enough. Just before my ex-wife died she was trying to persuade me to leave town and join her on a trip to Australia."

"But you didn't."

"No. Circumstances took over. And being a good father was more important than being a good boyfriend right then."

Nate said nothing.

"I know you probably think I'm a terrible father. But I didn't want to be. I was determined to take care of Ally and make sure she was okay." Grant nodded his head at the chair.

"Can you sit back down? Looking up at you is making my neck ache."

Grudgingly, Nate took his seat.

"I expect Ally told you that Marnie and I broke up soon after Ally came to live with us."

"She did."

"And did she tell you I never dated again?"

Nate blinked. "Never?" His voice was full of shock. "You didn't have another relationship?"

"No."

"I didn't know that. Why not?"

Grant gave him a half-smile. "Because of Ally. She and Marnie had clashed like crazy. It had made things so much worse for her. Her grades dipped at school, and then she dropped out of the athletics squad." He cleared his throat. "Did she tell you she used to run for state? There was talk of her going to the Olympics one day."

"I heard."

"Her dropping out was all my fault. If I'd been there for her more, spent less time with Marnie or at the café, then maybe she would have coped a little better. After I split with Marnie I didn't want to introduce anybody to Ally. Didn't want to upset her any more than she already was. So it became just the two of us, the two musketeers." He rubbed his chin with his thumb. "We were so close that people used to remark on it all the time. What a lovely family we were, what a great dad I was." Grant winced. "But I wasn't a good father at all."

"I'm not exactly running for father of the year myself."

"Do you know the biggest mistake I made?" Grant asked, leaning forward on the chair.

"What?" At some point in the last few minutes Nate had gone from wanting to walk away to needing to hear more.

"I forgot that part of my role as a father was to prepare

my daughter for the real world. To let her make mistakes. To let her face her fears. To let her feel sadness and learn how to deal with it. I thought I wanted to protect her, but really I wanted to protect myself from seeing her in pain or crying or anything else that every teenager has to go through whether or not they've lost a parent." He let out a sigh. "I made it so she didn't think she could live without me. She wouldn't even leave town to go to college, did you know that? She got a scholarship and everything, but on the day I was supposed to drive her up there, she started unpacking all her bags. And that was my fault. All mine. I let her down.

"I let myself down, too," Grant told him. "Because I neglected myself. Didn't think about my own needs. And eventually I became a prisoner of my own choices."

"That's why you left?" Nate asked, a frown pulling at the skin between his brows.

"Call it a late mid life crisis. Or call it being a bad father." Grant shrugged. "Or maybe even being a good father. It got to the point where the café was no good for me. I was desperate to sell it but Ally refused to let it go."

"So, you let *her* go." Nate swallowed, but the bad taste remained in his mouth.

"I did it all wrong. I should have talked to her more. Explained how I was feeling. But I had this stupid idea that she was my daughter and didn't need to know any of that. I didn't want her to think I wasn't strong. But then I did the weakest thing I could ever do and I ran away."

Nate looked at him. "You hurt her."

Grant nodded. "I know I did. And I'll regret that forever. But one good thing has come out of this. Ally's learned to see her own strength. She's realized she doesn't need me to get through life and that she can stand on her own two feet. She's the strongest woman I know and I'm damn proud of her for that."

"You should be proud." Nate's throat tightened at the thought of her. At the memory of how she'd felt when he kissed her. How they'd laughed together as they played that damn Echoes of War – and he'd been killed every time. Thinking about her made his chest hurt.

She might have been strong, but he felt anything but.

Grant shifted in his chair. "I'm not going to tell you how to raise your child. Nor am I going to tell you how you should be treating mine. But man to man I'm going to give you one piece of advice that I wish somebody had given me."

Nate raised an eyebrow. "Okay." He was too curious not to hear more.

"Don't assume anything. Not about what's best for your daughter. Talk to her and listen to what she has to say." He rolled his shoulders. "Good luck with the café. My happiest memories are here. I hope yours will be, too." He held his hand out, and Nate stood to take it. And once they'd shaken hands, he watched the older man walk out of the door, turning left and meandering along the boardwalk.

In spite of himself he liked Ally's dad. His honesty had touched Nate in a way he hadn't expected. And the questions that had been swirling around his head were joined by newer, deeper ones.

Would he and Riley be as happy here as Grant and Ally once had been? Right now Nate had no idea.

❧ 30 ❧

"Dad?" Riley's voice echoed through the hallway. Nate was sitting at his desk, staring at the spreadsheet that had been on his screen for the past half hour. He couldn't focus on the numbers. They seemed to be dancing on the screen, little inky blurs that made no sense at all.

"There you are." Riley was breathless. "I thought you were working in the coffee shop today."

Nate turned his head to look at her. "I had some work to do here." Urgent work, too. He needed to sign off on the proposals for the Coastal Café chain. The bank had agreed to extend a line of credit to make it happen, and his investors were on board, too. Five locations along the Californian coast had been earmarked for purchase. All it needed was for him to give the go-ahead.

"How was school?" he asked her.

"It was okay."

"And detention?"

She shrugged. "I got my homework done so that's good." She'd been in afternoon detentions since the day her principal had allowed her to go back to school, and she hadn't complained about them at all. If anything her relief at not being removed from another school had made her throw herself into it with enthusiasm. "I also volunteered to help out at the elementary school once a week." She held out a piece of paper. "But I need your permission."

"You volunteered to do something?" His eyes widened. "And with little kids?"

"I figure I have a year to make my college applications look good. Volunteering always pleases the recruiters, or so my teachers tell me."

Yeah, well it pleased him, too. A lot more than he'd ever tell his daughter.

"What are you doing?" she asked, walking over to where Nate was sitting. She leaned against the front of his desk and squinted her eyes as she stared at the screen. "Oh, numbers," she said, wrinkling her nose. "I thought it would be something exciting."

"It's the business plan for the new venture." Nate leaned to turn off his laptop, the screen flickering before it turned black. "But yeah, the numbers on their own aren't that exciting." He twisted in his chair until he was facing her. "What do you want to do for dinner?" he asked. "I have some steaks in the refrigerator."

Riley shifted from her left foot onto her right. "Um, I was going to ask you if I could go out tonight." She swallowed hard. "Laura asked me over for dinner."

"I thought you and Laura fell out."

"We did. But she apologized and I accepted." Riley shrugged. "And she and Leo broke up so I figured she's okay now."

"I don't know..." He leaned back on the chair, considering her request. It had been a few days since they'd come back from Boston, and she'd complied with every punishment she'd been given. He hadn't heard a word of complaint from her since they'd stepped back on Californian soil. And yet he had an urge to keep her with him. Not to punish, but to protect. Even if Laura and Leo weren't an item anymore, there would be somebody who would hurt her again, leaving him to pick up the pieces.

"Laura's mom said you can call her if you'd like. She even said you could come and eat there, too." Riley's eyes were wide. "But you won't, will you? Because that would be super embarrassing."

"No, I won't," he bit down a smile at her tone.

Riley's eyes lit up. "Does that mean I can go?"

"Yeah, you can go. But only for dinner. I want you home by nine."

"Sure." She nodded quickly.

"And you need to be in bed by ten."

"Of course."

He racked his brain to think of another condition but came up empty. She was complying with everything he'd asked. And more, if you counted her volunteering. "Okay, I guess it's steak for one here," he said.

"You could invite somebody over to eat the other one," Riley said, the smallest of smiles pulling up the corner of her lips. "Like Ally, for example."

"I'm pretty sure she'd say no. But thanks for the suggestion."

The smile slipped off Riley's face. "I miss her," she said quietly. "It's quiet around here without her."

Yeah, well he missed Ally, too. More than he'd ever tell his daughter. How many times had he lifted his phone to call her, or stood beside his car and thought about driving to her house and begging her to take him back?

But all he could remember were the words she'd said when she'd given him her resignation letter. That she didn't want him to contact her.

It was killing him to abide by her wishes.

"Are you sure you'll be okay on your own?" Riley asked him, still hovering by the desk. "I can stay and eat steak with you if you'd like?"

Her words made him think of Ally's father and the conversation they had. Of how he'd described the way he'd held Ally back. Nate didn't want to make the same mistake. "Of course I'll be okay," he said, forcing a smile on his face. "Now get out of here. I've got work to do."

She nodded and went to walk away, but then turned on her foot and walked back toward him. Before he had a chance to ask her what she was doing, she threw her arms around him and hugged him tight. "I love you, Dad," she whispered.

"I love you too, sweetheart." His throat tightened as she walked out of the office, her footsteps echoing in the hallway. Another half hour and he'd be on his own again. And that was okay.

Wasn't it?

Ally glanced around the restaurant until she could see Ember, Brooke, and Lucas already sitting at a large table. Ember's mom was there, too, along with Deenie Russell. Next to her was her husband, Wallace, and a few people that Ember worked with at school. Squaring her shoulders, Ally walked over with her crutches, painting a smile on her face as they all stood to greet her.

"Happy birthday," she said to Ember, holding a pink and silver gift bag out to her.

"It's so good to see you." Ember hugged her tightly. "Thank you for the gift, you sweet thing."

The next few minutes were taken up with hellos. When she'd greeted everybody, and exchanged pleasantries with

Ember's mom and Lucas' folks, Ally slid into a chair between her two best friends.

"How are you doing?" Brooke asked, her voice low. There was enough chatter at the table for nobody to pay attention to them. "How are things going with your dad?"

"Okay. He's moving back into his house tomorrow. I'm not sure whether I'm looking forward to it or not." The truth was she'd gotten used to having him around again.

"You could have asked him to come tonight. He would have been welcome," Ember added.

"It's fine. He dropped me off here and headed out to meet Lorne. The two of them are going to play pool."

"Are you enjoying working at Lorne's?" Brooke asked her. Ally had the feeling her friends were both skating around what they really wanted to ask, but it was all good with her.

"It's okay," she told them. "Different. Slower paced. Plus Lorne keeps everything in such a mess. If I try to tidy up after him he complains he can't find anything. I don't think it's a long term option for me."

"Did you put your resume in at the Silver Sands Resort?" Brooke asked, giving her a sympathetic smile.

"I loaded it up on the website yesterday, but I don't think they'll be recruiting for a while. They've barely started renovating the place."

"Bulldozering it you mean?" Brooke said, wrinkling her nose. "Every time I drive past it's like a sandstorm. I keep thinking of all the birds and animals that have made it their home. I hope they're watching out for them."

Ember and Ally exchanged an amused look. Brooke had always loved animals, ever since they were all in Kindergarten. It was typical of her to worry about them.

"So you're in limbo?"

Ally pointed at her cast. "I don't think I'm going to be doing the limbo any time soon."

The waiter came to take their orders. Their conversation was silenced as he went from one person to the next, writing down their starters and entrees. Lucas ordered some champagne and the next few minutes were taken up with toasts to Ember. She blushed as Lucas kissed her, hugging her close as he wished her a happy birthday.

"They're so damn cute, aren't they?" Brooke whispered, following Ally's gaze. "I keep wishing he had a brother or something. He's such a good guy."

Ally's heart contracted. She missed being held the way Lucas was holding Ember. Missed being kissed, too. But more than anything she missed *him*.

She shook her head. Tonight was supposed to be happy. Not spent moping over lost loves.

Lucas turned to smile at Ally. "How's the leg doing?" he asked.

"It's okay. I'm due to go back to the orthopedist next week for another x-ray. I'm hoping for good news."

"I bet you can't wait to get back in your running shoes," Ember said, sitting down with her two friends.

Couldn't wait was an understatement. The events of the past few weeks had put her whole body on edge. Every time she thought about Nate all she wanted to do was fling herself at the sand and run until it stopped hurting. But instead she was trapped with her thoughts. And no matter how hard she tried, they wouldn't be ignored.

"Yeah, but it may be a while before that happens."

"More champagne?" Lucas asked, pouring the sparkling liquid into Ally's glass when she nodded at him. He wandered around the table, filling glasses. His mom said something to him and he laughed, leaning down to join his parents' conversation. To her right, Ember was talking to her principal from school, her face animated as she described what had happened at recess that morning. And Brooke was talking to

Ember's mom, the two of them laughing at something Ember had said.

She realized she was the only one that wasn't speaking with somebody. Even worse, she didn't want to talk, because the one guy she wanted to talk with wasn't here.

Remembering she'd lost him made her hurt all over again.

Taking a sip of her champagne, she closed her eyes for a moment, trying to center herself. She was strong. She'd be okay. She really would. One day she'd even be happy.

But right now that day seemed very far away.

Nate checked his watch. How could it only be seven-thirty? He'd cooked himself a dinner that he'd hardly been able to eat, and stared at that spreadsheet again until the numbers started to swim in front of his eyes. That's when he found himself wandering around the house, looking for something to do other than think.

But everywhere he looked reminded him of *her*.

The dent in the sofa where she'd sat and played video games. The side of his bed where she'd curled up and held him tightly. The guest room that still smelled of her flowery scent, and the bed he still hadn't let the maid strip and remake.

Even when he closed his eyes he could see her. That long, blonde hair and those deep eyes that seemed to see right through him. What would he give to touch her one last time?

By a quarter to eight he was practically bouncing off the walls. He thought about calling Kirsten just to shoot the breeze, but then remembered she was three hours ahead and was probably heading for bed. He switched the TV on to see if there was something worth watching, then flicked it off almost as soon as the screen flickered to life.

Pulling his phone out of his pocket, he found himself pressing the number of the last person he should be calling in that moment.

Riley answered as soon as the call connected. "Dad? Is everything okay? I'm not late, am I?"

"No," Nate replied, shaking his head even though she couldn't see him. "I just wanted to ask you a question."

"Okay..." She sounded suspicious. "Shoot."

"Do you like Ally?"

There was silence, followed by laughter. "Oh, Dad, of course I do. I love Ally. That's why I think it's crazy that you won't talk to her. But it's your life."

His heart began to pound against his chest. "I think... I mean I thought..." Oh God, this was harder than he thought. What was it that Grant Sutton had said about connecting with his daughter? It was all about communication. Okay, then. He took a deep breath. "I thought you might resent her. That she was taking my attention away from you. And maybe that's why you left for Boston."

"Dad, hold up a minute. I'm going outside." He waited until she spoke again, her voice less muted now. "Okay, listen to me. I went to Boston because I'm stupid. I'm a teenager and I make mistakes. And yeah, I was pretty grossed out when I saw you and Ally, but what kid wouldn't be? I'd have been like that if I'd seen Mom with somebody, too. But none of this is Ally's fault. In fact, me feeling better is thanks to her and you. You guys made me feel like I was part of something again. Like a kind of family or something." She cleared her throat. "So, no, I didn't leave for Boston because of you and Ally. I left because I was stupid and sometimes I make the worst decisions."

Yeah, well that made two of them.

"I think that's the most you've said to me in a while,"

Nate said. His eyes were stinging and he blinked to try and soothe them.

"Yeah, well don't get used to it. I'm a teenager, remember?"

"How could I forget?"

"Was that all you wanted to ask me?"

"Ah, no. There's one more thing," Nate told her.

"What?"

"Have you got your keys? Because I might not be here when you get home."

❧ 31 ❧

Nate pulled his car into a gap between an old truck and a fancy black sedan and shifted it into park. The sun had almost slipped beneath the horizon, leaving only a ghost of orange blazing and dancing on the ocean waves, a contrast to the indigo expanse of sky above.

With the ignition off he could hear music coming up from the beach. Something with a heavy beat. Beneath it was a low level of chatter interspersed by the occasional tinkle of laughter that cut through the air.

She was here. Knowing she was so close made him feel relieved and anxious at the same time. But more than anything it made him determined – the same kind of determination that had made him search for her in the first place. He'd spent half the evening driving around town until he bumped into Lorne and Ally's dad at the bar, and discovered Ally was at Delmonico's on Paxton's pier, celebrating Ember's birthday.

He climbed out of his car, pressing the key to lock it, then walked over to the wooden pier that jutted into the ocean.

Delmonico's was full, diners spilling out onto the veranda

that circled the building. Nate glanced at them, but he couldn't see her anywhere – she must be inside. He pushed at the glass door, stepping inside, and looked around the tables.

He spotted her almost immediately, sitting between her two closest friends. There had to be at least twenty people at the table, drinking champagne and laughing together.

Ally was sitting in a dining chair, her leg stretched out in front of her, the cast resting on the wooden floor. In the gloom of the interior she seemed to shine like a star. Her blonde hair glistening, her skin glowing. His breath caught in his throat as he stared at her.

She was so beautiful.

She blinked as though somebody had called her name, even though everybody was busy chatting. Slowly she turned her head, the smallest of frowns pulling at her brow. Her lips opened as she looked over at him.

He could hear his pulse as it rushed through his ears. Ally's bottom lip opened a little more, the lines between her eyes deepened. But her eyes – those beautiful, expressive eyes – didn't move from his face.

Nate walked forward, moistening his lip with his tongue, his eyes never leaving Ally's face. "Hi," he said when he reached her.

"Hi." She blinked, her eyes full of questions.

"I was wondering if we could talk."

She glanced around the table, her eyes guarded. "I think our food will be out soon."

Ember reached out and curled her hands around Ally's wrist. "It's fine. I'll tell them to keep it warm."

Ally turned back to Nate, her face still impassive. "Okay," she said, grabbing her crutches and pulling herself up to standing. "You want to speak outside?"

"That would be good."

He had to clench his hands not to reach out and help her.

He knew how soft and warm her skin would be. How good she'd smell as he gathered her in his arms. How amazing her lips felt when they pressed against his.

The temperature was cooler outside, enough for Ally to shiver as the two of them walked over to the far end of the pier.

Nate shrugged his jacket off and tried to put it on her shoulders.

She shook her head. "I'm okay."

Folding the jacket in his hands, he took a deep breath and let it out. "Thank you for agreeing to talk," he said.

She shifted, waiting for him to say more.

"I, ah, I wanted to say I'm sorry for the way I treated you the day Riley left. The way I spoke to you on the phone was wrong. I should never have done that."

Those big blue eyes that seemed to haunt his dreams were full of pain. "You hurt me," she told him. "When I was trying to show you some support."

"I know. I'm an asshole."

A shot of laughter came from the beach, followed by a splash. Teenagers no doubt. But hopefully not his this time.

"You *were* an asshole. Not always, but that day you were."

"Do you think you can forgive me?" He knew it was too much to ask, yet here he was saying it anyway. "I hate that you hate me."

"I don't hate you. I'm mad at you." Little tendrils of hair were dancing around her face, lifted by the sea breeze. "And I'll probably get a little less mad every day. So yes, I'll forgive you. Eventually." She bit at her bottom lip. "It's getting cold out here. I should go back in. It's Ember's birthday."

Nate nodded. Somehow her eventual forgiveness wasn't enough to make him feel better. He wanted more, so much more. But right now wasn't the time. "Of course you should go." Even if he didn't want her to. Even if he'd be happy doing nothing more than talking with her tonight.

"Okay then." She gave him the smallest of smiles. "Have a good evening."

"You too. And wish Ember a happy birthday for me."

"I will."

He watched as she made her way back into the restaurant, staying in the same spot where they'd talked as he looked through the window to make sure she'd made it safely back to the table. As if she could sense his stare, she turned and looked over her shoulder, a frown pulling at her face.

First contact had been made. Now it was time to think about the second.

Ally was bleary eyed when she walked into Lorne's shop the next morning, thanks to the combination of too much champagne, and staying awake all night to try and work out what Nate was trying to say. Was he just feeling bad for being an ass or was he trying to reconnect with her? She wasn't completely sure.

"Morning." Lorne was in the stock cupboard, pulling bottles of sunscreen down from the shelves. "There's coffee on the counter for you."

She picked it up and took a big mouthful. "Thanks," she told him as she swallowed it down.

"I didn't make it."

She put the mug down on the counter. "Who did?"

"I think you can guess." He winked at her.

She smiled a little smile to herself, looking to her left as if she could see through the wall to the coffee shop beyond. There was only one person she knew who'd think to bring her coffee, and he happened to be the guy who ran the place.

"That was nice of him," she murmured.

"That's what I said. He left an envelope for you, too." He nodded at a brown letter sized envelope propped up next to the register. Ally took it, feeling the thickness. Intrigued, she opened the flap and pulled the pack of stapled paper out, biting her lip as she read the small black print.

"It's a contract," she said, frowning. Surely he wasn't trying to recruit her again? But as she skimmed the wording Ally realized it wasn't an employment contract at all. It was asking her to sell her intellectual property. Nate wanted to buy her idea for Coastal Coffee by Déjà Brew, and he was offering $10,000 plus a percentage of revenue.

"This isn't right."

"What isn't?" Lorne asked her.

She shook her head. "Nothing." Sliding the contract back into the envelope she took another mouthful of coffee. Right then she needed all the caffeine she could get. "Is it okay if I go next door for a minute?" she asked him. "I won't be long."

"Be as long as you like. We're not exactly swamped with customers."

It wasn't that busy in the coffee shop either. Brad was wiping the counter down with a cloth, and she could hear Jeff singing to himself in the kitchen. Then she turned her head and saw Nate sitting at one of the tables, his laptop open as he hunched over it.

"Hi," she said, walking over to him.

He looked up, his eyes widening at the sight of her. "Hey."

"Thank you for the coffee."

"You're welcome. You can expect one every day."

She bit her lip, not wanting to show how much she liked the sound of that. "I read this, too," she said, holding out the contract. "I want to talk to you about it."

"Take a seat." He nodded at the chair opposite him. Ally lowered herself into it. "Is there a problem with the contract?" he asked her when she was comfortable. "You can take it to a lawyer to make sure you're happy with it."

"You're paying me ten thousand dollars for an idea I came up with in a moment."

"Yes." His face was serious. "Is it not enough? Do you think I should pay more?"

She shook her head. "No. I don't want your money. It was just me thinking out loud."

"My lawyer insists I buy the idea off you." Nate shrugged. "He's worried that you'll sue me if I don't. Think of it as me mitigating my risk. That's all. This way everybody's happy."

"But it's not worth what you're trying to pay me."

"I disagree. And so does my lawyer."

Ally sighed. "I can't take this from you," she told him. "I just can't."

His expression was wary. "Can I ask you why not?"

"Because it feels wrong. Like I'm taking money I haven't earned." She breathed in a mouthful of air. "And to be honest, it makes me feel cheap."

"There's nothing cheap about you. Nothing," he said, firmly. "You have more class than anybody I know. This," he said, tapping the envelope, "is just business. Nothing more."

"I just can't. I'm sorry." She hated the way he was looking at her.

He blew out a mouthful of air. "Let's have dinner so we can talk about this."

"You want to take me out?"

"Yeah."

"But I ate out last night."

He shrugged. "Push the boat out, be a devil."

She tipped her head to the side. "Is it a business dinner or a date?" she asked him. The way he was looking at her took her breath away.

"Does it matter?"

"It does to me."

He pulled the laptop screen down so she could see his whole face, his eyes sparkling. "I'm hoping it's both," he told her. "That we can get the business done really quickly. After that, as far as I'm concerned it's all date."

It took a lot of effort not to smile. She was a strong woman, she shouldn't let him back into her life too easily. And yet the pull toward him felt as strong as ever.

Stronger maybe.

"Okay," she said, nodding slowly. "You can pick me up at seven."

He had no compunction about smiling. In fact, he was grinning ear-to-ear. "It's a date," he said, nodding at her

"Almost," she reminded him, unable to keep her face straight any longer. "It's partially a date."

❊ 32 ❊

"We're eating at the coffee shop?" Ally blinked, bemused, as she looked at the darkened café, turning to Nate to give him a questioning stare.

He shrugged and grabbed the keys from his pocket. "I figured we'd have more privacy here."

"It's the perfect place for a business meeting," Ally agreed, her voice teasing. Nate grinned and shook his head, opening the door and flicking on the lights. He gestured for her to walk in first.

He'd cleared all the tables and chairs away, leaving only one in the middle of the room. It was covered with a crisp white tablecloth and all laid up for dinner.

That wasn't the only thing that had changed either. There was new artwork – huge black and white canvases fixed to the dark blue walls.

It took her a moment to realize they weren't just random photographs. They were her photos, or her dad's anyway. Each canvas depicted a different time of her life. There was the one with her parents holding her as a baby, both of them proud as punch as they stood outside the café, the sun shining down on them all. Then there was an elementary school Ally — maybe seven or eight years old, deep in concentration as her dad taught her how to pour the coffee.

She felt her throat thicken as she took them all in. Her eyes fell onto the final one — of Ally standing behind the counter of Déjà Brew, laughing at somebody to the left of her. She had no idea that photograph even existed.

"Do you like them?" Nate's voice was soft.

Ally turned to him and nodded, her chest too full of emotion to be able to put how she felt into words. "There's a blank space," she said, her voice thick. "What's going there?"

"I don't know." He was eyeing her carefully, as though he was trying to gauge her emotions. "I guess that's up to you."

"*Me?*"

He nodded. "I want to take a photo of the café as it is now. But I want you in it."

"But I resigned."

"I know. And I want you back." He gave her the ghost of a smile. "I want a photograph of you, me and, Riley, all standing behind the counter. I want us to be as happy as you were in the last photograph."

She took a ragged breath in. "Nate…"

"You don't have to say anything now. Let's eat before the food gets cold." He walked over to the counter and opened the lid of a white insulated box. Inside were two containers. He carefully decanted their contents onto two white plates. Grabbing a bottle of wine from the refrigerator, he filled two glasses up, carrying the food and drink over to the table.

"Please sit down." He gestured to her. Ally slowly lowered herself into the seat and allowed him to take her crutches, resting them against the door.

She picked up the glass Nate had placed in front of her, taking a sip of the crisp white wine. She couldn't help but look at the photographs again, couldn't help but feel the connection to this place.

And to him.

Though the steak must have been resting for a while it still tasted delicious. "Did you cook this yourself?" she asked him as she swallowed a bite.

"Medium rare, the way you like it."

She smiled to herself. "Thank you for the photographs," she said, spearing another morsel. "They mean a lot. It's nice to know the old beach café is never going to be forgotten."

"I'm thinking we can do something similar with all the Coastal Cafés. Have old photographs of the local town, make people feel that the café is part of the history."

"That's a good idea." All she heard was 'we'. What did it mean? She took another sip of wine, trying to think things through. "I've signed the contract," she told him, trying not to smile at his look of surprise.

"You have?"

She fished the envelope out of her purse and pushed it toward him. Once again he slid the contract out, skimming the black type until he reached the part she'd written on.

"You crossed the zeros out."

"I'll take one dollar for the idea," she told him. "Nothing more, nothing less." She bit her bottom lip, waiting for his reaction. "I called a lawyer and he advised that would make this agreement binding. You just have to pay me something."

"A dollar?"

She nodded.

"I'll accept it on one condition." He raised an eyebrow, that crazily attractive smile curling his lips.

"Oh yes?" She leaned forward. "What is it?"

"I want you to come and work for me."

She put her silverware down on the plate and tried to

work out what he was trying to do. "You want me back as manager?"

"No. Not as manager."

"Then what?" She couldn't help but ask. She was so curious to know where this was going. It didn't help that the conversation between them was so easy, so light, it made her heart yearn for more.

"I want you to head up the Coastal Coffee brand. To oversee the redevelopment of the cafés and make sure they fit with your vision. You know the California beach trade so much better than I do. I know you have an eye for what works and what doesn't." His eyes twinkled. "I need you, Ally."

The way he said it, all deep and graveled, shot straight through her. A delicious pulse that made her want to shiver. "And if I say no?"

"You can say no any time you want and I'll respect it."

She inhaled a mouthful of air, thinking through the offer. It was everything she'd dreamed of. Something different and yet still connected to this café she'd grown up in. It would be crazy to turn it down – jobs like this came along once in a life-time. "If I say yes, will it be weird the two of us working together after everything that happened?"

"I promise not to make it weird."

"Okay then. Yes."

Nate grinned, his body visibly relaxing. "Thank God. I'll put it in writing with all the details."

"Is that it?" she asked, tipping her head to the side. "Is the business meeting over?"

"It is. But the date isn't."

Oh.

He reached for her hand, curling his fingers around her palm. "There's something else I want to talk to you about."

He ran his thumb up and down her wrist, sending electric waves up her arm. "Or tell you, really."

His eyes caught hers, and the way he was looking at her stole her breath away. As though every emotion she was feeling he was reflecting right back at her. "What is it?"

"I'm so sorry for talking to you the way I did when Riley ran away. I was a dick and I took my frustration out on you. I know you were only trying to help and I pushed you away." He gazed at her through his thick lashes. "I'll never do that again."

"I just wanted to make things right."

"I know. And I should have accepted that. I should have known that a problem shared is a problem halved. Instead I assumed you were thinking about yourself."

"I'd never do that. Not when it comes to Riley. She should always come first. She's your daughter and she needs your support."

"I know that. I think I always did, somewhere deep inside me. I was just too scared to see if it was true." He looked down, his brows knitting together. "I've not always had the best experience with girlfriends. My last one asked me to send Riley away."

Ally frowned. "What a bitch."

That made him laugh. He looked up with a grin on his face. "I know. Thank God I saw that before it was too late." His expression turned serious. "I talked with your dad the other day. He had some wise words for me."

"My dad?" Her brows shot up, surprise making her mouth fall open. "What did he have to say?"

"That there's more than enough love to go around. And part of being a parent is learning to let go. To let your child make their own mistakes. To show them how to be healthy by having your own life, too."

Tears stung at Ally's eyes. "Dad never did that," she whispered.

"I know. And I can tell you he regrets it. He told me not to end up regretting it, too." Nate ran his finger in a circle around her palm. "Riley and I have started family counseling again. I want her to have a safe place to be able to talk to me and tell me what she really thinks. What she needs. Without ever being afraid of upsetting me."

"That sounds wonderful," Ally said.

"We had our first session this morning. She told me she wanted me to date again. That she didn't want to worry about me being lonely whenever she went out." That smile was playing at his lips again. His eyes caught hers. "She wants me to date *you*," he said. "Which is pretty cool, because that's what I want to do, too."

"Oh." Ally felt breathless.

"I've fallen in love with you, Ally Sutton," he said, his voice strong and true. "With every part of you. And I know I'm not much of a catch. A single dad of a teenager with issues. You should probably run as fast as you can." He glanced down. "Or maybe hobble."

She grinned.

"I guess what I'm trying to tell you is that I shouldn't ask you to be mine, but I'm a selfish enough bastard to do it anyway. I want that last photograph on the wall to be the three of us. Because I can't imagine my life turning out any other way."

The tears that had been threatening for the past few minutes were spilling over. "That's the nicest thing that anybody's ever said to me," she whispered

"You better get used to it. I plan on telling you every day." He stood and reached for her hand, pulling her into his embrace. She closed her eyes as he pulled her in tightly, her face resting against his muscled chest, their bodies aligning as though they were made for each other.

He wiped away the tears from her cheeks then tipped her chin with his finger until she was looking up at him. "Will you date this old man?" he whispered.

"Yes." She nodded. "Yes, I will. Because I love you, too." She was smiling through the tears. "And I love your daughter, Nate. So much. I want nothing more than to be in both of your lives."

"Thank God." He dipped his head until his lips captured hers, his arms tightening around her waist. She could feel every part of him against her – his hard chest and stomach, and the burgeoning desire that lit a fuse inside her she wasn't sure would ever go out. She could spend the rest of her days in his arms and it still wouldn't be enough.

She could never get bored of this man, and from the way he was kissing her he felt exactly the same way.

And there was nothing she wanted more than that.

They'd been kissing like hormone-filled teenagers outside her apartment for the last ten minutes. "I should leave," he murmured against her lips, though he was reluctant to let her go.

"One more kiss," she whispered, pulling him in closer.

"I wish I could come inside." One of his hands was holding her waist, the other cupping her jaw so he could angle her face perfectly. Enough so he could plunder her mouth as she rested back on her apartment building wall. God, she tasted delicious. Everything about her was soft and enticing.

"I wish you could, too," she said, sliding her hands up until they reached the hard planes of his abdomen. His body tensed at the sensation.

"God I need you."

"I need you, too. I'm not going to sleep tonight."

He smiled against her mouth, loving the idea of her being so wound up with desire that she would toss and turn. "I'll call you when Riley's asleep. We'll see what we can do about that."

"You should go," she said, Riley's name making her blink her eyes open. "She'll be wondering where you are."

He sucked a deep breath in, trying to calm down, but it was no good. He was too tightly coiled for that. "Yeah, I'll go." He ran the pad of his finger from her temple to her jaw, loving the smoothness of her. "Are you sure you can put up with me having to go home and be a dad?" he asked her. "Making out like teenagers and having to go home all frustrated?"

She grinned at him. "You're worth it. And anyway, I kind of like making out like a teenager. Half the pleasure's in the anticipation."

"If you say so." He kissed her again, his lips soft against hers.

"You really should go," she said, her voice reluctant.

He pulled himself away from her, enough to leave a few inches of space between them. Immediately he missed the feel of her body against his. "I'll call you when I get home."

She smiled. "You do that."

He leaned forward and pressed his lips against hers one last time, using every piece of willpower he had to pull himself back again. It was late, he needed to get home. As much as he wanted to be with this woman forever, that need would have to wait.

"I'll see you tomorrow," she said.

"And the day after that," he told her. "And the next day and the next day..."

She laughed. "I get it."

"You will."

"Now go home," she said, grabbing her crutches and leaning on them. "I'll speak to you later."

"Goodnight, baby."

"Goodnight."

He watched as she turned on her crutches and walked into the lobby, pressing the button for the elevator. When the doors pulled open, she walked inside and lifted her arm in a wave.

He waited outside until he saw her living room light come on. Any other time he would have seen her up to her apartment, but his willpower right now was paper-thin. Instead he pulled his phone out and quickly tapped out her number.

"Hello?"

"I was just checking you'd unblocked me." He smiled, remembering how she'd admitted to blocking his calls earlier that evening, telling him she couldn't bear to hear his voice when they were apart.

She chuckled. "Yeah I unblocked you. For now."

"Glad to hear it. I'll call you in a bit."

"Drive safely."

"I will. Oh and Ally?"

"Yeah?"

"You better get used to me calling you. Because I intend to do it all the time when we can't be together. I can't get through the night without hearing your voice. I've tried it for the past few days and it's almost killed me."

"I like the sound of that." Her voice was warm. "And you'd better get used to me calling you, too."

He was planning on it, because everything about this woman was a breath of fresh air in his life. His heart ached for her, his body thrummed for her, and his mind craved her. He could spend the rest of his life talking with her and still never get enough.

"Speak to you soon, baby." He grinned as he ended the call and walked back to his car, sliding in behind the wheel. As the engine sparked to life he had to force himself not to blue tooth dial her again.

The rest of their lives were beginning. He could wait another five minutes to hear her voice again.

EPILOGUE

Ally walked out onto the beach in her bare feet, smiling as her soles sunk into the warm, dry sand. She closed her eyes to appreciate the moment, though not even her eyelids could block out the brightness of the sun. It was a perfect late fall/early winter day in Angel Sands – the only clouds in the sky were the wispy, barely-there kind that reminded her of a shimmering veil.

"How does it feel?" Nate asked. She opened her eyes to see him watching her, amusement curling up his lips. "You look like you're enjoying yourself."

"It's amazing." She wriggled her toes. "No itching, no crutches. Just me and the sand. I can't wait to run again."

"Hey, don't run before you can walk," Ember joked. Ally grinned at her. It was late afternoon and they were all gathered on the boardwalk next to the coffee shop, as though there was some kind of minor miracle going on instead of an ankle cast being removed. Her friends had all been waiting here for her when she and Nate had gotten back from the hospital. Ember and Brooke, Ally's dad and Lorne. And Riley of course. Even Frank Megassey had snuck out of the hardware store to make sure everything had gone okay with the removal.

"Did they use a circular saw?" he'd asked her.

"Just a little hand held one."

"Did you get a look at what make it was?"

She'd laughed and shook her head. It was such a typical Frank thing to ask. You could take the man out of the hardware store, but you couldn't take the hardware store out of the man.

"You want to go paddle in the ocean?" Riley asked her, slipping her hand into Ally's. In the few weeks since she'd come back from Boston – and Nate and Ally had begun dating in earnest – Riley had welcomed Ally in with open arms. According to her, Nate was so much easier to deal with when Ally was around.

"I can actually leave the house without worrying about him anymore," Riley had confessed one evening as she was getting ready for a study session at Laura's. "Tell me you're going to stick around."

"You can bank on it," Ally had promised her.

Riley and Nate were beside her as Ally walked down to where the ocean was lapping at the sand, rushing up then slowly receding, leaving the yellow grains wet and glistening. She leaned down to roll up her jeans, and wobbled for a second.

The next moment she felt warm, strong hands curling around her waist. She didn't have to look behind her to see who they belonged to because she knew. Just as she knew the sound of his breath, the fragrance of his skin. In the past weeks she'd gotten to know every single part of him.

The man never failed to take her breath away.

The water was cool as it lapped over her feet, rising up to

her ankles before it pulled away again. "That feels good," she said, leaning her head back on Nate's chest. He tightened his hold on her. Riley didn't seem to mind – maybe she was getting used to their public displays of affection.

Or maybe she'd seen the worst, and anything was better than that.

"I've got something for you," Nate whispered in her ear.

Ally turned her head, angling to look up at him. She raised a single eyebrow.

"Not that," he said, laughing. "Though now that you've mentioned it..."

"Enough! Seriously, you guys. I'm going to get a smooth-ie." Riley mock-stomped off, her eyes rolling at them, though Ally could tell she wasn't really angry.

When she was out of earshot, Ally grinned lasciviously at him. "You know, I was just thinking about all the possibilities now that the cast is off."

"It'll be like starting all over again."

"Are you free tonight?" she asked him.

"Always." He dropped his head to kiss her, his lips lingering on hers. "Or at least for a couple of hours before bedtime."

"That's all it takes."

It was his turn to raise his eyebrows. "With what I've got in mind, it'll take a damn bit longer than that."

"Promises, promises." The grin was still on her face. "Any-way, stop changing the subject. What have you got for me, other than... you know?"

"Come back up the beach. I'll show you."

Her friends were sitting at one of the tables on the board-walk. Brooke and Ember were drinking coffee, and Nick had a milkshake. Lorne and her dad were gossiping, and though she couldn't hear what they were saying she could tell they were having a great time. Through the glass windows she could see Riley leaning on the coffee shop counter, talking with Brad as he made her a drink.

A shot of warmth blasted through her. Everybody she loved was here. Some she was related to by blood, others by friendship, but they were all her family. Was there anybody as lucky as she was?

"Here it is." Nate reached for a large white box he'd left at the edge of the boardwalk. It had a sports logo emblazoned on it.

"You bought me shoes?"

"I owe you a pair, remember? I figured you could do with some new ones."

"Let's try not to throw these ones in the trash." She winked at him, her equilibrium returning. Slowly she prized the lid off, revealing a bright new pair of running shoes. She pulled them out, admiring them. "These look expensive," she murmured. "Thank you." She turned to put her arms around him, but he was already kneeling down on the sand.

"You want a hand putting them on?"

"Sure." She shrugged, not telling him he looked a bit weird kneeling next to her. She watched as he pulled the shoes out of the box, lining them up next to her feet. For a moment he stared down at them, then reached out to run his finger from her ankle to the tip of her toes, making them curl with delight at his touch.

He slid the first one on and tied the laces, then angled the second one on to her toes. Ally frowned when the sole of her foot scraped against something hard. "Is there a stone in there?" she asked, pulling her foot out. "Something about it feels weird."

"Take a look." Nate's voice was gruff. He was definitely acting strange. Still, Ally took the shoe and tipped it so she could see inside. Sure enough there was something there. It slid down to the heel, catching the light as the sun's rays shone down on it, and she realized it wasn't a stone at all.

It was a ring.

Nate watched as Ally slowly reached into the shoe, pulling out a gold band set with a square cut diamond. She looked at him, her eyes wide, and her lips trembling. "Nate?"

He was more nervous than he'd thought he would be. What if she said no? Ally held the ring between her forefinger and thumb and he gently took it from her, holding his breath as he held it to the ring finger on her left hand.

"You probably think I'm crazy," he said, his voice thick as his eyes met hers. "But I nearly lost you once and I never want to do it again. Since you came into my life it's like the sun finally came out, and bathed everything around me in light." He gave her a gentle smile, loving the way she was staring at him with those big blues, hanging on every word. "You're absolutely perfect," he told her. "You're funny, you're beautiful, and you have the biggest heart of anybody I've ever met. It would truly be my honor if you'd agree to be my wife."

"Yes," Ally whispered. Without saying a word he slowly slid the ring onto her finger. With his eyes locked on hers he lifted her hand to his lips, kissing her skin and the ring. His body flooded with relief and exhilaration combined. There was no way he was ever taking this grin off his face.

"You've made me the happiest man on Earth."

"Does Riley know about this?" Ally asked him.

"I spoke with her about it yesterday. She was so excited."

He looked up to see his daughter watching them through the glass window of the coffee shop, her grin wide as she clapped with delight. Ember, Nick, and Brooke were watching them, too. From the expressions on their faces they'd be quizzing Ally about everything very soon.

Then he looked over at Lorne and Grant – Ally's father and her almost-dad, the two men who had been the biggest part of her life until now. He hadn't asked them for her hand in marriage – Ally was nobody's to give away – but he had consulted them and asked for their blessing.

They'd given it willingly.

He probably had only one more minute before they all ran down to congratulate them. Sliding his fingers into her hair, he angled Ally's face until her lips were only a whisper away from his.

"You're my best friend," he told her. "My soul mate, my everything. I can't wait to spend the rest of my life with you."

He slowly pressed his lips against hers, closing his eyes to try and control the emotion that was bursting through him. Was it really possible to have everything? He thought it was. Only a few months ago he'd arrived in this town desperate to make a change.

And he'd found the woman who changed everything.

She kissed him back and it was as though nobody else was there. Just the two of them losing themselves in each other, and that huge sparkling ring on her finger.

When he opened his eyes they were surrounded. Ember and Brooke were almost jumping up and down with excitement. Riley was grabbing at Ally's hand to take a look. Lorne and Grant slapped Nate on the back as though he'd won something amazing.

Which he really had.

"Welcome to my world," Ally murmured, biting down a grin as she turned to look at all their friends.

"Thank you, baby," he said, smiling back at her as she slid her hand into his. He'd come to Angel Sands seeking a new start for his daughter, but in the end he'd found a new life for them both. And with this woman by his side, he'd found the kind of happiness he hadn't known existed. "I love your world," he whispered, brushing his lips against hers. "I can't think of anywhere else I'd rather be."

THE END

DEAR READER

Thank you so much for reading Nate and Ally's story. If you enjoyed it and you get a chance, I'd be so grateful if you can leave a review. And don't forget to keep an eye out for **SWEET LITTLE LIES**, the third book in the series, coming out in AUGUST

To learn more, you can sign up for my newsletter here: http://www.subscribepage.com/e4u8i8

I can't wait to share more stories with you.

Yours,

Carrie xx

ABOUT THE AUTHOR

Carrie Elks writes contemporary romance with a sizzling edge. Her first book, *Fix You*, has been translated into eight languages and made a surprise appearance on *Big Brother* in Brazil. Luckily for her, it wasn't voted out.

Carrie lives with her husband, two lovely children and a larger-than-life black pug called Plato. When she isn't writing or reading, she can be found baking, drinking an occasional (!) glass of wine, or chatting on social media.

You can find Carrie in all these places
www.carrieelks.com
carrie.elks@mail.com

ALSO BY CARRIE ELKS

If you'd like to get an email when I release a new book, please sign up here:

CARRIE ELKS' NEWSLETTER

CPSIA information can be obtained
at www.ICGtesting.com
Printed in the USA
LVHW031708200519
618472LV00001B/140

9 781094 778884